# DUALITY

Book 1

Melancholia

## Books by Elle Casey

### CONTEMPORARY URBAN FANTASY

*War of the Fae* (10-book series)
*Ten Things You Should Know About Dragons*
(short story, The Dragon Chronicles)
*My Vampire Summer*
*Aces High*

### DYSTOPIAN

*Apocalypse* (4-book series)

### SCIENCE FICTION

*Drifters' Alliance* (ongoing series)
*Winner Takes All* (short story prequel to Drifters' Alliance,
Dark Beyond the Stars Anthology)
*The Ivory Tower* (short story standalone, Beyond the Stars: A
Planet Too Far Anthology)

### ROMANCE

*By Degrees*
*Rebel Wheels* (3-book series)
*Just One Night* (romantic serial)
*Just One Week*
*Love in New York* (3-book series)
*Shine Not Burn* (2-book series)
*Bourbon Street Boys* (4-book series)
*Desperate Measures*
*Mismatched*

### ROMANTIC SUSPENSE

*All the Glory: How Jason Bradley Went from
Hero to Zero in Ten Seconds Flat*
*Don't Make Me Beautiful*
*Wrecked* (2-book series)

### PARANORMAL

*Duality* (2-book series)
*Monkey Business* (short story)
*Dreampath* (short story standalone, The
Telepath Chronicles)
*Pocket Full of Sunshine* (short story & screenplay)

# DUALITY

Book 1

## Melancholia

ELLE CASEY

## DEDICATION

*To Caroline, one of the strongest ladies I know.*
*Sometimes we don't know how strong we are*
*until the universe challenges us beyond our limits.*

# Chapter One
# Malcolm

FOR AS LONG AS I can remember I've brought nothing but misery to those around me. Pain. Sadness. A loneliness so bone-deep it smothers any thoughts of joy or hope that might try to seep in from reality.

I don't do this on purpose. In fact, I'd do anything to change it, this effect I have on people. Some kids might think they want to be an agent of darkness, so they dress up in black clothes and dye their hair and do drastic things to their wardrobes, shocking people with their angry, outlandish attitudes. But if they were to walk a day in my shoes, they'd change their minds in a second. They'd join the Latin club and study hard and do everything they could to make their parents proud. No one truly wants to be me; they just think they do.

I call myself that - the agent of darkness - but I don't really know what I am or what my problem is. What I *do* know is that it's real and it's nothing I can control. Believe me, I've tried. I've done everything from smiling entire weeks on end until my face ached with it, to hiding out in my house and cutting off contact with the outside world. But nothing works.

My own happiness and attitude have nothing to do with how others feel in my presence; I can be smiling like a Girl Scout who just offloaded a thousand boxes of Thin Mints for cold hard cash, and the Miserables would still dive into the depths of despair without a second thought after being around me for a while. That's what I call them - the Miserables - those people who *want* to be sad for some strange and entirely effed-up reason.

I'm not a Miserable. I'm immune to the sadness that I deliver in spades to the innocents around me. It's kind of a sick joke on me, how I can be working so hard at being happy while I make everyone around me want to jump off a cliff.

Hiding doesn't work. No matter how invisible I try to be and no matter how hard I try to stay away, the Miserables come and find me anyway. They seek me out and haunt me, refusing to leave without a fight. I'm rarely alone. Sometimes there are whole groups of them flitting around me like angry black butterflies, and other times it's just one person.

Case in point: my latest unwelcome acquisition, Caden Kucharski. His friends call him Kootch for short. I don't call him anything because I'm trying to get rid of him, but the kid is miserable with a capital M, and he wants nothing to do with happiness. He's been all over me like a fly on shit since last month.

"Yo, Malcolm. What's up, man?" He stood waiting for me at my locker. Again.

I just stared at him hard for a few seconds, wishing he'd take the hint and get lost. I spun the combination of my lock, focusing all my attention on it, hoping he'd see I was blowing him off. It was a wasted effort, though. It always is.

The problem with Miserables like him is they never get the hint. Sometimes it even seems to make them happy when I'm mean like this, which is really sick and twisted. Lots of times I have to force myself to be nice, when all I really want to do is scream at them to fuck off and leave me the hell alone. I mean that in the nicest way, though. I'm just trying to protect them from me, from the effect I have on them. I wish I could have friends. I just ... can't.

My hard look had zero effect. Caden smiled. "That good, eh? Yeah, me too. Just got out of Chem class. That asshole Pritchard is a real prickard. Get it? Prickard? Guy's a prick?"

"Yeah, I get it." I shut my locker and spun the dial on the lock. I sighed heavily, knowing I was going to be peppered with Kootch-isms all the way to my next class.

"So what's up after school? Going anywhere? Wanna hang out?"

"Busy."

"Oh, you're busy again, huh? That's cool. Seems like whenever I ask you to do something you're busy, but hey, you can't blame a dude for trying. I downloaded some new music to my nano, you should check it. Hardcore metal, man." He held out his mp3 player towards me.

I didn't even look down. "No, thanks. I don't like metal."

"Really? That's surprising. I figured ... well, who cares. I don't like it that much either. I'll probably delete it off today anyway. What music do you like? What's your favorite band?"

"Are you asking me on a date?" Sometimes if I play the homo card with guys it makes a difference and scares them off. I should probably feel bad about playing on people's phobias to save myself, but I don't. I know it saves them too.

"Ha! That's funny. No, man. I'm straight. I like the ladies and believe me, the ladies like the Kootch. Check this." He lifted up his hand and held it out towards a girl coming our way down the hallway. "Yo! Melissa! Give me some-a that sugar."

She scowled at him and walked by, making sure to stay far away from his outstretched hand.

I tried not to react, but I couldn't help it. I laughed.

"Bitch," he mumbled, letting his hand drop. "Chicks in this school are so friggin stuck up." He cheered up instantly. "But the chicks over at Eastman? They're hot and willing for the Kootch. All up on me and shit when I'm at the games."

"Whatever you say, Caden. Listen, I have to go to the bathroom. See you around." I made a sharp left turn into the guys' room and quickly locked the main door behind me. Luckily, no one else was in there.

The sound of Caden hitting his forehead on the door echoed out into the wall-to-wall tiled room. "Hey, man, did you lock the door? What'd you do that for? I need to take a shit." He laughed. "Nah serious, I don't need to do that, but I could take a piss. I got the urge to purge. Open up. And hey, you can call me Kootch, by the way. All my buds call me Kootch."

I dropped my bag on the floor and sat down, resting my head on my forearms crossed over my knees. This was the only thing that worked - waiting them out. Even the Miserables had to heed the call of the school bell. I've racked up a record amount of tardies in my high school career, but it's better than being molested in the bathroom by a million questions and one-sided conversations that made me want to drown myself in the toilet.

The bell rang, interrupting Kootch's inane chatter. He was quiet for all of two seconds. "Oh, dude, you're going to be late. Don't worry, I'll cover for ya. I'll tell Adams that you're constipated or something. Talk to you after class! Or you could text me in class. I'll risk it for friends like that. Later!"

And then he was gone.

I sighed and stood in front of the mirror, taking a few seconds to look at myself. I try to be unnoticeable. I dress average - not in fashion and not out. I don't wear black or paint my nails. I wear my hair in a boring cut, not too long or too short, and keep it the natural brown I was born with. I tried the emo thing for a while, dressed all in black and tried to look forbidding and dangerous so people would leave me alone, but the Miserables loved it. They ate it up. It attracted them to me in droves, so I had to stop. Now the name of the game for me is to be plain. Unremarkable. Invisible.

Grabbing my backpack off the ground, I sighed at what my life had become. Hiding out in the bathroom again, fending off the friendly advances of another Miserable soul. *So lame.*

I walked over to the bathroom door, counting to ten slowly once I reached it. I had to make sure I couldn't hear Kootch anymore before turning the lock. Miserables can be really persistent and tricky when they want to be. I've been hijacked by a few who held their breath so I wouldn't hear them. They can be freaky intense in their need to be unhappy sometimes.

When I was sure he was gone and the nearby hallway empty, I unlocked the door and walked out. I turned left to go to English Lit class, the wide corridor stretching out in front of me and beckoning me forward. It's a sick joke. The hallway calls me to something I can never have - a normal day in high school, filled with gossip, friends, jokes, and maybe even a crush on a cute girl. There will be none of that for the agent of darkness. None of it. I've given up on being sad about it. It's just my reality, nothing more, nothing less.

The second bell rang right next to my head. To me it's not just the sound of being late. It's the sound that reminds me I'll never fit in here or anywhere people are. I'll never have any friends. I'll never be able to live a peaceful life until I go so far, far away that no one will ever find me. I have three months left before my eighteenth birthday. Three more months before I can cut out of this place and disappear forever. I'm counting the days.

# Chapter Two
# Rae

ISMILED AT THE PLUMP lady standing behind the front desk. But not too much. I have to be careful not to smile too much. People get very attached sometimes, and then it's not good for anyone.

"We're thrilled to have Rae here with us at Preston High," said the principal, Mr. Tweeds. He was trembling, he was so excited. "Just thrilled. I've received nothing but glowing recommendations from everyone I've talked to about her." His smile revealed capped teeth and funky-colored gums.

The receptionist's constant, unwavering grin was putting me on edge. I had to turn my back to her.

Facing my parents now, I watched their heads bob up and down in response to the principal's glowing accolades.

"She's top of her class here just like she was at her previous school, and on track to be valedictorian," the principal continued. "We've already done the conversion of her transcripts. We're just pleased as punch to take her on. She'll be a credit to the school."

"Oh, she will," said my mother, so absolutely sure of her words, they practically sparkled as they came out of her mouth. "She's been number one in her class since her very first day of kindergarten. We've never had to worry a single moment about her grades."

I gritted my teeth in frustration. My parents. *Ugh.* They meant well, but *ugh* anyway. They refused to accept the fact that my perfect grades weren't the result of a brilliant mind but rather a side effect of something else entirely.

"It's other things that are a problem," said my father. He was being stern, like he always is when he talks about this part of my life. "We have to be absolutely sure she'll be safe here at this school. As I mentioned in my email and over the phone, she's had some ... issues before. And I don't want to see those issues repeated here." My father frowned at the principal as if the poor rotund man was personally responsible for the incidents at my last school.

Mr. Tweeds was shaking his head vehemently and holding out his hands like two stop signs. "You have absolutely nothing to worry about, nothing at all, I can assure you. We have a zero tolerance policy towards stalking of any kind, and that includes social media and other types of cyber activity."

"Good. But you have to remain vigilant." My father had his finger up and was pointing it in the man's face.

I nearly laughed at how comical he looked, all serious like that. I knew it was a big deal, but sometimes he took it too far. I rolled my eyes. I couldn't stand it anymore. Reaching out and taking his finger, I gently pushed his hand down to his side. "Okay, Dad, he knows. He heard you the first twenty times you said it."

My dad turned his concern on me, all his anger gone and replaced with fear - fear for my future. He always worries about my future - my next year, my next week, my next five minutes. It was suffocating at best and more like insanity in my darker hours.

"Rae, you know we have to be careful. People get ... crazy sometimes where you're concerned."

Anyone listening in on this conversation from a remote location would think we were all members of a looney bin, having a deluded discussion over a celebrity or something. But I'm no celebrity. I'm just Rae. And for as long as I can remember, I've had this problem. It follows me everywhere like a faithful dog at my heels. People who get near me become happy, too happy. They become so full of joy, they eventually get to the point that they can't *not* be around me. And in their need to be close, they get *too* close. They smother me. They scare me. They become a danger to everyone.

Or at least, that's what my dad thinks. The problem is, he suffers as much as the strangers do from the effects of being in my presence. He thinks he's just being a protective, loving father, but I know the truth. He's under my thrall. He can't be without me, just like my mom can't. Just like the kids at my last school and the one before it and the one before that one...

The only thing keeping my parents from homeschooling me on an island in the middle of nowhere is my threat that I'll leave them. It's a threat I have to reissue every time they pull me from another school. Eight times in the last three years, I've stared my parents in the face and warned, *"If you don't enroll me in a public school somewhere, I'm going to disappear and you'll never see me again. Ever."*

And so they enroll me, because they have no choice.

Neither of them wants me to leave. In fact, they both believe they'd die if I ever did. It's been a burden of mine that I've been unable to shake, try as I might, since I was old enough to understand what was going on. I hate to say this even just to myself, but one of these days, I *am* going to leave. I'm going to disappear forever and never look back. I'll go where no one can find me, where I'll be completely alone. Then I'll never have to worry about people gluing themselves to me and not wanting to let go. I'll finally be able to think and just breathe for a change. Maybe I'll get a dog to keep from being completely lonely.

"Here's your list of classes and a map," said the receptionist behind me.

"You don't need to give her a map," said the student helper standing next to her. She snatched the paper out of the older lady's hand. "I'll be happy to show her where to go."

The girl grinned at me with a thousand-watt smile. The orange and yellow of her cheerleader uniform went perfectly with her bouncy ponytail and miniature megaphone earrings.

*Uh-oh. A Rainbow.* That's what I call the people who can't get enough of me - people who want to overdose on happiness until they drown in its sweet depths. But no one can handle that much of it at once. It always manages to short circuit something in their brains. *Want* changes to *need*, and then I become the drug they're addicted to and can't live without. It's not a good thing to be someone's personal happy-crack.

I have to stay very far away from Rainbows whenever I can help it. It was a Rainbow at my last school who I now have a restraining order against. Jerry the Rainbow. Captain of the basketball team with hands as big as dinner plates. His joy was a scary thing to behold in the end.

"No, that's okay," I said, taking the map from her hands. "I like to find my own way."

"Nonsense, this is the first thing we always do," said the principal. "We give a tour and hands-on service for every new student or student in need." He grinned big at me. His front teeth looked like they were just balanced there, like they'd fall out at any moment. I tried not to stare.

A small snort came from across the room.

I leaned to the side so I could see around the fat principal. A girl with hacked up and dyed green hair sat there in a chair, waiting for someone. She was examining her fingernails, which I noticed were painted moss green to match her hair. Her torn stockings went perfectly with her scratched-up combat boots, ratty shorts, and loose shirt that hung off her right shoulder. Her bright red bra strap stood out in stark relief to her pale skin.

I smiled briefly. It was possible I was looking at a Neutral, which thrilled me to the bone. I'd only met a couple in my life, but they were like golden people to me - the few who weren't affected by me in any way. They either liked me or hated me on my own merits. Usually, it ended up in hate because being around someone like me can be very annoying, with the Rainbows there all the time. But still, for a few short moments in my life, I've had interactions with Neutrals, and I could recount their looks and mannerisms all in detail by detail even now.

Years later. Being me is a lonely business. I hang on to what I can and try to forget the rest.

"I'll get to you in a moment, Miss Butts. You can just wait your turn."

I lifted an eyebrow. *Her name is Butts? Holy bad luck.*

"Can't wait," she said, not looking up.

"How about if *she* shows me to my first class?" I asked. I'm not ashamed to admit I turned on the sweetness just a little. It doesn't take much for me to get my way.

"Are you sure that's a good idea?" asked my mom, frowning at Miss Butts. She leaned in closer to me and whispered really loudly. "I think maybe you'd be better off with the cheerleader, don't you?"

I whispered back at her, putting as much admonishment into my voice as possible. "Mom, geez, give it a rest. Please."

My mom got that expression on her face, like she was going to get all firm about it.

I looked at the principal. "Tell her it's okay, would you? She worries too much."

The principal was nervous. He looked from the rebel in the waiting room to the chipper cheerleader bouncing in her Keds and didn't know what to say.

"I ... um ..." Sweat beaded on his forehead.

"Please?" I smiled at him. "Just this once? I'd appreciate it. I'm sure your receptionist could use her assistant's help, and I'm anxious to get started." *Lies, lies, lies.* I just wanted to get away from all these people and out into the empty hallways. I took my moments of peace when I could get them. Maybe this Neutral wouldn't hate me all the time. Maybe we could be friends for two minutes before she got tired of the Rainbows.

"Well, if it's all right with your parents." He looked to my father for guidance.

I gave my dad the look. The one that said, *"Don't suffocate me."* He'd seen it thousands of times.

"Fine." He turned his head to look at the girl in the chair. "But you mind your Ps and Qs young lady. Our daughter is very special."

She looked up and scowled at him. "Who the hell are you to tell me what to do? You're not *my* father." She stood. "I'll take this special snowflake where she needs to go, but only so I can go have a smoke on the way." She grabbed the map out of my hands and the schedule from the assistant without hesitating. Looking down at it, she said, "Come on ... Rae. Let's go find your English Lit class with Mr. Adams." She walked out the door without waiting for me.

I patted my mom on the shoulder. "Bye, Mom. Bye, Dad. See you after school." My mom leaned in for a kiss, but I ignored it. It was better not to encourage her. She's been known to dissolve in tears over a simple goodbye.

"We'll pick you up!" shouted my mom.

"I'll get a ride!" I said from out in the hallway. I took several long steps to put some distance between us.

"That was lame," said the girl, clearly disgusted.

"Yeah. Sorry. My parents are seriously overprotective."

"Poor you," she said, just before blowing a big bubble with her gum. She popped it and then sucked it in, cracking the gum as she chewed it down.

"What's your name?" I asked.

"Jasmine. Jasmine Butts. Go ahead and laugh. Like I give a shit what you think."

"I like it. Jasmine Butts. Jazzy Butts." The smile came whether I wanted it to or not.

"Call me that again, and I'll kick you in the taco."

I burst out laughing. "Wow. In the taco? You don't mess around, do you?"

"No." She blew another big bubble and sucked it back in.

"So, do you like going here?" I asked.

She looked at me briefly and frowned. "Please hold all questions until the end of the tour."

I bit my lip and nodded, not trusting myself not to laugh again.

She gestured to the left. "This is the shitter on your left. If there's a chick on the door, you can use it. If it's got a man on the door, well, I don't recommend it."

A little farther down the hall, she gestured to the right. "That's the water fountain. If you don't mind drinking other people's loogies, go for it."

"Oh, sick." *Note to self: Bring water bottle.*

A door opened in the hallway farther up ahead and a boy came out, a backpack thrown casually over his shoulder.

She spoke in a quieter tone. "And that, ladies and gentlemen, is the elusive and mysterious Malcolm McNamara. Late to class as usual."

Something about the way he was walking caught my attention. I couldn't see his face, but the way he slouched over and slinked a little, it was as if he was sneaking down the hall, trying not to be seen.

"Who's he?" I asked, speeding up. I just wanted to see his face.

She put her hand on my arm to stop me from going too fast. "He's our resident ghost. Just leave him alone."

I shook her off. "Why?" We were stopped now, our bodies still facing down the hall, but heads turned to face each other.

She shrugged. "I don't know." She seemed mystified by her answer. She blew another bubble and then sucked it in. "Come on. You're already late." She started walking again.

"Why were you in the office just now? Were you in trouble?"

"You could say that. But then again you could say that I was in the process of actively thwarting the tyranny of the close-minded, too. It just depends on how you look at it."

"What'd you do?"

"I let everyone in the cafeteria know that our meatballs are tainted with horse meat."

I laughed, a little shocked to learn that about my new school. "Are they?"

"How do I know? But if it pushes a few more kids towards being vegetarians or at least thinking about what they shove in their stupid mouths, then it works for me."

"Okaaaay," I said, nodding while at the same time wondering what her ultimate goal was. Definitely not popularity. Friendship probably wasn't the plan either. The concept was a luxury to me, to actively shun friendship for no other reason than not wanting it. But maybe she'd change her mind after getting to know me; maybe she'd want to be friends with me. It wouldn't be terrible to hang out with her, even though she was obviously someone who worked pretty hard at getting people mad at her. Anything was better than being alone. Almost anything.

"So here you are," she said, turning the corner and gesturing towards the first door on our left. "Your very first class at Butt Suck High. Here's your map, here's your list, and here at the bottom is your locker combo and number, written in purple pen because Ashley Dumbass doesn't write in any other color *but* purple. You'll find it around the corner, back where we just were. When you get your books, you can load them in there and never look at them again like most of the students here do, or you can use them to study. I leave that up to you." She saluted and turned to go.

"Thanks, Jasmine. For your help and the tour."

She said nothing. She just waved over her head and popped another really loud bubble on her way down the hall.

I went over to the door and peeked through the narrow but tall rectangular window with wire mesh embedded in it, getting a partial view of the classroom's interior. Most of the students were looking at the teacher. The boy Malcolm was just sitting down in a seat near the back of the class on the far side, and a boy in the chair next to him was leaning over to say something to him.

I took a deep breath and grabbed the doorknob. "Might as well get it over with," I said, turning the handle and pushing the door open.

All eyes went to me, and the teacher stopped talking in mid-sentence.

## Chapter Three
# Malcolm

KOOTCH WAS IN THE MIDDLE of telling me how he'd given Mr. Adams some stupid explanation for why I wasn't in class, when she walked in. The new girl. I couldn't tear my eyes away for a full thirty seconds.

Kootch stopped whispering when he saw I was otherwise occupied, and when Mr. Adams quit talking in mid-sentence, he turned to see what all the fuss was about. "Daaaaamn," Kootch said quietly as his gaze took in the girl standing awkwardly in the doorway.

It wasn't difficult to see that he was speaking the mind of pretty much every guy in the place. She was cute for sure. But what struck me most about her was her outfit. I'm not really a guy who notices stuff like that, but her clothes were so ... plain. So was her hair. Most of the cute girls in this school went all out with their wardrobes, with skinny jeans and shorts so tight I could read their lips, and cleavage coming out of everywhere. They spent tons of time and money on their hair; I'd heard them talking about it. Even the girls without the means to do it found a way to be trendy and sexy. This chick looked like she'd just stepped out of a 10-year-old magazine ad for JC Penney instead of yesterday's Abercrombie advertisement. She looked like our librarian.

My mouth quirked up in a half smile as I realized I'd been trying for the same look myself when I'd gotten dressed this morning. *Fashion-challenged students unite!* Maybe she did it to keep the guys from hanging all over her. She definitely had Kootch drooling.

She caught me looking at her and smiled.

I quickly changed my expression to a scowl, breaking eye contact and looking down at my desk. The last thing I needed to do was take the new girl down nightmare alley. *Let her stay as far away from me as possible.*

"May I help you, young lady?" asked Mr. Adams, moving from behind his desk to stand in front of her. I looked up at his tone.

She handed him a paper. "I'm in your class. Today's my first day."

"Oh, wonderful," he said, looking down at it. "Rae Livingston. And where are you from?" He was grinning at her like a loon. I'd never seen him so happy before. Normally, listening to him talk was about as exciting as watching the antique road show on TV. *Oooh, look! An old-as-shit lamp!* But right now he sounded like he might be worth listening to for a change. He had some kind of energy in his voice that wasn't usually there.

"I'm from South Carolina. That's where I was last, anyway."

"I don't hear an accent," he said in a singsong voice.

*Is he flirting with her? Oh, man, that's gross.*

"I wasn't there long." She looked out over the class. "Do you have a spot for me anywhere?" It was like she was changing the subject or something. I didn't blame her. Mr. Adams was kind of creepy when he was acting excited. I suppressed a shudder.

Six guys stood up all of a sudden, making a horrible racket scraping their chairs across the floor.

"She can sit here!"

"Take my chair!"

"I have room!"

"No, Rae, sit here!"

The other two just stood there, dumbstruck.

"Oh, man," said Kootch, loud enough that everyone around him could hear. "Guess I'm out."

"No, Mr. Kucharski, you're not out," said Mr. Adams, wryly. "Please stand and come to the front."

The six guys who offered seats sat down, grumbling.

Kootch looked at me, his eyeballs practically dancing out of his head. "Dude!" he man-squealed. He stood and half-walked, half-skipped up to the front. "You want me to show her to her seat? You want me to carry her stuff for her?"

Never mind that she wasn't holding anything but a purse. Kootch's enthusiasm was embarrassing to watch.

"No." Mr. Adams frowned at him. "I want you to go to another classroom and get her a chair. We don't have any extra as you can see." He gestured out into the room.

Kootch calmed down considerably. "Oh. Yeah, okay. I can do that." He flexed his right arm for the class, earning a few giggles. "Be right back."

He nodded at Rae on his way out, walking into the door accidentally, apparently forgetting he had to open it first. Several students laughed as it shut behind him.

"Miss Livingston, please take Mr. Kucharski's seat. He can use the one he's bringing in."

My heart stopped beating for a few seconds. *She's going to sit here? Oh, shit.*

She looked scared. "Oh, no, that's okay. I don't want to steal anyone's spot."

Mr. Adam's waved her on. "It's fine, just go take it. He needs to sit up front anyway. It'll help him concentrate."

More giggles came from around the room.

*Dammit. Here she comes.*

All the eyes in the room followed her progress. I could swear I was hearing the music from the movie *Jaws* playing in my head.

*Duh-nuh. Duh-nuh.*

I wanted to shout at her to go away. To go sit somewhere else. But that would have been rude, and I really don't like being rude. She looked like the type that would cry, too.

*Duh-nuh-duh-nuh.*

She smiled at me and tucked a piece of hair behind her ear. She has a dimple in her right cheek, and her two front teeth stick out just the littlest bit. It made me like her more when all I wanted to do was hate her. Hating her was better for her health.

She was only three seats away now.

*Duh-nuh-duh-nuh-duhnuhduhnuhduhnuhduhnuhnaaaaaa!*

She sat down at the desk next to me, and her perfume or the fabric softener in her clothes wafted over and sailed up into my nose.

I rocketed to my feet. Before I could figure out what the hell I was thinking, my legs were moving. I strode to the front of the class, tripping over backpacks and purses on my way but still not stopping.

"Mr. McNamara! Please take your seat." Mr. Adams sounded as confused as I felt.

"I can't," I said, standing there in the front of the room in a panic, begging Mr. Adams with my eyes to let me leave.

"Well, sure you can. Just turn around and march your feet back in the direction they just came from." He waved a finger at me dismissively. "Go on. Sit."

Everyone laughed.

"I have to ... help Kootch. Kucharski. Caden. With the chair."

Mr. Adams actually rolled his eyes at me. "Mr. Kucharski can manage, I'm pretty sure."

I took more steps towards the door. "I'll just go check."

"Mr. McNamara!"

His frustrated voice followed me out into the hallway, but I ignored it. I ran. I had to get away. That girl is a nice person, I can tell. She isn't loud or showy or anything. Just nice. Smiling with that dimple. Plain but not plain. I couldn't mess her up like I'd messed up so many others.

I tried to calm myself down as I walked, looking for solutions where there probably weren't any. *Somebody'll take my seat next class, and I'll sit as far away from her as possible. That'll solve the problem. Distance. All I need to do is put some distance between us.* Skipping school was not an option. I had the State on my ass all the time, and they always came knocking when I didn't show for school. Until I was eighteen, they called the shots in my life. *Three more months. Three more months is all I need.*

Kootch came around a corner, lugging one of the heavy wood and metal chair-desk combo units at his side. "Dude, what're you doing out here? Coming to help me?"

"No. Mr. Adams wanted me to run an errand."

"Oh, okay. I'll see ya. I'll take notes for ya while you're gone."

I didn't say anything. Even a little encouragement was a bad idea. I jogged to the end of the corridor and ran down the stairs.

Pushing open the exit door, I realized I was in the smoking section of the school, outside under the overhang that protected the smokers from inclement weather - as much as it could anyway; the school didn't want to make smoking too convenient.

There was only one person out there. Jasmine is her name. She's one of those rebels without a cause, making herself look ridiculous just to cause a fuss. But I like her. She doesn't take shit from anyone, and she's also one of the people least affected by me. It's weird because she seems like she'd be a full-on Miserable the way she's always scowling, but she pretty much lives in her own world, not bothering with me or anyone else.

"What's the matter?" she asked. "Bullies after ya for your lunch money?" She blew smoke up above her head, kind of smiling. Her expressions always have a tinge of bitterness to them.

"No." I shoved my hands in my pockets, looking around and jumping up and down a little bit to stay warm. It wasn't yet summer and some days were still too cold for a t-shirt. I'd left my sweatshirt in my backpack, which was sitting by my desk in the classroom.

"Ass on fire?" she asked, sucking hard on her cigarette.

I looked behind me. "Not that I'm aware of."

"Good. I hate flaming asses." This time she blew the smoke in my face.

"Do you mind?" I scowled at her.

"What?" she asked, her face the picture of innocence.

"I don't smoke, and I don't particularly want to get cancer from your second-hand crap either."

She rolled her eyes and then pointed with her cigarette at the sign affixed above her head on the overhead support. "Then why are you hanging out in the smoking section, freak?"

I stared at the red sign for a few seconds, its bright white letters glaring out at me, calling me stupid. SMOKING SECTION. PUT YOUR BUTTS IN THE PROPER RECEPTACLE.

"I have no idea what I'm doing here," I said under my breath, turning and grabbing the door handle. I left the smoke to Jasmine's lungs and entered the dark stairwell, climbing the steps with little enthusiasm.

I was practically in slow motion by the time I got to the landing. I could have left my backpack in the classroom and just said screw it, but my poetry journal was inside, and I didn't want some idiot like Kootch getting his hands on it. I had to go back.

I really didn't want to return to that classroom and have to sit by that girl, though. She was trouble, no doubt about it. Maybe she'd even be like ...

*No. Do not go there. Focus on what matters now - the future. Stay away from the past.* I had to keep my head up and my nose clean, stay under the radar for just a little while longer.

*I can do this.*

I walked out into the hallway and took slow, measured steps to the classroom, hoping to get there just before the period was over. The only problem was my watch said I had thirty more minutes before that would happen.

I took a detour around the inside of the building, passing every set of lockers twice before I got back to the classroom. I was just reaching for the handle when the bell rang.

# Chapter Four
# Rae

THIS WAS ALWAYS THE WORST part - walking into a classroom of a new school on the first day. Twenty-odd pairs of eyeballs stared me down and searched my face, hair, and clothing, all the while making judgments. And if that was all it ever was, I'd probably be fine with it. But always, always there was the beginning of the Rainbow connection, too - the first tendrils of energy or whatever it was flowing out of me and into them. I'd been hoping today it wouldn't happen ... that today would be the first day I could walk into a room of strangers and not feel them warming to me instantly. But I knew immediately that today was not going to be that day.

Mr. Adams lit up the room with his smile, and from the expressions on the other students' faces and the giggling I heard, it wasn't his normal reaction to a new student. I resisted the urge to sigh. This is my life, and I just have to deal with it. At least for now. There was no point in getting mad at any of these people or the teacher; they couldn't help themselves.

No less than six boys stood and offered me their chairs. *No girls this time.* I gazed out across the room, hoping I'd see some

Neutrals there. Jasmine was an awesome find, right there on my first day before I even started classes. Maybe I'd win the lottery and stumble into a whole room of them. *A girl can dream.*

The happy faces staring back at me said, *no - no Neutrals in here.* I would just have to hold out hope that in one of my other classes I might get lucky. Everyone here was giving me the Rainbow vibe. Except ...

I frowned. There was a blank space in the Rainbow network, somewhere out there in the classroom. Someone who wasn't like all the rest was sitting there amongst the others. I scanned the room, stopping when I found the spot where there wasn't a feeling of need and want coming at me. *There you are. Got ya!*

It was a boy, the one who Jasmine had said was a ghost. *Malcolm Mac...something.* He was sitting towards the back of the room on the far side nearest the windows, looking at me. First he was smiling, but then he wasn't. I couldn't believe it when his expression turned sour, as if he'd smelled something nasty. And now he wasn't checking me out at all; he was staring at his desk.

I wanted to jump up and cheer, but I had to control myself. If I got too happy about being scowled at, everyone else's emotions would just get that much more amped up. I took a deep, even breath and let it out slowly. *Just chill. You can talk to him after class and see if he's a Neutral.*

I'd gotten distracted by my thoughts, and now realized I'd missed something. A boy was skipping to the front of the class, coming towards me with a goofy grin on his face.

"Oh. Yeah, okay. I can do that," he said, flexing his arm and pumping his bicep muscle for effect. It was pretty impressive, but I schooled my features to remain impassive.

"Be right back," he promised. But he was so focused on staring at me, he walked right into the door. I laughed along with everyone else; it was impossible not to. He left the room with the goofy grin still on his face.

"Miss Livingston, please take Mr. Kucharski's seat. He can have the one he's bringing in." Mr. Adams gestured out into the room.

I went into panic mode. I don't know why, but suddenly the idea of being next to the boy who might be a Neutral had me freaking out. I've never seen a Rainbow do what he did before, but neither have I seen a Neutral do it either. People either fawned over or disregarded me ... at least in the beginning. No one had ever gone from smiling to angry in such a short period of time. Usually it took Neutrals a solid couple weeks to start hating me.

"Oh, no, that's okay," I said. "I don't want to steal anyone's spot." I scanned the room, hoping I'd see another place open somewhere else. But the room was jam-packed. I wasn't even sure where he was going to put the desk the other student was bringing back.

"It's fine, just go take it. He needs to sit up front anyway. It'll help him concentrate."

I gave him a small nod and walked over to the seat, keeping my eyes glued on the guy who seemed mad at me. It was better than encouraging the others, and not as weird as staring at the floor the whole way.

He was focusing on the surface of his desk almost the whole time I came towards him, but then when I was just a few feet away, he looked up. He didn't smile, and he didn't frown. He just stared at me.

I grinned, suddenly shy. I so wanted to know what he was thinking at that moment. *Does he want to be my best friend like everyone else in here? Or could he just ignore me without a problem, like Jasmine? Is it possible he's someone I could be near and not worry about my safety or his?*

Before my butt was completely in the seat, he jumped out of his and stumbled to the front of the classroom. Suddenly he was in a huge hurry to get the heck out of the room, like he'd forgotten he had a very urgent appointment somewhere far away. Or like I was a disease and he didn't want to catch it.

Mr. Adams told him to sit down, but he ignored the teacher and eventually ran out, giving up on asking permission.

I stared at the empty space where he'd been sitting, at a total loss about what had just happened. No one had ever reacted like that being around me. Maybe it should have hurt my feelings to be so completely and obviously dissed, but all it did was make me more curious about him.

No one else seemed to be concerned at all with his reaction. The kids sitting near me just smiled at me and nodded hello, acting like Malcolm hadn't just run out of there like a bat flying out of hell. The boy in front of me turned halfway around in his seat and whispered, "Hello."

I gave him a watery smile and looked again at the desk next to me. There was an old, battered and partially torn navy blue backpack on the floor next to the seat. It looked mostly empty, sagging almost flat. I couldn't help but wonder what the boy who acted like a ghost kept in his school bag.

I settled into my chair, putting my purse over the back of the seat before turning to face the teacher. He had moved back behind his desk and was speaking about something, but I didn't hear any of it. All I could think about was the boy who'd run at the first sign of being near me. Maybe Jasmine was right. Maybe he was a ghost that just wanted to be left alone.

But ghost or not, he's one of the cutest guys I've ever seen. He isn't flashy handsome like a lot of the guys in the room. He's more understated hot - like bad boy hot. I think his eyes are brown, but I could be wrong about that. He was wearing light-colored jeans, well-worn and torn at the knee, with a dark green long-sleeved cotton shirt. His hair was just plain. Nothing about him said he was interested in anything but blending in. I smiled to myself when I thought about how he and I had that in common.

I make it a point to never be fashionable. It attracts attention that I'm already trying to avoid. My hair always just hangs straight in the most basic of styles. The only thing I ever do to it is sometimes put it in a ponytail when it's hot or wear a hat over it when the temperature drops. It's easier to be plain than stylish and it's definitely cheaper for my parents. But I wish I could do things differently sometimes. I see things in the store with bright colors and wild patterns and dream about putting them on. I always walk away, though. The few times I'd stepped outside the box of plain vanilla that needs to be my life, it had been disastrous. Everyone is better off with me looking like a dork.

The door opened with a bang, and the guy whose chair I took was there, shoving a desk through the door. "Got it! Had to go two halls over, though." He sounded like he was expecting a medal.

"Thank you, Caden. Could you please just add it to that row right there and then take a seat in it?"

He stopped his furniture moving and looked over at his old seat. "But..." He gestured at me with his chin.

"You can go get your things, but I want you up here near me."

"Aw, Mr. Adams. Come on, man."

"No arguments." He looked at the class. "As I was saying..."

I blocked out the lesson, watching Caden maneuver the desk and then make his way over to where I was sitting. I looked up when he stopped next to my desk.

"Sorry," I said, feeling bad about getting him moved to the front.

"No prob. I'll just get my stuff." He grinned at me and bent over to grab his backpack from the floor next to me.

I expected him to turn around and go, but he didn't. He kept his eyes on me and sank down in the desk next to me, not fitting very well since he'd gone in on the wrong side, where the desk attached to the seat. His legs were squished together and he had to hunch into himself to fit in the small space. "So. Where're you from?"

"Mr. Kucharski!"

My mouth fell open, but I wasn't sure what to say, so I remained silent. I looked at the teacher and then back at Caden.

"I'll sit here, Mr. A. Malcolm's out running your errand for ya." Caden didn't even look at the teacher. He just kept grinning at me.

"Mr. Kucharski, if you don't get up from that desk right now and take the one I've assigned to you, you're going to find yourself in a week of detention. Right now! Snap to it!"

Caden rolled his eyes and then winked at me. "Catch you later," he whispered. And then in a louder voice, he said, "I'm comin', I'm comin'. Don't get your Calvins in a bunch."

"That'll be five days detention," said the teacher sourly, pulling a pad of paper from his desk drawer. "Would you like to double down or are you good with this?"

"Nah, man. I'm good with the five." Caden sounded defeated, shuffling to the front of the class with his bag hanging at his side.

The whole class laughed.

"Excellent. Now we can get back to Dickinson. Let's talk about how her isolation may have contributed to her verse..."

My mind wandered again. I'd read some of Emily Dickinson's poetry in my last school, too. Normally, I'd find the discussion worthwhile, but now I found the idea of a boy who couldn't stand to be near me much more interesting.

## Chapter Five
# Malcolm

I RUSHED INTO THE CLASSROOM and down the first aisle of seats, ignoring the students gathering their things and standing to leave. The room was filled with talking and laughing, giving me the perfect distraction I needed.

"Mr. McNamara!"

Or so I thought.

I looked up at Mr. Adams and waved, letting him know I'd be there to talk to him once I had my things. I kept my gaze low after that, hoping that new girl would be gone by the time I got to my desk. I took it easy, giving people extra time and space to get past me so I could delay as much as possible.

I finally arrived at the end of the last aisle as the noise in the room was dying down. The dark form of my backpack was clearly visible on the ground just up ahead. Zeroing in on it, I made my way past the few stragglers who hadn't yet left the spots next to their seats, trying not to touch any of them on my way.

Just being in my presence is enough to get people feeling the darkness, but touching me was a whole other level of awful, especially for the most sensitive ones. The Miserables usually figured that out pretty quickly and then did whatever they could to touch me as often as possible. It's why I wear long-sleeved shirts, even in summer. I have zero hope of ever having a tan, but it's better than the alternative.

I was almost within reach of my bag, and I was stretching over to get it from the seat behind, when it sailed up over the top of my chair and desk. My hand grasped only air near the ground.

"I got it for ya, buddy," said Caden. He was standing in the next aisle over, blocking people from leaving in his enthusiasm for helping me out. Or in his enthusiasm for getting in the new girl's face. It was kind of hard to tell what his goal was the way he was standing there hugging my backpack to his chest and grinning at the girl who stood immobile in front of him.

I walked farther up the aisle, keeping the row of desks between us. I avoided looking at the girl at all.

"Hand it over." I held out my hand, trying to grab the handle on top.

Caden twisted to the side a little, keeping me from being able to reach it. "What you got in here?" He acted like he was going to unzip it.

"Don't," I said, reaching over farther to grab it.

My fingers accidentally brushed over his, and he let go of the bag with that hand like he'd been burned.

"Dude." He stared at me, his other hand just barely keeping a grip on it.

"What? Just give it." I yanked the bag away and let it fall to the chair between us.

Caden stood there, looking confused. And then he glanced down.

That's when I saw that the new girl had her hand on his forearm.

"I was just trying to help," Caden said. He sounded lost.

"My name's Rae."

I didn't know if the girl was talking to Caden or me, but I didn't stick around to find out. I started walking, pulling my bag out of the chair as I went. When it was free, I used the momentum to sling it over my shoulder.

"Where are you going?" asked Caden. "Wait up! I'll go with you!"

I moved faster. I had my eyes on the door, and I was totally focused. *Get the hell out. Don't look back. Get away from both of them.*

A hand closed over my shoulder and held me back.

I yanked myself sideways, ready to yell at Caden to leave me the hell alone, but found myself facing Mr. Adams. I slapped my lips shut, stopping myself from doing something really stupid.

"Malcolm?" he said, tentatively. "You okay, son?"

I blinked a few times, trying to get my head on straight. I wasn't used to adults being that nice to me. "Uh, yeah. I'm fine."

"Do you want to explain your disappearance, perhaps? Try and convince me I shouldn't give you detention?"

"Uh ... yeah?"

He raised an eyebrow at me. "Well? I'm all ears."

"I ... uh ... had to take a smoke break?"

"Wrong answer." He walked back to his desk and wrote out a detention slip. "See that you come on time. Oh ... and plan to stay for the entire period next class. You take off like that again, and you'll be spending some time in the principal's office."

I took the detention slip from him with a frown. "Sorry. I won't do it again."

"See that you don't. Be in detention hall starting tomorrow."

I looked down at the paper, my eyes bugging out of my head when I read what was printed there. "*Five days* of detention? Are you *kidding* me?"

Mr. Adams gave me a mean smile. "Consider it an early Christmas present."

"But it's March!"

"I could advance you an Easter gift too, if you'd like."

I sighed in defeat. "No. Christmas is good."

"Fine. See you Monday." He gave me a fake smile before returning to his desk to shuffle some papers around.

*Asshole.*

I walked out of the room, not looking back. Other students were coming out and going in at the same time, most of them looking down at cell phones to send or receive text messages. I let them push me around and jostle me out into the hall.

*What a dick. Five days of detention? That's total bullshit. All I did was leave. What if I was sick or had to take a crap? People shouldn't get detention for that.*

"Dude, you got shit on too." Caden was at my side and obviously feeling very happy about my situation.

"Yeah, thanks, I didn't realize it until you pointed it out." I sped up.

"Hey, I got five days too! That's cool, right? You and me can hang out." He kept pace with me, knocking into people and ignoring their cries of annoyance.

I said nothing.

"So, what about that chick, Rae? Pretty sweet, huh?"

"If you say so."

"Don't tell me you're not into her. That'd be a fucking lie, man. She's hot as shit."

"Sounds attractive."

"Don't be such a downer, dude. You know she's cute. Why don't you just admit it?"

I looked over at him sharply. Miserables never tell me to cheer up. They like it when I get pissed.

"What'd you say?"

Caden punched me. "You heard me. Don't be a douche. Come on, let's go. We're doing basketball in gym today, and you're on my team. Yo!" He held up his hand for a high five, and I responded without even thinking about it. The crack of our hands echoed over the heads around us.

It was so strange to see him happy and all lit up like this around me, I forgot to try and ditch him. Or frown. I smiled all the way to gym class, listening to him cut up about Mr. Adams and the gnarly hairs that were always climbing out of our teacher's nostrils and ears.

# Chapter Six
# Rae

I WAS HOPING SINCE IT was my first day that I'd be able to skip out of phys ed, but no such luck. The husky P.E. teacher handed me a pair of sweatpants that were two sizes too big, a t-shirt with the school's logo on it, gray socks, and a pair of used kicks in my size.

"There you go. Everyone dresses out. And don't come here crying to me about being on your period, either. Everyone participates, every class, every week, all year long. End of story." She looked at me with a curious expression on her face before smiling. It was pretty clear this wasn't a normal thing for her. She seemed surprised by the fact that her teeth were showing, hurrying to cover them with her lips after a few seconds.

"Okaaaay," I said, taking the clothes and turning slowly towards the locker room.

"I don't mean to be rude," she said at my back as I walked away.

I waved over my shoulder, saying nothing.

Someone laughed. "Did I just hear The Hatchet apologize to you?"

I looked to my left. Jasmine was standing there wearing her gym clothes, a modified version of the ones I had in my arms. The sleeves had been cut off her shirt, and some words were written in permanent marker on the front of her pants.

"I guess." I said, shrugging. The teacher's name was Hatcher, but her nickname seemed pretty appropriate. She had a pretty severe face and very short hair that could very well have been cut with an axe.

Jasmine threw an article of clothing into her locker before slamming it shut. "Somebody write that shit down. *The Hatchet apologizes*. Wonder what the occasion is. Maybe she got laid last night or something."

"Isn't she a lesbian?" asked a girl just down the bench from Jasmine.

Jasmine rolled her eyes and shook her head. "Somebody put that girl out of her misery, would you please?"

"What? What'd I say?" The girl looked around and then gave up on finding an answer. "Shut up, *Butts*." She stormed off while the other girls standing nearby giggled.

I walked over and put my things down on the bench next to Jasmine, relieved she and I had this class together. I like sports, but school gym class was pretty much universally lame, no matter what district or state I'd been in. "Do we have assigned lockers?"

"Nope. Just bring a lock and use whatever's free."

I held out my purse that was still hooked over my shoulder, wondering what I should do. I hadn't brought my lock, which was stupid because I knew better. Several of the schools I'd been in before had the same policy. Most of them gave me a few days' grace period, but still. I should have known. A girl doesn't go through eight different high schools and not learn a few basics.

"Use mine for today or until you get one." She opened her locker again and gestured to the inside before sitting down to tie her purple high-top basketball shoes. The ragged pieces of multi-colored cloth tied on her wrists flapped around as her hands moved.

"You don't mind?" I put my purse down on the bench and used my toes to pry off the back of my other shoe, balancing by holding onto the wall of lockers. I'd worn short black boots with black socks and jeans - nothing that would work for gym class, so I was stuck with the loaner outfit the teacher had given me. I looked at it with distaste. It was hideous, but would probably be perfect for keeping people away. At least it smelled clean.

"I offered, so I guess the answer is no, I don't mind." She reached in the locker and pulled out a pack of cigarettes.

I watched her, wondering if she was going to light one up in here. I couldn't imagine the Hatcher lady just ignoring that.

Jasmine caught me staring. "What are you looking at?"

"You with that cigarette. I was just wondering if you were going to smoke it in here."

"Are you an anti-smoking campaign on legs too?" She tucked the cigarette behind her ear.

"Um, no. I don't smoke, but if you want to that's your business." The truth is I think smoking is dumb, but I wasn't going to offend the only friend I might ever have in this place by telling her that.

"Good, because I like smoking. It calms my nerves."

"Good." I smiled at her. I was anxious to change the subject, so I smiled and said, "Sorry if my shoes stink."

Jasmine looked down at my feet. "You're putting smelly shoes in my locker?"

I grimaced. "I might be. I was nervous today. First day and stuff."

She sighed. "Fine. But you owe me one. And if you get any of that stink on my stuff, I'm going to be pissed."

I refrained from telling her that her smoke smell was getting all over *my* stuff. Beggars can't be choosy about stink. "Deal." I shoved my shoes in on top of hers and then put my purse in above them on a hook. I was dressed in the borrowed clothes in less than two minutes and cinching up the drawstring when I heard people laughing.

I turned around to see what they were doing and noticed a group of girls standing in the doorway, looking out into the gym.

"What's up with them?" I asked, folding my clothes and putting them in the locker.

Jasmine shut the door and attached her lock, turning the dial to make sure it wouldn't open. "Who knows. Probably some dumb-shit acting stupid. Chicks around here dig that stuff."

We walked over to join them. "You don't?"

"No. I like more mature guys. College guys."

"Do you have a boyfriend?" We walked out of the locker room and into the big basketball court area. There was one full-size court going length-wise and two smaller ones going the other direction, with a total of six basketball nets around the periphery. Bleachers were accordioned in around most of the gym, but one set was pulled halfway out, and it was there that some of the students were gathering for the start of class. The sounds of sneakers squeaking on the court and the echoing of basketballs bouncing all over came at us from every direction.

Jasmine talked louder to be heard over all of it. "Not right now. I don't have time for guys. I'm too busy with ... stuff."

"What kind of stuff?"

"Stuff stuff." She walked ahead of me and took big steps up to the top of the bleachers, sitting down well away from the others.

I looked at my options and decided pretty quickly to follow. Several girls were smiling at me in obvious invitation, but I didn't want to encourage them. They'd be on me soon enough.

I got to the last row and walked over to join Jasmine. Sitting down, I gazed out across the gym. Groups of guys were standing around below us on the court, some of them busy taking turns at making baskets. A few others were walking on their hands, seeing who could go the farthest across the floor before falling down or knocking into someone else.

One of the guys was making everyone laugh.

Jasmine shook her head and breathed out a sigh of annoyance.

"He was in my last class," I said.

"Kootch. Total dumbass goofball."

"Kootch? I hope that's a nickname."

"Yeah. It's short for Kucharski. Polish or something."

"Do you know him?"

She looked at me with a frown. "Why, you interested in him?"

"No," I nudged her a little with my arm, "not at all. He was just really funny in my last class too, so I was just wondering about him is all."

"He lives next door to me, so yeah, I know him a little."

I looked from her to him, wondering if there might be something to the way she'd said that. "Boy next door, huh?"

"Ew. No. Don't say it like that."

"Why not?" We watched as he walked on his hands and then fell over into a somewhat graceful cartwheel. "He's got a nice body. He seems nice."

"Yeah, he's all muscle and dumbassedness and no brains."

I laughed. "Dumbassedness? New word."

"Don't try to deny it makes total sense."

"Oh, I won't. I get it completely." I smiled, loving this feeling of two girlfriends talking about guys. It felt so normal, and normal for me was so *abnormal* it was like a gift. I would cherish it as long as it lasted.

Kootch took that moment to try and do a breakdancing move that didn't work out so well. The sound of his head hitting the floor made me flinch.

Jasmine gestured casually. "Exhibit A. Kootch face-plants into the wood floor. Total fail. Dumbassedness in action."

All the guys jogged over to see if he was okay - all of them but one. The lone unconcerned classmate only caught my eye because he was standing off to the side by himself, stopping himself from going over to check on his friend with obvious effort. He took a half step out towards the court and then turned back around, shaking his head.

"There's that guy again," I said, mostly to myself.

Jasmine turned her attention away from Kootch and was staring at Malcolm now. "The ghost. You still on him?"

"I'm not *on* him, I'm just ... curious."

"I told you, he's a ghost. You're not going to get to know him so you should just let it drop."

"That sounds like a challenge to me." I don't know why I said that. I shouldn't have been trying to get to know anyone at this school, least of all a boy who's bigger and stronger than me. A Rainbow's want and need can be such scary things when paired with superior strength.

"Go for it. If you think you can get him to even give you the time of day, when he's turned down pretty much every girl at this school, then he's all yours. Trust me, no one gets through to that guy. Many have tried. All have failed. Crash and burn. Horrible to watch, really."

I shrugged, acting like it didn't matter to me. "No, I'm not interested in him like that. I was just wondering what his deal is."

"His deal is that he's a ghost." She stood, knocking me in the arm with the back of her hand. "Come on. Let's go shoot some hoops."

"I'm pretty good at basketball, you know." I made sure to put the challenge in my voice as we walked down the bleachers.

"I'm better." She walked out onto the floor, stealing the first ball that came her way, ignoring the cries of the offended guys and walking over to the farthest net. She stopped when she was at the free-throw line, bent down, and put the ball between her legs, launching it at the net granny-style.

I laughed when it went in.

Jasmine made a gesture with her hand, imitating the ball going in. "Swish. All net, bitches. Let's see you beat that." She turned around and blew me a kiss.

"What are we playing?"

"I have the letter D. First one to spell the word wins. You have to make a shot from where I did or you don't get a letter."

"What are we spelling?" I asked, taking my spot and aiming the ball, using the technique my dad had taught me many years ago.

"You'll see."

I launched the ball up, putting just the right amount of backspin on it. *All net. Oh, yeah.* "Swish. Letter D for me too."

Jasmine nodded. "Respect. That wasn't half bad. But can you do this?" She did a lay up, once again managing to throw the ball up from between her knees and getting it in the basket. It was so not graceful.

I couldn't stop laughing.

"What? Jealous?" she asked, bouncing the ball as she walked over my way. She switched from dribbling with her right to her left.

"Jealous of your granny action? I don't think so."

"Hey, Rae!"

Jasmine and I looked over at the same time as Kootch came jogging up to us, dribbling a ball at his side.

"Check it," he said as he cruised by, throwing the ball up in a casual toss as he went under the net. It bounced off the rim and out into the court where someone else snatched it up.

"Nice moves, Kootch. Been practicing a long time?" Jasmine snickered.

He stopped jogging and turned, walking back in our direction. Gym class had barely started, but he was already sweating. "Don't be jealous, JB. You know you want this." He stroked his hands from the top of his chest down to his waist.

She feigned retching and then swallowed hard. "Oh, man. I just vomited in my mouth."

Kootch stopped in front of me. "You'll have to forgive little JB there. She's had the hots for me since she was five. Poor kid. I had to let her down easy like eighteen times so far."

Jasmine stared daggers at him. "Kootch, get your stank-ass jock off my court before I have to school your stupid dick in front of all those girls." She jerked her head over to the gaggle of them sitting on the bleachers. They'd moved down to be closer to the court. Several of them were looking over at us.

"Oh, you wanna play, JB?" He started moving back and forth, pantomiming dribbling an invisible ball or something, staring at her no matter where his body went.

"Stop calling me that idiotic name." She stared at him, her expression clearly saying she thought he was a complete fool.

"What? JB? But that's your name. Come on, let's do this. Two on two."

Jasmine snorted. "Your math skills are blowing my mind, Kootch. I count three." She gestured to me, her, and him.

I held up my hands. "Don't count me in on this. I'm just watching. Do one-on-one."

"No, you're not, Rae-Rae. You're in. And I got my wingman over there." Kootch gestured to the far corner of the room.

Jasmine and I looked over.

*Malcolm.*

The idea of playing basketball with him got my blood going. I spoke before I could think too hard about it. "Okay, I'll play if you can get him over here."

Jasmine frowned. "He won't play with us. He never plays. He takes a zero for anything but soccer."

"Why only soccer?" I couldn't help but wonder what made that sport different.

"I don't know. I guess he likes to kick the shit out of things." Jasmine grabbed a ball that was rolling by. "Go get him, and we'll play. Otherwise, beat it, Kootch. We're busy." She crouched down and launched a granny shot at the basket. When it went in she did a funky dance, not caring who watched. "Swish-it. Swish-it real good." When she was done shaking her hips a few more times, she walked over and retrieved the ball from under the net where it was still bouncing weakly.

Kootch took off towards Malcolm, waving as he went. "Come on, man! I got us a game going!"

Jasmine brought the ball over and handed it to me. "He's not going to come. Your turn. I have letter O."

I spared one last look for Malcolm who was busy shaking his head no, before walking over and lining myself up at Jasmine's last point. The ball was just leaving my hands when Kootch let out a big whoop and threw me off. The ball bounced off the rim and came flying back at me.

"Bummer for you," said Jasmine, taking the ball away from me. She turned to say something and froze with her mouth hanging open, staring at a point behind me.

I turned to see Kootch and Malcolm coming towards us. Malcolm didn't seem at all happy about the situation.

"Well, well, well ... would you look at that," said Jasmine, her tone low so only I'd hear her. "The ghost is coming to play b-ball with us. Huh. Wonders never cease." She nudged me in the back. "Maybe he likes you or something."

# Chapter Seven
# Malcolm

I SAW CADEN COMING FOR me, and I should have taken off. But I stood there like an idiot, and then before I could do anything about it, he was jumping up and down in front of me all hyped up about something. His voice was a couple notches higher in pitch than normal.

"Dude, come on! It's two-on-two with the new girl and Butts."

"No, thanks." I tried to move around him to go sit on the bleachers. I was happy taking a zero as my grade for non-participation. Basketball tended to be a contact sport in my experience, and when people mixed physical contact with me and the natural competitiveness of sports, it usually ended up being a pretty potent combination of anger and drive. I've seen plenty of bloody noses in my time. Way more than I should have in basketball.

Caden blocked my progress. "Whaddya mean, no thanks? You're not going to take another zero are you?"

"Yes, I am, actually." I stepped to the other side, but Caden blocked me there, too.

"Dude, stop being such a lame-ass pussy all the time. Come on, I like this girl. Be my wingman. Keep Butts busy while I make my move."

I battled with myself. Being near the new girl was a mistake. I knew it was. I wasn't so worried about Jasmine; she didn't seem all that bothered by me either way. But the new girl had a chance at staying happy if she could just keep the hell away from me.

The only thing I couldn't shake was the idea that if I could get Caden to fall for her - and her to fall for him - maybe he'd finally detach himself from me. And then he could have a chance at being happy. As long as he was stuck to me like this, he was doomed to be a Miserable for life.

The risk was worth it. It was only one game. *How much trouble can I cause with a single game of two-on-two?* "Fine. One game and that's it."

Caden jumped up really high and whooped so loud it echoed all over the gym. "Whoot! *Yes!* Come on, dude. I already got warmed up. You need to take a few shots before we start." He snagged a ball that was rolling by and bounce-passed it to me. "Come on, take a shot over there."

He pointed to the basket next to where the girls were playing.

I dribbled the ball very unenthusiastically over towards the net, and when I was about ten feet away, I launched the ball up without aiming. It completely missed the backboard and banged into the closed bleachers behind. Several people turned around and laughed.

Caden just stood there staring at me, arms hanging at his sides. "Is that why you sit out every period? 'Cause you suck balls at sports?"

I couldn't help but laugh. "Fuck you, Kootch. I'm just cold, that's all."

Truth is, there's no point in me getting competitive and trying too hard because it's too easy for me to win. When I turn up my emotions, they overwhelm people and throw off whatever concentration they might have, making it possible for me to win without even trying. I'm actually pretty good at basketball, but it's better when I play stupid and let other people have the glory.

That way no one gets hurt. I'd given up long ago on the idea of being a superstar. Superstars live in the limelight, and I have to stay in the shadows.

Caden grabbed the ball and passed it hard to me. The force of it stung my hands.

"Stop being a homo and throw the damn ball like you're s'posed to."

"A homo? Come on, man." I frowned at him, bouncing the ball a couple times, my shoulders moving up and down with the rhythm.

"Yeah, you're right. Calling you a homo is an insult to homos everywhere. Stop being a chick and throw the ball like a man."

"Wow. I wonder how the new girl will feel about that one."

"She's gonna love me. Now throw the fucking ball in the god-damn net before I come over there and take your man-card away."

I stared at him long and hard for a few seconds. And then I threw the ball up without even looking at the net. It bounced once off the backboard and went in.

Caden nodded his head in respect. "Well, all right. Now *that's* what I'm talkin' about. Come on, dude. Let's go wipe the court with their sweet asses." He loped over and grabbed the ball. After dribbling it in my direction a few steps, he turned and faced the girls, waiting for me to catch up.

Caden had his game face on now, and for the first time this period he had his voice low enough that only I could hear it. "Okay, now, here's the plan. We'll go in there and act like we suck a little. It'll be an act for me, but you can just go ahead and suck like normal. And then when they think they have us bending over and kissing our own asses, we give it to 'em."

"Give it to 'em?" I raised an eyebrow at him.

"Yeah. We cram the ball down their throats and show 'em who's boss."

"Your knowledge and skill around members of the opposite sex is a wonder to behold, Caden."

"If you don't call me Kootch I'm gonna get pissed. Caden's a stupid name."

"And Kootch is ..."

"Fucking cool."

"Okay, Kootch it is. But just in case you weren't aware, some girls call their hootch a kootch. So maybe it's not as cool a name as you think."

"Dude, shut the fuck up."

"Yeah, okay." I had to stop. Messing with him was fun, but it was too much like friendship to be safe. I was a little bummed about having to blow him off all the time, because as obnoxious as he was, he was at least amusing. Taking the zero in class always made the time go so much slower, watching students run around and have fun while my butt got numb on the bench.

"Now, let me do all the talking. I don't want you to mess this up," he said as we got closer to the girls.

I said nothing, instead focusing on looking at anything but the new girl.

"Okay, chicks," announced Kootch, "the men have arrived. Get ready to lose this two-on-two in a matter of fifteen minutes, max."

Jasmine was all about getting down to business. "What're the rules? I don't want you crying later when you lose that we broke some imaginary rule."

"There will be no crying unless it's by you two, but here are the rules: First team to five wins. No elbows, no touching the jewels, and no leaving the half-court here."

"Jewels?" asked the new girl.

"The nads. Testicles. Man muffins. You know, jewels. Hands off the merchandise."

"Wow, you guys play rough here," she said.

Jasmine snorted. "He wishes. He keeps laying that rule out every week hoping to tempt someone into actually touching them, but so far no joy."

"Shut up, *Butts*. What do you know about my nads? They get touched all the time."

"I know nothing, thank the Lord. And no, before you decide to volunteer the information, we don't want to know who's been touching your junk other than you. Come on, are we going to play or stand around talking about your hairy bean bags all day?"

I laughed. I couldn't help myself. Glancing up, I caught the new girl's eye. She was laughing too. *Damn. That dimple again.*

I looked away and snagged the ball out of Kootch's hands. "Come on. We got the ball."

I dribbled it over to the half-court line and waited for Kootch to get in position.

"I'm open!" he yelled, moving over to stand to the right of the basket.

Jasmine ran over and stood between him and me, blocking his access to my pass.

"Aw, come on, Butts. Go get Malcolm. Rae's got me covered over here."

Rae was standing closer to me, not doing much of anything.

"Play basketball and shut up," Jasmine said, arms flapping all over the place. The ripped pieces of cloth that served as her bracelets looked like tiny banners flying in the wind, a rainbow blur covering Kootch's face.

Kootch tried to run around her, but she checked him with her hip and sent him flying.

"Hey! Foul, man! Butts is using her butt to block me!"

"Can't hack it? Stay off the court," she responded, turning around and flapping her arms in his face again.

The new girl - Rae - started coming for me. She looked so innocent and sweet jogging over in those huge baggy sweatpants and funky sneakers, it distracted me or something. It was only after she dove at me and slapped the ball away that I realized she might know more about the sport than I'd given her credit for.

"Hey!" I shouted as the ball spun out of my hands and she ran by, recovering it and turning it into a nice dribble by her side.

"Yes!" yelled Jasmine. "Go, Rae, go!"

Rae dribbled the ball towards the net, leaving me in the dust. She was totally focused on her goal of getting that first point; I could tell by the determined expression on her face. Her tongue was stuck out in concentration.

But Kootch had other ideas. He spun away from Jasmine and lunged towards Rae.

She saw him coming and screamed, launching the ball up into the air.

It sailed over his head and arched towards the basket, but the force she'd put on it wasn't enough to get it all the way there, and it angled down a foot away from the rim.

Jasmine had already moved and was standing under the net. She caught the ball and granny-shot it up onto the backboard, earning their first point.

"Yes! Take *that*, Kootch!" Jasmine strutted over and high-fived Rae.

"Thanks for covering for me," said Rae to Jasmine. She grabbed the ball off a bounce and passed it to me.

Kootch punched me in the arm. "Come on. Half-court. Time to stop fucking around." He wasn't laughing anymore.

I rolled my eyes, knowing we were in for a serious game now. Kootch wasn't the losing type, especially when there were girls on the other team.

I passed him the ball and walked parallel with him to the net.

He was doing all kinds of fancy moves with the ball, passing it between his legs, spinning around, juking-out no one at all. The girls just stood back and watched him, shaking their heads.

"You want a piece-a this? You want a piece-a this? Come on now, girls. You got lucky once. You aren't gonna get lucky twice. Unless the Kootch decides to *let* you get lucky."

He accidentally bounced the ball off the top of his toe, and it went rolling straight over the court to Rae.

She picked it up, pivoted, and tossed it up into the net.

"That's what we call a swish, bitches." Jasmine held up her hand for a high-five and Rae slapped it without even moving her feet.

"That's two," said Rae, looking back at us and grinning. She caught my eye and turned to face me. Reaching up, she tucked some hair behind her ear. "Ready to surrender?" she asked.

My heart stopped beating for a second, and then it raced to catch up. Before I could answer, Kootch was there in our faces.

"Surrender? You must be outta yo' mind, woman. Never surrender! Never say die!"

"I think I heard that in a movie once," said Jasmine, staring at him with no expression on her face.

"Yeah, best movie ever. I wrote it. It's called *Kootch Is Going to Fucking Win This Game*." He snagged the ball out of Jasmine's hands and ran to the half court line. "Come on, Malcolm! Get your ass in gear! You're giving them the game!"

I jogged over, the whole time wondering if that double meaning in Rae's question was intentional or if I was just imagining things. It had to be me just dreaming, because there's nothing to surrender. There is no game or challenge or anything like that between us, other than this stupid basketball match. She's just naturally sexy or something. She acts like she doesn't even realize it about herself. She's totally going to take Kootch down, and he'll have no idea it's happening until it's all over. Hopefully, she'll be gentle with him. He's a dipshit a lot of the time, but underneath it all, I think he's a good guy.

Kootch gave up on the whole idea of teamwork and took a shot after walking two steps. It wasn't pretty, but it went in.

"Yeah! Three points!"

"One point, dumbass. You get one." Jasmine walked over and took the ball.

"It's just an expression, Butts. And don't call me a dumbass."

She was dribbling the ball and chewing her gum really obnoxiously, walking backwards to the half-court line. "I call it like I see it, *dumbass*."

"Listen, Butts, I'm not the one with the word *ass* in my name, okay, so just put your shit away."

"Why don't you come over here and *make* me put my shit away, Kootch? Or should I call you Hootch?"

"Listen, Buttface, I'm warning you..." Kootch started walking towards her.

"Uh-oh," I said softly to no one in particular.

"What? What're you going to do?" Jasmine was totally taunting him now and she knew it. She was actually smiling, and she didn't do that very often. "You gonna throw a rock at me again?"

ELLE CASEY

I frowned. Rae had been walking over and she stopped next to me.

"What's she talking about?" Rae asked.

"I have no idea."

Kootch threw his arms up. "I told you I didn't throw that fucking rock!" He was roaring mad now.

I took off after him without thinking too hard about it. I was just afraid he was going to do something really stupid, and I wanted to stop it before it went too far.

Rae apparently had the same thought, because she ran right next to me. We both reached Kootch, just as he was getting in Jasmine's face. His jaw was bouncing as he held in his anger with gritted teeth.

"Yes, you did!" Jasmine yelled. "It was totally you, you prick! And I still have the scar from it, too!" She jabbed a finger towards the corner of her eye.

"Yeah, well, it's an improvement. You should *thank* me."

She shoved him in the chest.

He didn't even budge, but he did roar. And then he squatted down and grabbed her around the waist, picking her up about a foot above his head as he squeezed her to his chest.

Jasmine screamed in either fright or surprise, beating him about the head and shoulders. "Put me down, you fucking lunatic! Ahhhh!! Get him off me!!"

Rae was on him in a second, trying to pull his arms away from her teammate. But Kootch was much stronger than her, and she looked like a little mosquito buzzing around him, having no effect whatsoever.

Kootch started spinning around in a circle, making it impossible for Rae to help her friend. "Say you're sorry!" he yelled.

Jasmine poked him in the eyes on purpose. "Sorry for what?! Telling the truth! Never!"

I stepped over to help, worried either someone was going to get hurt or we were going to get busted by the teacher. I was trying to grab him by the shirt sleeve, and I did get a grip on it, but his movement carried me sideways when I didn't let go. I accidentally slammed into Rae, knocking her off her feet.

I had a split second thought that I needed to help her not fall on the hard floor, but only succeeded in going down with her. We landed in a tangle, me on top of her and Kootch and Jasmine spinning just above us.

"Owww! Those're my eyes, Butts!" he yelled.

She slapped him in the face, first one cheek and then the other. "Good! See how you like it!"

I struggled to roll away from Rae. I was freaking out that touching her was not only feeling way too good, but it was going to hurt her in ways that were too awful to think about. She was going to get attached and sad and then terrible things would happen.

"Hey! Hey! What's going on over there?!" Mrs. Hatcher the gym teacher had finally decided to make her appearance. The slapping of her feet on the wood floor reached my ears.

Kootch took one step back and got his foot caught in my legs. "Ahhhh!! Buuuuuutts!"

He went down in slow motion, Jasmine high above him and still in his arms.

Everyone screamed, including me.

# Chapter Eight
# Rae

EVERYTHING WAS GOING SO WELL, and then Jasmine and Kootch had to get into it with each other. One second they were arguing, and the next thing I knew Malcolm and I were running over to break them apart. I nearly had a heart attack when Kootch grabbed Jasmine and lifted her up, spinning her around. If I hadn't heard the angry words between them, I might have thought he was just being playful; and if I hadn't seen her slapping and poking him, I might have thought she was his girlfriend being swung around in fun. But that was definitely not the case with them, and I had to rescue my new friend.

I was reaching up to grab Kootch's arm and stop him from spinning anymore when Malcolm slammed into me.

I was so stunned, I didn't realize what had happened until I was on the ground and he was on top of me. All the air had been pushed out of my lungs and I couldn't breathe for a few seconds, but that didn't stop me from feeling every inch of his body as it lay on mine.

He was heavy and warm. I could smell his scent - not cologne exactly but something definitely male. Some of his hair tickled my cheek as he rolled to the side. Part of me wished he had stayed right where he was, but a girl like me can't have that kind of contact without terrible things happening later. Unfortunately, I think it made me want it that much more.

An adult's voice shouted out across the gym. "Hey! Hey! What's going on over there?!"

*The teacher. Oh no!* I scrambled to get my arms and hands under me so I could get up.

And then the mountain that was Kootch started to fall.

I screamed, and so did a bunch of other kids around us. Even Malcolm yelled, holding up his hands as if to stop it all from happening.

The full weight of Kootch holding Jasmine landed across my middle, and I grunted hard. I continued with frantic wheezing as all kinds of scrambling was happening on top of me.

"Let! Me! Go! You complete idiot assjockey!" yelled Jasmine.

"I'm trying! I'm trying! Ow, stop kicking me you nutbag!"

"All of you get up! Get up right this second! Do you hear me?!" Mrs. Hatcher had joined the fray, leaning in to try and grab bodies.

I just laid there trying to get my breath back as everyone rolled away and kicked around in their attempts to get free.

The teacher grabbed Kootch's shirt and hauled him to his feet. "Detention! All of you have detention, do you hear me?! Physical violence is *not* tolerated in my class. That is bad sportsmanship! Bad sportsmanship!"

She pulled Jasmine up by the wrist next, taking her by the shoulders when she was standing finally and setting her off to the side, away from Kootch.

Jasmine glared at Kootch as she straightened her t-shirt and pants.

Everyone was on their feet now but me. I looked up at Malcolm, finally able to breathe again.

He held out his hand to help me up, staring at me with a strange expression on his face.

I took his hand and used the leverage he provided to stand. His fingers were really warm, and I didn't want to let them go when I was up. Something about him made me want to hold on ... to cling. He was like a life raft and I was lost at sea.

But he dropped my fingers like they were burning him, and turned away.

I let my arm fall to my side, staring at the floor as the teacher continued to lecture us.

"What were you thinking, Caden? You know you can't touch girls like that. I thought you knew better. Maybe I should call your parents."

"Aw, no, Mrs. Hatcher, please don't do that. If you call them ... just don't. I'll clean out the locker room. I'll wash all the towels or whatever."

"The janitor does that work, but believe me, it's tempting. No. I'm giving you two weeks of detention."

"Are you sure you can't just make me clean some lockers or toilets or something?" he asked in a pitiful voice.

"I'm sure. Now go get dressed. You're done for the day."

Kootch walked off, his head hanging low and his feet shuffling on the dusty wood.

"As for you, Jasmine ... how many times have I told you that your mouth is going to get you in serious trouble?"

"About eighty?"

"Don't be a smartbutt with me. Just go get changed, and think about how wrong this could have gone for you if it hadn't been here in this gym with all these witnesses around. A boy as big as Caden in a dark alley could mean big problems for a girl like you."

"Kootch wouldn't have hurt me even if it was in a dark alley. He's not like that." Jasmine sounded offended on his behalf. I was kind of proud of her for sticking up for him like that, even if I wasn't sure if it was true or not.

"You don't know that. You don't know him at all. Everyone has secrets, and most of them things you don't want to know about. Now go." Mrs. Hatcher pointed to the locker rooms.

Jasmine was mumbling as she walked away, but I couldn't hear any of the actual words.

"And you two..." Mrs. Hatcher was staring at me and Malcolm.

Neither of us said a word. We looked at each other for a couple seconds and then at the floor. My heart skipped a beat. *He is so cute. And he doesn't seem to be affected by me. Maybe he's a Neutral! How can I get him to talk to me so I can find out? I can't believe I could have two Neutrals in one class. That would be a first.*

"Malcolm you finally decide to participate and this is what you do?"

"I told you ..."

"Yes, yes, yes ... you've told me ... it's better if you don't participate. But I don't agree. It's better if you *do* participate and be a part of a team. You can't be a loner your whole life."

He looked up sharply at that, sounding angry when he responded. "Yes, I can."

"No. You *can't*." She fixed him with a stern look. "*Everyone* needs people. That's how we're wired. I don't care what color you are, where you're from, or what your sexual preferences are ... everyone needs someone. And you aren't going to find that someone by sitting on the sidelines of life all the time."

Malcolm looked like he wanted to say something, but he just clenched his teeth together, making his jaw stick out at the corners.

She turned to me. "And you, young lady. It's your *first day*, and you're already involved in a physical altercation. I cannot imagine your parents would be very proud of this kind of behavior."

I was almost happy she was mad at me. No one stayed mad at me, not even for a little while. *Could she be a Neutral too? But she'd been so weirdly nice in the locker room...*

"Um, yeah. They'll probably be mad." It was a lie, because even my parents couldn't get mad at me, but it felt normal to say it. Normal is awesome.

"And here I was listening to all this talk around the teachers' lounge about our new valedictorian." She pointed a finger in my face. "If you mess up your gym grade, I'm not going to be responsible for you losing that honor."

"No, ma'am." I tried really hard to look chagrined, not sure I was pulling it off. I wanted to jump and cheer over the idea that she was mad at me, like I was a regular kid in her class who'd messed up.

"Make sure you bring your own uniform tomorrow. You can buy the shirt you need in the main office. Wear any color sweats or shorts, but not too short. I don't want to see any butt cheeks in my gym."

"Okay." I couldn't stop smiling.

"I don't see what's so funny here, Rae. A first impression is very hard to change. If you set yourself up here as a trouble-maker, you'll have a hard time living that reputation down."

"Yes, ma'am." I should have been cowed and worried, but I was thrilled. *She's mad! She's angry at me! She's treating me like everyone else!*

The teacher rolled her eyes. "I don't know what to do with kids these days." She stared us down again. "Two weeks of detention. All four of you. Starting today after school."

We both nodded at her, saying nothing.

She gestured towards the locker rooms. "Go. I don't want to look at you anymore. When you're back in street clothes sit on the bleachers. Apart. I want all of you separated for the rest of this class."

We walked around her without another word and moved towards the locker rooms in silence. It was only at the door that separated the girls' locker room from the boys' that Malcolm finally spoke.

"You're on track to be valedictorian?"

I shrugged. "I guess."

"Oh, man. That sucks for Jasmine." He pushed the door open.

"Why?"

"Because until you showed up, that was her crown."

He disappeared inside, leaving me with a sinking heart and a sick feeling in the pit of my stomach.

## Chapter Nine
# Malcolm

I JOINED KOOTCH AT THE lockers where our stuff was stored. He was already standing in his boxers, pulling out his clothes.

"Can you believe that shit? Totally unfair." He slammed his locker door closed. The happy-go-lucky jokester was gone and in his place was the Miserable I'd been trying to ditch for weeks.

"Yeah." I removed my lock and opened the locker. As I took out my clothes and dropped them on the bench, I realized I was twice as bummed now as I had been before. For a little while there I'd actually been thinking I could hang out with Kootch. Now I knew it was just a fantasy.

"That Butts ... she's the one who caused all this." He pulled on his jeans but left them unbuttoned.

"No she didn't, man. You did. You're the one who picked her up and swung her around." I frowned, keeping my eyes on my clothes and not him. I didn't want to fight, but I couldn't let him blame Jasmine for what happened.

"Did you hear what she said? She's still blaming me for that bullshit with her eye. It was years ago. *Years.*" He yanked his t-shirt on over his head and pulled the bottom of it down.

I looked at him. "What was that all about, anyway?"

Kootch sat on the bench and pulled on one of his socks and then one of his hiking boots, letting his pant leg bunch up at the top of it. "When we were kids, she got hit with a rock that went flying over my fence into her yard. That part was true. But it wasn't me who threw the fucking thing, so she's blaming the wrong guy." He banged his foot down a few times, getting the boot on all the way.

I thought about that for a few seconds as he picked up his second sock. "Who threw it?" I finally asked.

Kootch froze in the middle of pulling on his second boot. He stared at the locker doors, saying nothing.

I laughed a little. "Hello? You in there?"

He went back to pulling on his boot. "Yeah, I'm here. I don't know who threw it."

"But it came from your yard?"

"Yeah." He sounded defensive.

"And you were in your yard when it happened."

"Yeah!" Kootch stood up and opened the locker door so hard it banged back against the others. "So?" He scowled at me for a second before going back into the locker.

"So ... you must know who threw the rock, right?"

"Yeah, I know." Now he just seemed sad. He pulled out his backpack and dropped it on the ground. Then he buttoned and zipped his jeans, not looking at me.

"Hey, if it's a big secret, no big deal. I was just curious." I quickly got undressed and grabbed my jeans.

After a long pause, Kootch finally responded. "It was my asshole dad, okay? *He* threw the fucking rock."

My pants were only halfway up, but I stopped trying to get them on as I processed that bit of information. I wasn't sure I understood. "Your dad?" I pulled the jeans the rest of the way up, securing them as I stared at Kootch.

He shrugged. "What can I say? Guy's a dick."

I grabbed my shirt and fumbled around with it, trying to find the opening for my head. "He threw it on purpose? At a girl?"

"Nah, man. Not at Jasmine. At *me*." Kootch looked up, a flash of pain in his eyes. It made me feel sick to my stomach for him. His status as a Miserable suddenly became a lot easier to understand, assuming I was reading his expression right.

"Your dad threw a rock at you, missed, and it flew over the fence and nailed Jasmine in the eye."

"Next to her eye. But, yeah. That's pretty much what happened."

"Holy shit. Talk about being in the wrong place at the wrong time."

Kootch smiled without humor. "Yeah, tell me about it. I felt like shit. Still do, and it was like ten years ago or something."

I pulled my shirt on over my head, not looking at him anymore on purpose. There was no need to get things heavier than they already were. But I had to say something. Kootch was obviously torturing himself over the whole thing. "It wasn't your fault."

"Yeah, well, it felt like it. Maybe I shouldn't have ducked or something."

"That's stupid. No one takes a rock to the face if they can help it."

Kootch stood, apparently done talking about it. "Want me to wait for you?"

"No. Hatcher wants us sitting apart on the bleachers. I'll see you out there."

"Later." Kootch grabbed his backpack and left the locker room.

I sat down on the bench and pulled on my socks and shoes, thinking about what had happened. For some reason out on the basketball court, Kootch had dropped the angry Miserable act for a while and livened up. He was actually laughing and teasing the girls, which was so not like him; usually he was too angry to do anything but make sarcastic or rude remarks to people. But then when we were in the locker room again he was back to being unhappy.

He must really like that Rae girl. That was the only explanation. Maybe being around her made him forget how unhappy he was when he was around me. I guess it's possible that love can be stronger than any power I might have over someone's emotions, even though I don't remember actually seeing that in action before.

I decided then and there that I had to encourage that connection between them. Kootch was one of the hardest guys to shake; he'd hung on to me no matter how much I blew him off or was rude to him. And over the weeks he'd been around me, he'd slowly gotten more and more depressed, his moods darkening to the point that I was really starting to worry, hence my hiding out in the bathroom earlier today. Maybe if I could help him fall in love with Rae, he'd lighten up and not want to be around me so much. And not be as sad and depressed. I couldn't have another kid's suicide on my conscience. One success and two near-misses were more than enough, thank you very much.

I jerked the laces of my shoe really hard, making the knot as tight as I could. It seems stupid, but I always made sure that nothing could slow me down, not even untied laces. When it's time to run, I have to be ready to run. A shoe tripping me up could be the difference between getting away and having an out of control Miserable going ballistic on my ass. That was never fun.

I got up and took my backpack out of the locker. After pulling my lock off the door and dropping it into a side pocket of my bag, I left the room and went out into the gym. I walked over to the bleachers and took a spot halfway up, about six rows down from Jasmine. Before turning to face the court, I gave her a nod. I meant for it to be an apology, but I wasn't sure she took it that way. She scowled at me and stuck out her tongue.

My plan was to sit there and zone out for the rest of the period, dreaming of the log cabin I was going to live in up in the mountains one day, when my thoughts were interrupted by a wad of paper hitting me on the side of the head.

I turned to my right. Kootch was gesturing from down the bench, pointing at the crumpled up paper at my feet.

I rolled my eyes. Apparently he was back to being Happy Kootch and now wanted to chat.

I bent over and picked up the paper, opening it up and smoothing it out over my leg.

*Meet me after class. We need to plan this detention.*

I just faced forward and shook my head, *No*. The only plan I had was to take off as soon as that bell rang so I could disappear in the crowds. I had three more classes before the end of the day, all of them without Kootch or Jasmine in them. Hopefully, I wouldn't see that Rae girl either.

Another wad of paper hit me, this time in the chest.

I whipped my head sideways and scowled at Kootch. "Stop!" I whispered loudly.

"Mr. McNamara!" Mrs. Hatcher was yelling across the court. "Eyes front! No talking!"

I waved at her and bent over, picking up the paper casually and waiting until she was turned around before opening it.

*U have to help me w/R. Do it. Don't B a pussy.*

I flipped Kootch off, not even looking at him.

A minute later another piece of paper hit me, this time in the side of my nose. I let it drop to my feet, ignoring it and Kootch.

"Dude!" he whisper-yelled. "Better pick it up!"

I sighed heavily. Reaching down, I grabbed the paper and opened it.

*Wait 4 me or I'll tell everyone u were checking out my junk in the locker room.*

I laughed. I couldn't help it. Kootch was totally mental. I looked over. "Fine. Dick."

He smiled enthusiastically and gave me a thumbs up.

I sensed a movement out of the corner of my eye and looked over. Rae was sitting above us, several rows back. She was staring at me.

I turned away, but not before I caught her smiling.

My face burned bright red. I could feel it on my ears too, so I leaned over and put my forearms on my legs, lowering my head down so she wouldn't see me. The last thing I needed was some Miserable hooking herself to me when Kootch was hot on her tail.

*Why does life have to be so friggin complicated?* I twisted my arm and stared at my watch, willing time to go slowly for a change. I really didn't want to go to my next class with Kootch next to me, listening to him plan how he was going to get Rae to go out with him. All I could think about was how soft her body had been under mine, when I landed on her like a completely uncoordinated moron. I'd felt her soft chest push up into mine for a few seconds, and she'd smelled like flowers. The memory of it made my blood stir and my body heat up.

*Oh, shit. Think un-sexy thoughts, think un-sexy thoughts! Old ladies! Mrs. Hatcher! Smelly dogs! The fat lady next door!* It wasn't working. Images of Rae beneath me assailed my mind. I had to shift in my seat to get comfortable as my jeans grew too tight in certain places.

I don't know what made me do it. I should have just stared at the fugly gym teacher and gotten control of myself. But I was stupid and looking for trouble apparently, because I turned around again.

Rae had her hands folded under and propping up her chin, her elbows resting on her bent knees. She smiled again when she caught me looking and waved her fingers at me. The dimple caved in and she winked.

I turned around fast. *Oh, shit. I'm in trouble.*

I jumped up without thinking and grabbed my bag, holding it in front of my waist to hide my shame.

"Where are you going?" Kootch whispered loudly.

I didn't respond. I just leaped down the benches in front of me, banging them loudly as I went, and took off running when I got to the gym floor.

"Malcolm!" Mrs. Hatcher was yelling.

"Gotta go, Mrs. Hatcher!" I shouted as I ran out the double doors and into the hallway. "Emergency!"

Throwing my bag over my shoulder, I pumped my legs and ran as fast as I could through the lobby area and towards the main doors leading into the school. I had to put some distance between Rae and me. She was so pretty, so innocent, so nice. And Kootch liked her. I had to make sure she stayed safe, and the only way I could do that would be to keep her the hell away from me.

I kept going until I got to the bathroom nearest my next class. I shut myself up into a stall and hung my backpack on the hook inside it. I sank down onto the toilet seat and leaned against the wall of the stall.

Reaching up to trace some graffiti there, I contemplated my current situation, trying to figure out how I was going to avoid Rae when I had two weeks of detention in the same room as her, not to mention at least two classes.

Nothing was coming to mind.

# Chapter Ten
# Rae

I WAS SO HAPPY, I had a really hard time not smiling my head off. In all the schools I'd gone to, this was the first one where I'd had such amazing luck right off the bat. I had not just one, but possibly two Neutrals in classes with me, and they were already my friends. Maybe even three Neutrals. It was kind of hard to tell with Kootch. But even so, Jasmine and Malcolm ... it was too awesome to think about; if I did, I was bound to get all excited, and then the Rainbows would get crazy. *Deep breath. Relax.*

Malcolm took one look at me and went running out of the gym. I have no idea what I did to make that happen, and truth be told it did sting a little to be so obviously rejected; but it was good news, because it meant he wasn't attaching himself to me.

I sighed at myself, admitting that of course the one time a guy didn't glom onto me I suddenly felt the need to have him do exactly that. I guess I'm destined to be miserable, no matter what happens. People attach, I hate it. People run, and suddenly I want to date them.

*Date them? Do I really want to go out with Malcolm?* My face burned at the idea. Having him touch me *had* been just a little amazing. And seeing him close up and unguarded like that had shown me that he's actually really, really cute. There was something about him that was so attractive to me, but I couldn't put my finger on what it was. Probably it was the fact that he was the one guy in the whole school who wanted nothing to do with me.

Mrs. Hatcher blew three short blasts on her whistle. "That's it! Bring it in! Put your balls away and get dressed."

Several students laughed when a guy yelled, "You heard her ... put your balls away!"

I got up and walked down the bleachers, catching up to Jasmine as she strolled towards the doors leading into the lobby area.

"So where do we go for detention?" I asked. I was secretly thrilled to be punished like this. I'd never received detention before, no matter what I'd done.

"There's a big classroom for all detention given to people in our grade, right next to the library. You have your schedule?"

I dug into my purse and handed it to her.

"You have Fine Arts as your last class. I'm just down the hall from you. Meet me outside the door, and I'll walk you there."

I took my schedule back and slipped it into the outside pocket of my purse. "Thanks. I was a little worried I'd get lost."

"Don't thank me now. You'll probably wish you were wandering the halls instead of being in detention later."

"That bad, huh?"

"Boring. Mind-blowingly dull. You can actually feel yourself aging as you sit there. There's no talking, no breaks, no eating. Nothing but sitting there and studying."

"Sounds like you've been there before."

"I like to speak my mind. Some people don't appreciate it like they should. Doesn't affect my grades, though, so I can't complain too much."

Her comment reminded me that I wanted to ask her about the valedictorian thing, but I lost my nerve. This friendship was so new and fragile, I didn't want to do anything to mess it up. Besides, if I worked really hard at it, it's possible I could screw up my grades enough that she'd be back on top where she belonged.

That was the only fair thing to do. I didn't deserve to be number one when most of my grades had just been handed to me.

I resolved then to do whatever I could to bomb a few of my classes. Starting with Phys Ed. I'd take a page out of Malcolm's book and go for the zero. *No more basketball for me.*

"What are you so happy about?" Jasmine asked, glancing at me before she grabbed the handle leading into the main area of the school. As she pulled the door open, the bell rang signaling the end of class. "We have two whole weeks in detention, thanks to Kootch and Malcolm. Trust me, that's nothing to smile about."

"Malcolm didn't do anything wrong."

Jasmine looked at me sideways as she joined me in the hallway. "Hmmm, feeling a little defensive for Malcolm, are we?"

Doors opened and kids filled the halls. We had to talk louder to be heard.

"No. I'm just saying ... it was all Kootch pretty much. He's the dope who picked you up and swung you around."

"Yeah, well, I knew it would get him all riled up to mention the eye thing. That always pisses him off." She smiled.

"Why? Why is he so sensitive about it?" A guy running down the hall bumped into me, sending me crashing into Jasmine. She just ignored it and kept walking. She gave no indication that she felt the energy that flows through me.

"I have no idea. But it cracks me up to see him get his shit in a wad, so I mention it a couple times a year just for fun."

"What happened?"

Jasmine shrugged. "I don't know. It's stupid really. A few years ago ... maybe five or six ... I was standing out in my back yard, and all of a sudden this big-ass rock comes flying over the bushes and smacks me in the face." She turned and pointed to the corner of her eye. "Just barely missed hitting me in the eye and blinding me. I'm scarred for life."

"It's really small. I can hardly see it." I said, squinting for effect.

"Don't tell Kootch that. Next time we're around him, make sure you mention how big and hideous it is."

"You really like messing with his head, don't you?"

"He's been my next door neighbor for most of my life. We used to play all the time when we were little, and then one day he just decided he didn't want to anymore and that was the last time we hung out." She shrugged. "He deserves it."

"Oh, he totally does," I said, nodding. I was getting the sneaking suspicion there was more to the story, but I wasn't going to push. At least not today.

We were inside the main building now, in the area where several halls converged. It was like the Grand Central Station of the school, and the crowds were flowing around us, pushing us down the middle hall and jostling us around.

"That's my room just over there. You're down there and to the left," said Jasmine, pointing down a perpendicular hall.

"So I'll see you after Fine Arts?" I asked.

"Yup. See ya." She left me standing there and disappeared into the crowd.

I followed her instructions and found my next class. I spent the next couple hours avoiding looking people in the eye and changing the subject when teachers tried to engage me in conversation. All I could think about was getting through my last class, Fine Arts, and then over to detention. This was the best day I'd ever had in high school, and I didn't want anything to ruin it.

The bell rang, and I stood, putting my purse strap over my shoulder.

"Do you need help getting to your next class?" asked a girl who'd been sitting next to me.

"No thanks," I said over my shoulder. "I have a map." I left her standing there, blocked in by students gathering their things. I could tell she wanted to walk with me, but she was stuck. I shoved past a couple kids to make sure I could get away before she was free.

In my hurry to escape, I carelessly allowed my forearm to rub up against a large guy's arm. He stopped in mid-sentence and looked down at me. "Hi." He smiled, revealing perfectly straight, toothpaste-commercial-worthy teeth.

"Hi," I said, dropping my gaze to the floor. "Excuse me, I'm just trying to get by."

"What's your hurry? Rae, right?"

"Yes, it's Rae. I'm meeting someone." It was a lie, but he didn't know that.

"Who are you meeting?" He shifted to be even more in my way.

I opened my mouth, but nothing came out.

"Or is it a big secret?" His tone had gotten softer, and he'd leaned down to say it closer to my ear.

I leaned back away from him, trying to keep him from touching me again. "No, no secret. I just ... can't remember his name."

"Well, I don't want to get in the way of you and your meeting." He stood straight and turned to the side. Stepping over his chair, he put himself in the next aisle over and gestured for me to go. "See you later, Rae."

I nodded and walked by, not making eye contact.

"Hey, Brody, what's up?" asked a girl in a breathless voice. She bumped into me from behind. "Oh, sorry, Rae. Didn't realize you were still here."

The girl who'd tried to walk with me earlier was there, pulling a chunk of hair out of her mouth. She was smiling excitedly and breathing fast.

"Hey, Courtney, what's up with you?" asked the guy - Brody, I guess. "You got a secret meeting too?"

"What?" She frowned at him.

"Never mind. Ignore me. I'll see you later. After school, right?"

"Yes, sure. After school." She waved him off and then grinned at me again. "Sure you don't need some help getting to class?"

"She's meeting someone, Courtney," Brody offered.

"Oh. Who is it?"

*Uh-oh. Rainbow alert.* I could already sense the desperation settling in. I had two choices here: I could either totally cut her off and be over-the-top rude or I could just shine her on a little and then play the avoidance game. That was definitely the nicer way to go, even though it involved a lot of ducking into bathrooms and closets.

"I just need to get to Fine Arts. It's not a big deal."

She grabbed my arm. "You have Blakenship? *I* have Blakenship!" She looked like she was about to do a cheer, with pom-poms and everything.

"Oh. Goody."

"Come on, I'll show you! It's so lucky we were in this class together, isn't it?" She was practically squealing she was so excited.

I didn't bother answering because she'd just ignore the *No* I was going to respond with.

"Bye, Court. See ya, Rae." Brody climbed back over his desk as we cleared the aisle.

"Bye," I said, not nearly as enthusiastic as everyone else in our little party.

"Later, Brody!" said Courtney, pushing me forward. "Come on, let's go. I want to get there early and help you find a seat."

I rolled my eyes. No way was I going to sit near her.

We made our way through the crowded hall and went into the classroom she pointed out. "That's it right there. Two-oh-nine. Blankenship and the wonderful world of Fine Arts. You'll like him. He's an easy grader and hardly ever gives homework."

We walked into the room, and Courtney stood with me next to the teacher's desk as I waited to get his attention.

"May I help you?" he finally asked, looking up from a stack of papers. Some of them were being held down with lumps of fired clay, most of them in the shapes of animals. I quickly counted two ladybugs, one turtle, and something that might be a warped koala bear.

I handed him my schedule. "I'm new today. I'm in your class this period."

He took the paper from me in a paint-stained hand and frowned as he read it through some reading glasses perched on the end of his nose. "Hmmm... Rae Livingston." He looked up. "Our new valedictorian, yes?"

I shrugged.

"Oh em *gee!* You are *not*," gasped Courtney. "Wow, that's amazing. *Ha!* Jasmine thought she had that one in the bag. I can't wait to see her face when she finds out." She sounded way too happy about bursting Jasmine's bubble.

"It's probably not right," I rushed to assure her. "They haven't transferred all my grades yet. There are some low ones in there."

Mr. Blankenship interrupted Courtney's next words. "Hmmm ... okay, go sit down in the first roowwww ..." He checked a page in a thin book on his desk. "... Seat number eight."

I raised an eyebrow at his organization. This was the first class that I'd been in at this school with assigned seats. Everything else on his desk was a complete mess, papers stacked haphazardly with some of them even on the floor in various piles. His table at the front of the room didn't look any better. It was covered in lots of different paint bottles and water cans with brushes sticking out of them.

"I was kind of hoping you'd put her by me," said Courtney, pouting.

"I'm sure you were," he said, looking at her over his glasses. "Find your seat, Courtney."

She looked like she was going to argue, but then Malcolm walked in and I stopped paying any attention to what she was doing.

As he moved into the room, I stared. I couldn't help it. His jeans fit him so well, and he somehow managed to make that green long-sleeved shirt sexy. He was one of those guys who didn't try at all to be hot, but just managed to be amazing anyway. He wasn't overly muscled, but he wasn't a wimp either. And his hair was messed up from either the wind or the stress of our awful gym class, completely unlike the artfully arranged and gelled hairdos of the guys around us. He was cute and genuine and mysterious ... maybe even a little dangerous; everything I should avoid in a guy. And that just made me want to be near him more. *This is not good.*

"Take your schedule, Rae. And please find your seat."

Courtney had already left and was happily conversing with a group of girls near her table. She'd gone from wanting to be my best friend to acting like a complete stranger in a matter of seconds.

*Weird.* Normally it took a lot more than a seat assignment to shake a Rainbow.

"Is this the first row?" I asked, pointing to the one to the right of his desk.

"Yes. Seat number eight is at the fourth table down. Next to Malcolm McNamara."

I couldn't stop the grin from spreading across my face.

The teacher raised an eyebrow. "Is there anything else I can do for you?" He sounded a tad annoyed.

"Uh, no. Thank you." I took the paper with my schedule on it from the top of his messy desk and turned to go down the aisle between the large, black art tables.

Malcolm was standing behind his chair, the one nearest the wall, and had dropped his backpack in front of him on the table-top. He was reaching into one of the pockets and pulling out a notebook when I walked over.

He looked up and stopped in mid-unpacking. "What are you doing here?" he asked. His tone was flat.

"This is my new seat." I pointed to the chair next to him.

"No it's not." His expression went from bland to slightly panicked.

"Yes, it is. Mr. Blankenship just assigned it to me."

He glanced up at the teacher. I followed his gaze over to the man who was standing at the front of the class looking out over the students distractedly.

"You can't sit here." Malcolm pushed his bag over to rest in front of the aisle seat I was just about to claim.

I frowned, a little hurt that he was being kind of rude. "Well, the teacher told me to, so I think I can."

He sighed, almost angrily, before leaving the table and going to the front of the room. When he walked by me, he seemed to be taking great pains to not touch me.

It made me want to smell my armpits, but I refrained. I did blow my breath up into my nose, wondering if maybe I was all garlicky or something, but I didn't notice anything wrong there either.

I stood there confused as Malcolm had an animated conversation with the teacher. His arms were flapping up and down, making it clear he was upset.

The longer I watched, the more awful I felt. He really, really didn't like me. He was like a Neutral who'd finally gotten sick of all the Rainbows smothering me and treating me like a princess. But it so wasn't fair. He hadn't even had a chance to see any Rainbows acting nutty, so why was he so angry at the idea of being near me?

The teacher shook his head no, so I took the liberty of pushing Malcolm's backpack over to the seat where he had been standing, and put my purse down in the spot in front of my place.

I tried to catch Malcolm's eye as he walked down the aisle, but he refused to look at me. He walked around behind my seat and sat down in the one next to me, staring straight ahead. I could practically feel the coldness coming off his body. He really, really didn't want to be near me.

The thought of it made me want to cry. My happy bubble burst, and now all I could think about was how embarrassing it was going to be having to be with him in detention for two whole weeks, plus sitting next to him here.

Maybe his behavior should have made him become ugly to me, but I wasn't having any luck there either. I looked at him out of the corner of my eye, and my heart spasmed over how handsome his profile is. There was some stubble growing on his face, but not enough that he could ever grow into a beard. His lips were a dark red and just begged to be kissed.

My last experience with kissing a boy had been a disaster from the word go, so the idea of being able to do that with Malcolm was making me crazy.

I tried to stop looking and thinking about it, but it was very difficult. Only the teacher launching our next art project saved me from making a fool of myself and saying something stupid. It had been on the tip of my tongue to ask Malcolm why he hated me so much when he hadn't even taken the time to get to know me.

"Take one of these and pass the rest back," said Mr. Blankenship.

When the stack got to me, I took two watercolor papers off the top for both me and Malcolm and passed the rest to the guy at the next table. My fingers brushed against his during the exchange, but he didn't even flinch or look at me. He acted like nothing had happened.

I slid Malcolm's paper over to him without looking in his direction. *What the heck is going on in this place? Did I step into an alternate dimension or something?*

I stared at my blank paper, considering everything that had happened over the last few hours. Suddenly everyone was acting all weird, and after almost eighteen years of people acting exactly the same, no matter where I went or what I did, it was freaking me out. I pretty much hated my life and couldn't wait to change it, but that didn't necessarily mean I wanted to be thrown in the deep end of a completely different one either; mainly because with my luck, it would turn out to be even worse then the one I was already stuck in.

I chewed my lip as I considered the possible outcomes of a different life. None of them were coming up good in my imagination. I'd found a Neutral for a friend, but with the way things were going now, this could be the shortest stint I'd ever had at a school, and then I'd lose her. Back to the drawing board. Another move, another town, another group of kids to fend off. No more friends for me.

Luckily, the teacher announcing the instructions for our project today pulled me out of that murky place and set me on a happier course. Today I would be painting an impressionistic watercolor that represented my life, while I sat next to a boy who wanted absolutely nothing to do with me - a boy who caused me to have more than just a slight ache of yearning in my heart.

## Chapter Eleven
# Malcolm

I COULDN'T BELIEVE MY TERRIBLE luck. There were thirty or more classes going on right now in senior year, and Rae had to end up in *my* Fine Arts class and be seated in the spot right next to *me*. The Fates were out to get me. That's the only explanation. Or maybe they were out to get her.

Glancing at Rae out of the corner of my eye, I could see my darkness already working its magic on her. She'd gone from happy to sad in the space of seconds, and now looked like all the other Miserables who came calling.

She left the table and came back less than a minute later with a watercolor paint box. We were supposed to share, so she put it in between us along with the can of water and a pile of paper towels she held in her other hand.

"Start with your background," said the teacher, speaking to the whole class as he wandered down the aisles. "Use a lot of water and just wash the color over the paper. Think about what you want to paint and get the colors behind your main content right."

Rae was taking great pains to not look at me. Her chin was tilted slightly up in defiance. She was probably mad at me for trying to get rid of her, but it was for her own good, so I wasn't going to feel bad about it. At least, that's what I kept telling myself. The guilt snuck in anyway.

I dipped my brush in the water and wiped my paper down with it, getting it good and wet before I started.

Rae was being more precise. She'd started with a big orange circle right in the middle of her paper.

I dipped my wet brush in the blue and then the black, making a big puddle of color in the plastic lid of the paint box. Filling my brush, I brought it over to the bottom edge of my paper and started swiping it back and forth, covering the bottom with the darkest blue that I could get. I added more black when it wasn't quite dark enough.

Rae dipped her brush into the yellow and then red, using this bright color to draw circles around the one she already had. Her paper looked like what someone having an acid trip would see.

I added more blue to my next stripe, just above the really black one. I brought the end of the line up and turned it into a big wave that went to the top of the paper and then crashed back down to the bottom. *Turmoil. Drowning in darkness. This is my life.*

Rae used purple next, putting splotches of it all over the place. It looked like she was having a butterfly parade in the sun.

I knew it was ridiculous, but something about her color choices made me angry. We were supposed to be doing an impressionistic painting of how we saw our lives. Looking at her work was like looking at a lie. Here she was, a nice girl coming near me, smiling and acting like she wanted to be next to me - a Miserable of the worst kind - and yet she was pretending like her life was a big, giant confetti explosion in the middle of a tripped-out sun.

"You hate it that much, huh?" she asked. Her paintbrush was tinking around in the water can as she cleaned it off.

I looked back at my own paper, embarrassed that she'd caught me staring angrily at her painting.

"Yours sure looks cheery," she said.

I shouldn't have looked at her, but I did. She was smiling.

I said nothing. I just loaded my brush up with red paint and put a big red X in the middle of the wave.

"Two more of those and maybe you'll get a buzzer to go off somewhere."

I frowned at my paper and then at her. "What?" She was making no sense. I got the impression she was having a good laugh about something.

She pointed at my X. "That looks like those talent shows where the judges can X a person off the stage. Just two more and you're done. You're off the show."

My nostrils flared. This was no stupid gameshow. This was my messed up piece of shit life. I dipped my brush in the red paint and put two more Xs down.

"Eeerrrr," she buzzed. "Game over. Time to go home."

"What a great idea," I said, dropping my brush into the water can and bending over to get my backpack.

"Where are you going?" she asked, sounding mystified.

"Game over, remember?" I walked around her chair and moved out into the aisle.

My grand plan to exit using the steam of my anger as momentum ended the second she put her hand on my arm.

*Stupid, stupid, stupid! Why didn't you put your sleeves down before you left?!*

Her skin was touching mine, and the feeling that came up my arm and into my chest through her fingers was nothing less than mind-blowing.

I yanked my arm away, breathing fast in panic.

"Did you feel that?" she whispered, her face a mask of excitement and confusion all muddled together.

"No." I stepped back, my butt banging into the table next to ours.

"Yes, you did," she whispered in a more subdued tone. "I know you did, don't deny it."

"Static electricity. The air's dry."

"Bullshit. Don't leave."

I hesitated, one foot poised in front of the other, my heart beating like mad. I was literally stuck in place as my brain warred with my heart.

*Go! Don't stick around here and damage this girl any more than you already have!*

*Stay! She's drawing pictures of rainbows and butterflies for shit's sake! Maybe you won't kill her!*

But my heart was an idiot and had gotten people seriously hurt before, so I ignored it in favor of my brain. "I have to go."

I left her there at the table, and cruised to the front of the room. Mr. Blankenship was so busy with his own artwork, he didn't even notice me walking in front of him and out the door. The other students were laughing and having a good old time with their projects, so they paid me no attention either.

Once out in the hallway, I put my backpack over my shoulder and contemplated my options. I could skip the rest of school and detention altogether and go home, or I could go wait out the rest of this period and show up in detention right before the bell sounded. That way I'd be able to pick a seat far away from everyone else.

I got to the bathroom nearest the detention hall and went inside. Skipping the punishment would get me in deeper shit than I was already in, and I didn't want to expose myself to students any more than possible. Three weeks of forced studying at a table with three other students was bad enough, but missing it meant adding more time to my sentence. I had to just get it over with and hope it went smoothly.

I was sitting in the far stall when the bathroom door opened about fifteen minutes later. I quietly stepped up, putting my feet on the seat so whoever it was wouldn't catch me skipping class and possibly tattle on me. Mr. Blankenship was such a space cadet he probably wasn't going to notice I was gone at all.

At first all I heard were footsteps, but then there were voices. It immediately struck me as strange because at least one of them sounded too adult to be in the student bathroom.

I kept my breathing as even as possible, hoping they wouldn't notice me in here before they left.

"Did you see her?" This guy was a student, but I didn't know if he was someone I knew or not. He didn't sound like anyone I'd been in class with before. I knew he wasn't a Miserable; I heard their voices enough to recognize them easily.

"Yeah, I saw her." The second voice sounded familiar. A teacher, maybe. Or possibly someone who worked in the Main Office.

It was weird that a teacher and student were discussing a girl or a lady together in the bathroom in the middle of class. It made me want to stay hidden so I could hear more.

"Is she the one?" asked the student. He sounded excited and serious at the same time.

"All signs point to yes. But I can't be sure until we get her alone."

*Oh, shit. This teacher wants to get a girl alone? That's messed up. That can't be good, right? Why would he want to do that?*

"How are we going to get her alone?"

This voice definitely belonged to a student - a guy and someone who'd already gone way past puberty. His voice was deep but still youthful.

I wanted to get a look at him to see if I recognized him. I shifted ever-so slightly so I could try and look through the crack of the door, but they were both too far to the right of me to see them. All I could catch from where I was sitting were a couple of sinks and a mirror.

"I leave that up to you. Make friends. Play nice. Do what you have to do, but keep it clean. We don't need anything scaring her away before we can get the program online." Whatever they were talking about was seriously important to this guy, that much was clear from his tone.

I figured they must be talking about a student, since the teacher was telling the other guy to get to know her instead of doing it himself. At least this guy seemed to be advocating no violence, or a temporary no-violence period. Whoever this girl was, she needed to be warned. And this teacher should probably be reported. But who would I report him to? And what would I tell them? That a teacher was talking in the bathroom with a student about getting a mystery girl alone? I'd sound like a lunatic if I said anything like that.

"Got it," said the student. "I'll start today. She has detention."

"I'll get you in there. How long?"

"Two weeks."

"Whoa, two weeks. How in the hell did she get detention? She never gets detention." It was weird hearing an adult swear like that. Teachers always seemed too uptight and by the book, but this guy sounded seriously stressed. Like, beyond uptight.

The pool of potential candidates was shrinking. They were talking about a student who had two weeks of detention who didn't normally get in trouble.

Jasmine and Rae were the first students who leapt to mind because I knew they had just gotten two weeks; but that was stupid. There would probably be fifteen girls in there today. The chance that it would be someone I kind of know wasn't that great. Besides, I was pretty sure Jasmine is a regular in the detention hall, and the guy just said that whoever it is never gets detention. Today is Rae's first day, so it couldn't be her either.

"Not sure how it happened," answered the student. "I didn't see what went down, I just heard about it."

This guy sure seemed to know a lot about this girl. She must be in one of his classes. A goody-goody from the sounds of it, since she never got detention. It wasn't that difficult to get in my experience. I'd probably know her as one of the girls who wanted nothing to do with me. A truly happy person. That made me mad, to think they were going to take some happy girl and mess with her somehow.

"Well, find that out, too. I don't want any surprises."

"I got it handled. Just relax, all right?" The student sounded annoyed.

"Impossible," said the teacher, angry now. "Do you have any idea the pressure I'm under?"

"Yeah. The same pressure I am."

"It's not the same for you. You can make mistakes. I can't."

"No one can make mistakes. Don't fool yourself, old man."

*Old man? What teacher lets a student get away with that?*

"Just see that you get her alone and to me. I'll take it from there."

"I can check her out without your help, you know." The student sounded offended.

"Are you sure you want to be the one to submit the report?" The teacher paused before delivering his condescending response. "No, I didn't think so. Just get her to me, and we'll work on her together. I supervise, though. Deal?"

"Deal."

My legs were seriously cramped, and I really wanted to stand up a little and get a look at them. I shifted to the right, thinking I'd lift my eyes up over the top of the stall, but I accidentally banged my knee into the toilet paper dispenser. I froze in a squatting position.

"What was that?" asked the teacher. His voice shifted into an angry whisper. "Didn't you check in here before we came in?"

Footsteps moved closer to my stall. They hesitated once, twice, and then a third time. Now one of the guys was standing outside the door of the stall I was in. I could see his Vans, the toes just peeking under the edge. One of them slid back and came off the floor a little as he leaned over and looked under the door.

"There's nobody in there. I checked under all of them." The Vans disappeared.

If he'd just put his head a little closer to the bottom of the door, he would have seen me in here. I wondered what they would have done if he had, shuddering at the idea. I had a strong feeling it wouldn't have been anything good.

When the student returned to his meeting, the teacher said, "You can't just check under them, idiot. You have to open them."

"Jesus. Paranoid aren't you?" The student was obviously annoyed at being ordered around.

The first door banged open.

My blood pressure sky-rocketed.

Then the second door banged open. It rattled the dividing wall between my stall and the next.

The third door banged open. It sounded like he was using his fist to punch them back.

The bell rang.

Shoes hesitated in front of the stall next to mine.

The sounds of students filling the hallway reached my ears and my blood pressure evened out. I caught myself about to exhale loudly in relief.

"Dammit, I have to go," said the teacher. "I can't be caught in here with you."

"Go ahead. I'll stay. I have to take a piss anyway."

The main door opened and the squawking of students got louder for a few seconds before the door swung shut again.

Splashes inside a urinal came next. And then the main door opened again and a group of guys came in, bringing a bunch of noise with them.

"Yo, what up, man?" asked someone from the group.

"Nothing much. Takin' a piss. Going anywhere after school?" This came from the student who'd been planning with the teacher.

"Mickey D's," answered someone. "You in?"

"Nah. I have detention. Two weeks."

"Two weeks? Holy shit, that fuckin' sucks."

"Yeah, tell me about it."

"Who's the bitch?"

"Not a bitch. Try dick. Holder gave it to me."

"Holder *is* a dick. I don't trust that guy. Creepy. He was just in here, wasn't he?"

"Yeah, he was. Talk about a dick. Had the nerve to say hi to me in here, acting like he didn't totally screw me over."

Someone banged the door shut next to me. My face burned with the fear of being discovered. I slowly lowered my feet to the floor and sat on the toilet seat. I was afraid to take off while the guy was still in there, sure he'd see me and know I'd heard everything.

"You see that new chick? Rae?" said a different voice.

"Yeah, I saw her," said the guy who'd been talking to the teacher -- Mr. Holder, apparently. It was killing me that no one was saying the student's name, and he was still over by the urinals nowhere near my door. There was no way I could see who he is unless I stood on the toilet.

The voices were moving towards the exit. The person in the stall next to me started grunting.

Someone shouted out some encouragement. "Just relax, man. Let it flow."

"Fuck you," said the guy in the stall. He was very unhappy.

The main door opened and the sounds of the hallway came into the bathroom again. I waited until they went silent and the room emptied of all sounds except the ones of pain coming from the stall next to me, before moving from my hiding spot.

"Jesus, God, remind me never to eat the burritos from the cafeteria again," said the guy next to me.

I pushed out of the stall and walked quickly to the door.

"Hey! Who's in here?"

I ignored the guy and went out into the hallway, looking left and right, trying to figure out who'd been talking about getting a girl alone and also who'd been talking about Rae.

There was no way for me to know, though; it could have been anyone. There were groups of guys all over the place, and none of them looked guilty of anything more serious than checking out girls' asses as they walked by wearing short skirts.

I gave up on my hunt and turned right, following the hall that would lead me to the detention room, totally lost in thought. *Who are they trying to get alone? And what are they going to do when they get her there? Whoever it is, she has detention and I'm going to see her in a matter of minutes. I wonder if I should bother saying anything to anyone.*

I laughed bitterly at the idea of telling someone in the Main Office what I knew. I hadn't exactly set myself up as a credible source of anything at this school, the way I was always disappearing into the bathrooms and running out of class. They'd probably send me to another psychologist or something if I announced there was a grand conspiracy to attack a girl being put together by a chemistry teacher and a student in the bathrooms during class.

That the teacher was Mr. Holder, one of the chemistry teachers, was pretty clear - at least from what the student had said about his detention. But who was the student?

I decided my best plan was to just keep my eyes and ears open. If I saw anything bad happening, I'd tell someone. Otherwise, I was just going to mind my own business and hope it was my overactive imagination turning a totally innocent thing into something sinister.

# Chapter Twelve
# Rae

I WAS PUTTING AWAY THE paint set and water can when the bell rang. Quickly rinsing out the container and brushes, I stacked them up next to the sink with all the others and went back to my desk to retrieve my picture. We were supposed to hang them up to dry on lines the teacher had set up along the sides of the classroom. Each of us had assigned spaces on the line, and they went in order of our table layouts around the room.

Malcolm's picture was still sitting on the desk. I grabbed it along with mine and hung it next to our table in a hurry. I had to get outside soon or Jasmine would probably leave without me. Most of the class was already gone.

I clipped his painting up first and then mine. As I was stepping back to pick up my backpack, I sensed someone behind me.

I turned around and found the teacher there. He wasn't preoccupied or grouchy anymore; he was smiling brightly. I caught a glimpse of the last student leaving the room.

"Excellent work, Rae." His teeth were those of an older man - slightly stained from the coffee he drank and worn on the edges.

His mostly bald head was shiny, little wisps of white hair hovering over the top of it.

"Thank you," I said, measuring the space between him and the table behind me, wondering if I'd be able to slip by without touching him. It was doubtful. I waited to see if maybe he'd leave soon.

"Whose is that next to yours?" He pointed at the dark landscape with the Xs in it.

"That's Malcolm's."

The teacher stared at our paintings for a few long seconds. I could hear the ticking of the clock on the wall at the front of the class. I wondered if I was about to have a Rainbow event with him. My heartbeat picked up its pace. It really sucked when it was an adult who was the Rainbow. They could be much more intimidating.

"Interesting, isn't it? How you sit at the same table and yet your work is the polar opposite of one another's."

I shrugged. "I guess. It's just what we see about our lives, and our lives are different probably."

"Yes, but look around you. Sitting next to someone influences students and what they draw. I see it all the time."

I looked up on the drying line, and as my eyes roamed down the line of drying watercolors, I could definitely see what he meant. I could almost tell who was at a table with someone else. It helped that everyone had hung his painting next to his tablemate's, though. Maybe I was just imagining things.

But then I looked at mine and Malcolm's, and it was almost shocking how different they were. Malcolm's wasn't the only dark one in the room; in fact, it was weird how the paintings started out dark at our end of the room and got lighter and lighter as they went down the line. By the time they were the work of students sitting near the door, they were more like mine - full of color and life.

My heart sank a little. If I hadn't figured it out before by Malcolm's behavior, it was really being made clear to me now. I didn't belong here. I didn't fit in. Not with Malcolm anyway. I should be sitting across the room from him.

So why did that make me want to be with him more? I shook my head at my ridiculousness. Rejection was apparently a very powerful aphrodisiac in my screwed-up life. Maybe I should have used darker colors on my painting myself, but the thought of it was too depressing. I had enough of that in my life that I didn't want to focus on it.

"Good work, today, Rae. Just wanted to let you know I'm happy to have you in class." He had his hands behind his back and was rocking up on his heels.

"It's nice to be here. I have to go, now, though. I'll see you tomorrow."

"No, actually, you won't. We don't hold Saturday sessions in this district."

I face palmed myself. "Oh, yeah. Friday. Forgot." I gave him a weak smile, not wanting to encourage him too much.

"Hey!" came a voice from the doorway. "Are you coming or what? We're going to be late."

Mr. Blankenship turned around, and I used the space he created to squeeze by and run around the back of the room. "See you next week, Mr. B!" I said, skipping up the aisle on the far side of the room.

I reached the doorway and pushed Jasmine out.

"Hey, watch the grabby hands," Jasmine protested, slapping me away half-heartedly.

"Thanks for the rescue," I said, breathless with the excitement of gaining my freedom. Mr. Blankenship hadn't done anything threatening, but being too close to people like that made me nervous. They reminded me of Jerry.

"What was that all about?" Jasmine asked, staring at me with a funny look on her face.

"He was just welcoming me to the school and being nice."

"Man, what is *up* with people today? Is it April Fools and someone forgot to tell me?"

Fear seized my chest as I wondered if I was going to lose my friend on the first day. I tried to blow it off. "I don't know, maybe. It's Friday, so that always makes people crazy, right?"

"I guess." Jasmine didn't sound all that convinced.

"So... detention!" I said with all the cheer I could muster.

"Yeah. Wow. Detention. Hold me back."

I nudged her with my elbow. "It won't be bad. We can sit together and pass notes."

"Be still my heart. I'd rather text."

"I'm cool with texting. I need your number, though." I pulled my phone out of my purse and unlocked it.

Jasmine snatched it out of my hand before I could say anything. She punched in her number while she talked. "Phones are confiscated at the start. Some smart asses bring old phones and hand those over so they can use their real phones to text. But that's just asking for more jail time as far as I'm concerned. They don't pay much attention to paper notes, so we can do that." She handed my phone back to me.

I pressed the green button and called her. "Now you'll have my number in your caller ID."

Jasmine ignored the ringing in her bag. "Good."

We reached a door that a few kids were going into ahead of us. I recognized one of them.

"Oh, hey, Rae." He smiled big and held the door open for us.

"Hi. Brody?"

"Yeah, Brody. Good, you remembered me." Another smile came beaming out at me.

"Hello, Brody," said Jasmine with a saccharine sweet voice. "How's the weight room treating you?"

"You tell me, Butts." He lost some of his smile.

"Looks like you need to lay off the juice," she said, walking past him and into the room.

"Says you." He scowled at her but then smiled at me again as I walked by.

"What'd you do to get in here?" he asked.

"I'm not exactly sure," I said. I wasn't all that excited about telling people I got into a wrestling match on the floor of the basketball courts. That was just a little too embarrassing.

"Doing anything after?" He walked with me to the back of the room where a group of tables were set up in rows. This was the largest classroom I'd been in so far here, and there was nothing on the walls. It was very institutional and cold.

"Going home, doing homework." I walked faster, trying to keep up with Jasmine and leave him behind.

"Maybe I'll catch you after," he said, no longer walking.

"Maybe," I responded, getting to Jasmine's side.

"Brody Carstairs? Ugh," said Jasmine.

"What? He's nice. I think."

"Yeah, he's nice as long as he wants to get in your pants. Then, not so much."

I didn't know what to say to that, so I didn't respond. Besides, Kootch was sitting at a table next to Malcolm and was waving his hand at us like a goofball. He had a backpack and a book in front of the two empty seats across from him and Malcolm.

"Are we sitting with them?" asked Jasmine, slowing down as she stared at the table.

"I don't know. What do you think?" Part of me wanted to go there and sit by Malcolm. The other just wanted to never see him again, so I wouldn't have to deal with him being rude. I was playing tug-of-war with myself and both sides were equally matched.

"Might as well. Kootch is a pain in the ass, but at least he's entertaining. Plus, maybe I can grab a ride from him when we're done."

"You don't have a car?"

"Let's just say I'm transportationally challenged at the moment."

"Me too. Meaning I don't have a car at all."

"Good. Let's go suck up to the guy with the wheels, then." She picked up the pace and made a beeline for Kootch's table.

I followed along behind, ignoring the stares that bore into me as I went. I was really looking forward to losing the new girl label that was taped across my forehead. It was pretty tough to be invisible and avoid Rainbows when my presence was this obvious.

"Here you go, Rae," said Kootch, moving the book that was in front of him. "Sit here."

Jasmine took the seat he'd been apparently holding for me. "Hey, Kootch. How's your ass?" she asked.

He frowned at her. "Hey, that seat was for Rae."

"Oh really?" She looked behind her and ran her hand along the wood of the chair. "I don't see her name on it." She turned back around and smiled sweetly at him.

I took the other seat across from Malcolm, secretly pleased that she'd taken the one in front of Kootch. I hadn't realized it before, but now I was starting to think Kootch might be crushing on me, and that could be dangerous for both of us. He has muscles. Maybe not as big as Brody's, but big enough.

"You guys got fake phones?" asked Kootch.

"No. We have paper," I said.

"I have homework to do," said Malcolm, pulling a notebook out of his backpack.

Kootch punched Malcolm lightly on the arm. "Dude, don't be lame, okay? You're at my table, and my table's for passing notes. Homework is for pussies."

"Spoken like a true honors student," said Jasmine.

Kootch didn't even glance at her. "Blow it out your tits, Butts." He was looking at me. "Tell him, Rae. Tell him not to be a lame-ass pussy."

My mouth dropped open, and I looked from Kootch to Malcolm. I wasn't sure how to react.

Malcolm was staring back at me, a very slight grin turning up one corner of his mouth. "Well?" he asked.

I knew then what I had to do. I smiled, taking him up on his challenge. "Don't be a lame-ass pussy, Malcolm. Do your homework at home."

"Ha-haaaaa!" Kootch held his hand out across the table. "Now that's what I'm talkin' about. Give me some skin on that."

I leaned over and tapped his palm lightly.

"Okay, people!" came the teacher's voice. "Detention has officially started! When the paper comes around, please print and sign your name. Do *not* sign any name other than your own, do *not* write so messy I can't read it, and do *not* put a cartoon character's name in any of the blanks, or I will find you and I will give you more detention. For any repeat offenders, you will find yourself with in-school suspension. Do I make myself clear?"

Someone called out in a whiney voice, "Yes, Mrs. Hannigan." Several students giggled. I wasn't sure if that was really her name or they were just quoting the movie line.

She made her way to the front of the room and was staring at our table, a very unhappy expression on her face.

I grinned hugely, feeling like I was personally being threatened with being kicked out of school. It was a first for me.

"Don't be so happy about it," whispered Kootch. "She's not kidding."

"Care for another week, Mr. Kucharski?" the teacher yelled at the back of his head.

He ducked down but answered loudly. "No, I do not care for another week, Mrs. Dickcheeser!"

"That's Deckchester, Caden. *Deckchester.*"

"Yeah, sorry."

Several students giggled again.

"No talking, no texting, no doing anything but homework. Put your phones out on the table so I can collect them."

We all put our phones together at the edge of the table nearest Malcolm.

"Dude, you told me you didn't have a phone," whispered Kootch, sounding offended.

"No talking!" yelled the teacher right behind Kootch, making him jump.

Malcolm ignored Kootch's tantrum as he dug through his backpack, acting like he didn't even hear him. He took out a pen and opened up his notebook, dropping his backpack to the floor at the same time.

The teacher came by and took our phones, putting them in a shoebox.

Jasmine slid a piece of paper over to me, hiding it behind a pile of books she'd set out on the table. Her handwriting was very jagged and artistic, almost like a fancy font from a computer.

*Where do u live? Maybe K can give u a ride 2.*

I took a pen out of my purse and wrote my answer.

*In the Highlands. Do u know it?*

She raised an eyebrow before writing: *How could I not? Ritzy shitzy.*

I smiled as I wrote back. *Not as shitzy as u think.* My parents always chose a community with gates and alarms. We'd learned the hard way that being without them was too risky.

Kootch pushed a paper over to me.

*Want a ride home?*

I wrote out my answer, *Me and Jasmine, yes,* and slid it back to him. He frowned at Jasmine but nodded eventually. He slid the paper over to Malcolm.

Malcolm acted like he was going to blow him off, refusing to look at it at first. But Kootch jabbed him several times with his elbow and forced him into it.

Malcolm looked down and shook his head, *No.*

I kicked him in the shins.

He looked up at me sharply and frowned.

I grinned, taking the paper from in front of him and writing out a message. *I told u already ... stop being a lame-A, P-word.*

I pushed the paper over until it hit his notebook.

He stared at me for a few seconds and then finally dropped his gaze to read it. A smile quirked up the corners of his mouth. He took his pen and scratched out a response and pushed it over to me.

Jasmine leaned in and read it with me.

*Careful. You could get yourself in big trouble calling a guy like me a lame-A, P-word.*

I felt a flush in my cheeks start. *A challenge for sure.* His handwriting was so cool. So much like a guy. Messy, careless. I wanted to fold the note away and put it in my purse and keep it so I could stare at it in my bedroom later, re-reading it about a thousand times, maybe more. *Geez, what is wrong with me? I'm acting like a lovesick fifth grader.*

I was going to write a response, but Jasmine took the paper from me before I could. She wrote something out and passed it back to Malcolm.

He read it and smiled, pointing to it and looking at me with a big question mark on his face.

I took the paper and read what she wrote.

*Trouble is her middle name. Bring it.*

I snorted. I couldn't help it.

"No talking! Did you hear me over there! Table Kucharski!"

"Hey, it wasn't me!" yelled Kootch. "I'm just sitting here all innocent, studying and shit."

"Add a day to your detention for that language, Caden!"

Kootch got a mutinous expression on his face. He was opening his mouth to say something back when suddenly he jumped and a look of pain crossed his features. He glared at Jasmine for a few seconds before grabbing the paper from us and writing on it furiously. He shoved it over to her.

I leaned over and read it with her.

*That's physical abuse! Now we're even! Keep ur pointy boots to urself!*

She smiled all evil-like and wrote a response. I caught most of it before she slid it over. She followed it up by pointing to the corner of her eye.

*U almost blinded me. Not even....*

Kootch read it and rolled his eyes, dropping his head in his arms in surrender.

Jasmine opened up a book and acted like she was studying.

I looked at Malcolm again, expecting him to be reading or writing in his notebook, but he wasn't. He was just looking at me with those deep brown eyes of his.

A shiver went down my spine. I could feel my pulse in my neck. All he had to do was look at me to get me feeling all hot and bothered. It was sad, but oh so very exciting. I hadn't felt this alive in a long, long time. So much of my life was about keeping my head down and not connecting with people. And here he was, getting under my skin, making me think a lot of things I shouldn't.

He pushed a paper over to me.

*Ride with Kootch.*

ELLE CASEY

I answered him back. *I will if you will.*

He read it and frowned.

His next note made me want to scream. *It's better if I don't.*

I shrugged, keeping it cool. *Then I won't either.*

His nostrils flared. *You're stubborn and frustrating.*

I gritted my teeth. *You're the master of that, I'm pretty sure.*

He shook his head, smiling again like he'd given up on being mad at me. He wrote a message and slid it over. *I'll go. Just one time.*

I felt like I'd triumphed in a serious business negotiation or something. I couldn't keep the grin off my face as I took one of Jasmine's books and pretended to read it.

The rest of the hour flew by. I got nothing done other than looking around the room and passing a few notes with my new friends. Malcolm had been really fun at first, but after he agreed to ride with us, he stared at the people sitting at other tables as if he were measuring them up. I tried not to be jealous whenever his gaze landed on another girl, and it made me feel better that he never smiled at any of them. But still, I wondered why he kept doing that and why he seemed so intense. His eyes would narrow as they landed on someone, and I could see his mind racing with something. What I wouldn't give to know what he was thinking...

I was really looking forward to the ride home, especially now that I knew Malcolm would be going with us. He was trying to keep me away, but for now, I wasn't going to let him. As long as he wasn't acting like a crazy Rainbow, I wanted to get to know him better and find out why he'd drawn such a dark picture of his life. The danger of it was luring me in, and I ignored the alarm bells going off in my brain telling me to just walk away.

## Chapter Thirteen
# Malcolm

I DON'T KNOW WHAT POSSESSED me to say I'd ride home with Rae. She's trouble with a capital T. Jasmine hadn't been joking when she called her that, even if she'd thought she was.

What kept messing me up is the fact that Rae isn't like any other Miserable I've been around. She's always smiling, she has nothing negative to say about anything, and that picture she painted with all those colors and brightness ... none of it made sense. She was like a Miserable in the way she was wanting to be near me, but the opposite in the way she was inside.

I scrubbed my hands against my hair in frustration. She was looking at me again, but I didn't want to make eye contact. Every time our gazes met, I felt like I was going to have a heart attack and my body got all hot and sweaty. Somehow she managed to turn up the temperature in any room she was standing in.

"Okay, time's up," said the teacher. "Collect your phones before you go. Don't leave anything behind. I'm not responsible for lost items." She put the shoebox of phones down on a table near the door and wandered over to her desk were she sat down and began typing something out on her own cell. Apparently her job was over and she had no more interest in what we did.

"Finally," said Kootch, dropping a pen into his backpack. "That was the longest hour of my life. You ready to go?" He might have been talking to all of us, but he was looking at Rae.

"Show us the way to the beast," said Jasmine.

Kootch glowered at her. "Don't make fun of my car, Butts. She's sensitive."

"Dude. It's a car." Jasmine stood in the aisle next to the table waiting for Rae.

"If you can't respect her feelings, you can't ride in her." Kootch went around the chairs to stand next to Rae.

"Does that sound really wrong to anyone but me?" asked Jasmine, leading the way to the exit.

"It does sound a little off," agreed Rae. "But I appreciate the ride, so I'll give her the respect."

"Thank you," said Kootch, sounding mollified. "Finally. Someone who appreciates a fine piece of machinery."

I snorted, knowing exactly what his machinery looked like. I've never been in it, but it managed to announce its presence to the whole school easily enough.

Kootch turned around and walked backwards so he could face me but not leave Rae's side. "Dude, you've turned me down every single time I've offered you a ride. I'm glad you finally agreed to come, but if you mock her, I'm going to leave your sorry ass in the dust and you can just walk home."

"That's fine with me," I said, not really sure if I meant it. Walking through the halls and then out to the parking lot with three people who weren't acting like they wanted to slit their wrists any second was really nice for a change. Even Kootch seemed to be in a good mood. He hadn't acted angry about anything since early this morning. Just before Rae walked into our classroom for the first time.

"Okay, now remember," said Kootch, taking his keys out of his pocket. "She's sensitive. So just compliment her when we get close, okay?"

Jasmine laughed quietly.

"Butts, I'm not kidding. One word against Geneva and you're done."

"Geneva. You named the car Geneva. I don't know which is sadder, the car or you."

"Neither of us is. You'll see, Rae. It suits her perfectly." He lifted up his key and pressed on the key chain, but no sound came out.

"What are you doing, fool?" asked Jasmine. "Your POS doesn't have enough juice in her shoe-sized battery to power an alarm."

"We like to pretend that she has auto locks, not an alarm." He stepped up to the back of the smallest, ugliest car on the lot, a satisfied smile spreading across his face.

"We? Kootch, you are a seriously lonely guy, you know that? Please tell me you don't take her out on dates." Jasmine was giving him a feigned frightened look.

"Sometimes we go for a shake at MickyD's. Now shut up or you'll be sitting on the curb all afternoon."

He walked around to the side of the vintage Gremlin and opened up the driver's door. "Chicks in the back. Malcolm, get in front with me." He stroked the top of the car, using the side of his fist and some spit to remove something from the paint.

I held the seat forward so Jasmine could climb in. Rae got in on Kootch's side. Once the seats were back in place, Kootch and I took the front seats. The door on my side made a hellaciously loud squeak as I tried to shut it. I had to pull on it a few times to build up enough momentum to get past whatever was making it stick. It slammed shut on the last attempt.

"Damn, I feel like I just got shut into a can," said Jasmine in a low voice.

Rae giggled.

"Last warning, Butts. Last warning." Kootch adjusted his rearview mirror so he could smile at Rae before putting it back. "Okay, who's up for a shake?"

"Me!" Rae said without hesitation.

"I gotta get home," I said. It wasn't true, really. At least not from a parental supervision perspective.

"Bullshit. You can go for a shake." Kootch reached over and tried to pound me on the leg, but I was too fast for him.

I moved to the side and knocked his fist away. "Hands off," I said, mostly unfazed. "I've got homework. Just take me home, it's not far." I did have homework but it wouldn't take more than thirty minutes to do.

"Nope. Mickey D's first, then home. If you don't like it, you can walk."

"If he doesn't want to go, you can't force him," said Jasmine.

"Watch me," said Kootch, looking up into the mirror and grinning like a mad man at the girls.

"Stay with us, Malcolm," said Rae. "It'll be more fun if you're there."

Her voice slid over me like ribbons of silk. Tickling. A little scary, especially since I wasn't in the habit of letting anyone get close enough to me that their words could affect me.

Kootch changed the pitch of his voice to match Rae's. "Yeah, Malcolm. Stay. We'll just die of broken hearts if your handsome face isn't there to drooool over." He sighed in an exaggerated style and batted his eyelashes a bunch.

I punched him in the leg. "Dick." I looked out the window, trying to think of one good reason to say yes. *Rae.* "Fine. I'll go. A shake and that's it. If you don't take me home after I'll walk."

"Jesus, you are such a chick sometimes," said Kootch, back to smiling and using his regular voice.

"I take exception to that comment, Kootch," said Jasmine.

"You would," he responded, snorting laughter at his own come-back.

"Where's MickeyD's?" asked Rae. She leaned her head in between the seats and looked at me.

I could smell her hair. It reminded me of flowers and sunshine.

"Just a few blocks up," answered Kootch. "They like to take advantage of all the student wallets around here."

He tried to shift gears, and the car bucked a bunch of times, throwing Rae forward more. Her hair swung up and hit me in the face.

*Flowers. Sunshine. Heat. Girl. Sexy.*

I turned my head and looked out the side window, moving away from her to the far edge of the seat as inconspicuously as possible.

"Whoa, bucking bronco," Rae said, sliding back into her seat.

"Geneva gets a little sensitive in her gears sometimes. Just like *all* girls."

He jammed the stick shift a few times and some horrible clanking sounds came from the car's engine somewhere.

"Yo, grind some for me while you're down there," said Jasmine. "And since when did you become such an expert on women?"

Kootch was growling at the car and trying to coax the shifter into position. "Shut up ... Butts! I just ... gotta ... get it ... there we go."

The car took off, surging forward a few yards before Kootch got it under control again. He turned to grin at us. "See? Runs like a dream, purrs like a kitten."

I waited for Jasmine's response, but none came. She probably had too much whiplash to speak, or maybe she knew she'd reached the limit where Kootch would go from good natured to angry at her.

I frowned as I thought about how happy he'd been recently. It was so unlike a Miserable to go from wanting to wallow in darkness to being like Kootch had been all day today. Maybe his crush on Rae was temporarily cheering him up. I'd never seen that happen before, but that didn't mean it was impossible. Maybe love does conquer all.

The idea of Kootch actually loving Rae someday made me a little sick to my stomach. My reaction made me mad at myself. Kootch had every right to feel that way about her, and I didn't. But that wasn't making it any easier; I still didn't like it for some reason.

We drove along listening to the music coming out of Kootch's pretty decent stereo, and Jasmine and Rae sang along to a Rhianna song. Kootch tried to join in, but it didn't work out so well. Jasmine reached up to the front and patted him on the shoulder. "That's cute. But better stop before you attract a female turkey vulture."

Kootch was about to turn around and let her have it, but the entrance to the restaurant was coming up and he had to wrestle the gears again to pull into the parking lot.

Just as we were slowing down to go in, a bright yellow sports-car zoomed past the Gremlin and cut us off. Kootch had to slam on his brakes to avoid hitting the other car, and the girls screamed. My hand flew to the dashboard and a weird non-word came flying out of my mouth. "Gaaaarbdah!"

The car lurched to a stop in the street and for about two seconds it was dead silent in the car. Then Kootch spoke.

"Garbdah? We're about to die, and the best you can come up with is *Garbdah*? What does that even mean?"

The girls giggled.

My face heated up. "I think it means I'm about to piss my pants, but I'm not sure."

Kootch laughed along with the girls, and I couldn't help but smile too.

"That asshole's gonna pay," said Kootch, sounding very determined as he shoved the stick into first. "Fucking Brody buttdart." He drove into the parking lot and purposely took the space next to the canary yellow Porche whose doors were opening. He barely missed hitting the driver's side door, forcing Brody to yank it back just in time. I stared through the window at Brody's angry expression.

Kootch laid on the horn, yelling, "Geneva's in da houuussse!" The horn wasn't any better than the rest of the car. It sounded like a dying duck or something.

"Hey, dick!" yelled Brody through the crack in his door, over the sound of the weak-ass horn. "Do you mind? I'm trying to get out here!"

Kootch yanked up the parking brake, turned off the engine, and scrambled out of the car to stand just at his door and look over the hood at Brody. "Yeah, I mind, you crazy *fuck!* You almost hit my car back there! What's your friggin' hurry? Steriods got you in a munchie mood or what?"

I looked through the passenger door window at Brody pointing his finger over at Kootch. "Better watch your mouth before I come over there and teach you some manners."

I opened my door and got out, hoping to get between them if Kootch decided to get stupid. Brody had to close his door again to keep from hitting my door. I pretended not to notice I'd blocked him in.

I looked down at the girls, worried they were going to get involved. Rae reached through the space next to the front seat and put her hand on Kootch's arm.

"Don't," she said simply.

Kootch had just opened his mouth and was about to shout something back at Brody, but then he just stopped. A range of emotions traveled across his expression; anger changed to confusion and then resignation.

"Yeah, whatever," he said in a defeated voice. "Come on Rae. Butts. Let's go get a shake."

Rae withdrew her hand and grabbed onto the seat in front of her to gain the leverage needed to get out of the car.

"Oh, hey, Rae," said Brody, squeezing out of his half-open door. "Didn't see you in there. Can I buy you a burger?" He walked around to join the rest of us at the back of the Gremlin.

"No, thanks," she said, sounding none too happy to see him. "I'm just going to get a shake."

My heart swelled with pride for her. She wasn't fooled by his good-looking face and football player reputation. She was sticking by her new friends, which said a lot about her. She was looking less and less like a Miserable with every hour that went by.

"My treat, then," he said, standing right in front of her. His buddy Derek was coming up to join him at his left.

Kootch stood off to the side. He seemed to be wrestling with something, as if forcing himself to stay quiet. I decided to keep away; my presence would only heat the situation up, not help it.

"No, thanks. Really," said Rae, "I like to pay my own way."

"Yeah, she pays her own way, Brody. Do you mind?" Kootch lifted his chin at Jasmine. "Come on, Jasmine ... Rae. Let's get that shake."

Jasmine didn't say a word. She just rolled her eyes at Brody as she walked by.

"Yo, Butts," said Derek.

"Yo yourself, Derek. Jerk move in the parking lot." Jasmine looked over her shoulder and frowned at him.

He shrugged. "I wasn't driving. Blame the driver, not me."

"That POS you're driving shouldn't even be allowed on the road," said Brody, walking into the restaurant behind Kootch.

I followed all of them, keeping some distance between us.

"Brody, why don't you just shut it?" Jasmine had turned around and was facing off against him.

He laughed in surprise. "What are you gonna do, Butts? Fight for your man?" He puffed out his chest a little, emphasizing the difference in size between them.

Her face turned beet red. "No. I'm just going to kick you in the beanbags because you're such a hose and walk away."

"Wow, you play dirty." He didn't sound all that unhappy about the idea.

"Yes, I do. Don't forget it." She turned around and pushed through the doors, two steps behind Rae and Kootch.

I waited until they were all in before I entered, just behind Derek. "Grab me a shake," I said to Kootch as he walked up to join the end of the long line, handing him a five dollar bill. "Get whatever you want."

Kootch looked down at the five. "I guess we're talking Happy Meal here."

I grabbed the five and slapped a ten in his palm. "Here."

Kootch smiled. "Sweet. Gas money, get in my belly." He turned around to look up at the menu above the workers' heads.

I left him to go to the bathroom. I felt partially responsible for the mood that had darkened the parking lot and wanted to put some space between them and me. Part of me wanted to just walk out and go home on foot, but a bigger part of me wanted to stay and sit at a table with Rae and watch her laugh with Kootch and Jasmine. This was like a dream moment, and I wanted to capture it and enjoy it before it disappeared. Because it would for sure disappear as our time together slowly pushed the misery into their hearts and made them want to leave this world.

# Chapter Fourteen
## Rae

BRODY HAD SEEMED SO NICE before, but he was quickly becoming more obnoxious than anything else. I didn't want to be rude to him, but neither did I want to encourage him. He's big, and I could only imagine what it would be like trying to get away from him if he decided to get persistent.

His friend Derek seemed much more relaxed. He looked uncomfortable sometimes and rolled his eyes when Brody was puffing out his chest like a rooster. I took that as a good sign but wondered why he'd hang out with someone who annoyed him.

Malcolm disappeared into the bathroom without saying anything. I was standing in line next to Jasmine considering the milkshake flavor choices when Kootch started joking about it, distracting me from my evaluation of Brody and Derek's friendship.

"I think he has a bladder problem or something. I swear he spends half his life in the bathrooms at school."

"You counting how many times Malcolm uses the bathroom?" I asked, teasing him a little. Kootch did seem particularly desperate to be Malcolm's friend, but I guess I couldn't fault him for that. I was feeling a little that way myself, but I was pretty sure it was for different reasons. Flashes of Malcolm's almost tortured brown eyes staring me down in detention flitted across my memory and made me blush.

"I don't have to count. There's a normal amount and a *not* normal amount, and he goes a not normal amount." He looked up at the menu. "Should I Super Size my shit or what?"

"Please don't," said Jasmine, not even looking at him.

I laughed. They were so funny together. I swear Jasmine knew exactly what buttons to push with him to make him crazy, and she definitely liked watching him go crazy. I couldn't blame her for pushing them though; I kind of enjoyed it too.

"Listen up, Butts. You could find yourself riding home with Brody if you're not careful."

"Still talking about me?" asked Brody from behind us.

"Please. I wouldn't waste my breath," said Kootch, not even looking at him.

I turned around to diffuse the situation. Derek nudged Brody in the arm and Brody smiled at me. "Want a lift home?"

"No, thanks. I'm getting a ride with Kootch."

"Ever been in a Porsche before? I'll let you drive."

Kootch turned around. "You'd let her drive? Man, you're brave."

"He's not brave. He's just deluded about how much girls care about cars," said Jasmine, facing the menu again.

"I'll bet Rae likes fast cars."

I was about to answer that I really couldn't care less about fast cars when someone bumped into me from behind. I looked around and found myself staring at Malcolm. He was watching me closely

"Sorry," he said after a few seconds. "You order yet?"

"No, we were just getting ready to."

I looked back at Brody. "Thanks for the offer. Maybe another time."

"What kinda shake you want?" asked Kootch, looking at Malcolm.

"Chocolate. I'll go get a booth. Unless we're not staying."

"No food in Geneva. We eat here," answered Kootch, still under the delusion that his car wasn't a Gremlin.

"You wouldn't want to spoil her upholstery," said Jasmine, trying not to laugh.

"No, I wouldn't. Thank you for understanding that, Butts." Kootch didn't look at her, he just walked up to the counter and placed his and Malcolm's order.

Jasmine stepped over to the register that came open next to Kootch's and ordered us both a shake.

I handed a five to the cashier. "My treat," I said as Jasmine reached into her purse.

"I'll get you next time," she said, giving me a flash of a smile before dropping back into her regular morose look. She pulled out a white and red box from her purse. "I'm going to go have a smoke before we eat. Be right back." She left the line and went outside, lighting her cigarette when she was standing next to the butt can by the door. I watched her take a drag and let out a big stream of smoke.

I moved away from the cash register after I had my change in hand.

"You don't smoke, do you, Rae?" asked Kootch, standing off to the side with me as we waited for our orders.

"No. It makes me sick to my stomach."

"I don't like it either. Nasty habit. Butts needs to stop."

"Better not tell her that." I could just picture her reaction to Kootch bossing her around. A rock would probably fly over the fence between their houses in the other direction.

"Oh, believe me, I do. Every chance I get. Last week I emailed her a picture of a black lung. At this point I think she might be smoking just to spite me."

I laughed at how put-out he sounded. "I doubt that."

"No, seriously. I know this for a fact. She wakes up every day, stands in front of the mirror, and says to herself: Hello, Jasmine. What are we going to do today to piss Kootch off?"

"I really don't think she's that focused on it," I said. It was entirely too easy to get Kootch all freaked out. I really didn't think Jasmine had to consciously think about it. It came natural for her.

"Well, for someone not focused she sure is good at it."

"Maybe she likes you," I said, pretty sure it was a distinct possibility. Jasmine tried to act mad at Kootch or like she was mocking him, but her defense of him in front of Brody said a lot.

"What? You're nuts. She's hated me since we were like five. Kindergarten. One day we're best buds playing in the mud and shit and the next ... bam. I'm out and I suck. No explanation. I had to play with Richie, the retarded kid down the street, for a whole year."

I had to laugh. He sounded so offended. "She told me *you* stopped playing with *her*. And that's not very nice, you know."

"Ha. That's bullshit. Don't fall under her spell, Rae. She's a liar. And Richie's cool. He was fun. But he knows he's retarded. It's not like that's news to anyone."

I play-frowned at him. "You don't really mean that, do you? About Jasmine being a liar?" I wasn't even going to get into it about his complete lack of political correctness. I had a feeling I'd be wasting my breath.

He looked uncomfortable. "Maybe not the liar part, but the spell part? Yeah. She's a witch. Or a voodoo guru. I'll bet she probably has about five Kootch dolls at her house, and all of them have pins in the ass."

"Number thirty-eight!" yelled out an employee standing at the counter with a tray in front of him.

I held up my receipt. "That's me. See you at the table." I took the tray with two shakes on it and left Kootch standing at the counter with his conspiracy theories.

*Jasmine a witch? Ha.* Something told me if that were true, Kootch would have already been turned into a toad.

I glanced back to make sure I hadn't offended Kootch by just walking away, and noticed Brody and Derek were walking over to join him. I hesitated halfway to the booth, wondering if I should go back and keep the mood happy between Kootch and Brody, but when I saw Malcolm sitting all by himself over in the corner, I couldn't *not* go. Whenever we were alone he ran, so this was my chance to try and talk to him without Kootch constantly interrupting.

I put my tray down on the table and stood at the end of it. I was going to take the seat across from him, but I had a flash of boldness and sat down next to him instead, forcing him to slide over. Now he was trapped into a conversation with me. *Perfect.* I smiled, pleased with myself and my slick move.

As our bodies touched on the sides, I instantly felt the warmth from his leg and arm move into me and spread towards my core. And then I smelled his cologne or maybe it was his deodorant, and it reminded me that he is all-guy. I breathed in the scent of him and smiled at how all these sensations added up to an absolute thrill, just being able to sit by him. It struck me for a split second that maybe this was what other people felt when they came near me. Before my mind could go any farther down that path, Malcolm spoke.

"You can sit over there if you want," he said, looking across the table.

"You'd rather sit next to Kootch?" I raised an eyebrow.

"Uh, no. Good point." He gave me a half smile.

I put my straw to my lips, hesitating for a moment before I took a sip. I swallowed the little bit of ice cream I'd managed to work up the fat straw and said, "So what's the deal? Why are you always so anxious to get away from me?" *There.* I said it. I clamped down on the straw again and sucked for all I was worth, trying to distract myself from my boldness with the job of making thick ice cream move.

I had no idea where my sudden bravery or this recklessness were coming from. Things were somehow making me forget that getting close to people is and always had been dangerous. I should run. I should leave this place and my shake behind. But I wasn't going to. Just for now, I was going to go with the flow. Some weird vibe was telling me to engage, to fight the fear and ignore the feeling that told me this was going to be a bad, bad decision with terrible consequences. I must be losing my mind.

He scoffed at me. "Right. What? Afraid of you? You're nuts." He grabbed Jasmine's straw off the tray and banged the end on the table, forcing the wrapper off. He put the end of the straw in his mouth and chewed on it, not looking at me.

"No, I'm not. See? ... Even now you won't look at me."

He huffed out a breath and turned to face me. "I'm looking at you. See? No big deal." His face turned pink, and he turned away.

"Do it for fifteen seconds," I dared him, my breath coming faster. I didn't know why this felt so risky. I was just asking him to look at me. What's the harm in staring into each other's eyes, dreaming of a life where things could be different and I could actually...?

"That's dumb," he said, looking down at the table, chewing on the straw like he was planning to ingest it at any second.

"Then do it." I lowered my voice. "Unless you're afraid." *Challenge proposed.*

He slowly turned his head to look at me. "Maybe I am." But he held my gaze and drew the straw out of his mouth.

*Challenge accepted.*

The white and yellow striped plastic slid out of his mouth through his dark red lips. His tongue came out to lick the tiny droplet of spit that the straw had left behind.

I don't know what made me do it, but I started to lean in towards him, not even knowing what the heck I was going to do once I got close. It was like something else was in control of me, making me forget every risk that ever followed on my heels, every dangerous thing that could happen as a result of letting someone fall under my spell.

Malcolm didn't move back like I expected him to. He just stared first into my eyes and then at my mouth. His tongue came out to lick his bottom lip nervously when I was just inches away.

"I haven't played the death stare game since third grade," said Jasmine, dropping into the booth across from us. "Kootch never could win at it. Too freaked out about people being close to his face."

I jerked back away from Malcolm, smiling and fake-laughing past the awkward moment. It is very possible that I might have actually kept going and kissed Malcolm if Jasmine hadn't come along when she did. Right in the middle of the McDonald's. *What was I thinking? I'd have to move from this town in less than a week! A new record of awfulness!*

I shook my head, trying to get the mist out of it. *What in the heck is wrong with me? Do I have a death wish or something?* I could turn him into a Rainbow with one touch and screw everything up with everyone. No more hanging out in gym. No more trips for milkshakes. No more anything. I scooted towards the edge of the seat, trying to be as casual about it as possible. *He's trouble. He's a death wish. Stay away from him.*

Kootch arrived at the table and took the spot next to Jasmine, dropping the tray down with a clatter, totally oblivious to the tension and fear that was pulsing out of me in waves. He pushed Jasmine over with his hip, not even looking at her while he did it.

"Here you go," he said, taking a shake off the tray and putting it in front of Malcolm. "Chocolate shake for you and Meal Deal for me." He hurried to open up his hamburger box. Lifting out the monstrosity inside, Kootch stared at it for a few seconds, an expression of great anticipation lighting up his face. "Now that's what I'm talkin' about." He dove in and took a huge bite. A combination of ketchup and mustard oozed out around the sides of his mouth, some of it dripping to the white box below.

"Oh, geez, Kootch! Hello, table manners? Ever heard of them?" Jasmine threw a few napkins in his general direction, clearly disgusted.

"Wha? Whaff's da probwom?" A piece of lettuce fell out of his mouth and landed on the edge of the tray.

I giggled at Jasmine's horror.

"I can *see* in your *mouth*, Kootch," she nearly growled. "And trust me ... it isn't pretty."

He turned to face her and opened his mouth wide, talking and flapping his jaw way more than necessary. "What? No, you can't. I dunno what you're talkin' about."

She punched him in the leg, and he feigned being in great pain, leaning over and fake-choking.

"Owwww, d'you see that?" he cried, trying to force tears but failing. "More physical abuse. Someone call the cops. That's assault with a deadly weapon."

She snorted, going back to her shake. "What weapon?"

He grabbed her hand from under the table and held it up for our benefit. "This! Boney knuckles and a pirate ring! I'm bruised for life!" He dropped her hand and rubbed his leg. "Seriously, keep your kung fu chop suey to yourself."

"Learn some manners and I will," she said, smiling at me. It was the happiest I've seen her look since I'd met her this morning.

Kootch frowned but went back to his burger and fries, grumbling under his breath but not loud enough that I could tell what he was saying.

I tried really hard not to laugh, but in the process of doing that I mangled my straw by biting it so hard that I could barely get the shake through until it melted most of the way down.

We all watched Kootch as we finished our shakes. It was a weird form of entertainment, slightly gross and entirely fascinating. It's possible he broke a few records sitting at the table with us that day: one for fastest eater and one for biggest bites taken without choking to death.

He let out a gnarly burp when he was done. "Buuuurrrrappp! Oh, man. That hit the spot." He patted his stomach and grinned at all of us.

"Can we go now?" asked Malcolm, clearly not impressed.

I'd been avoiding looking at him since getting caught staring him down and almost kissing him, but I turned my head in his direction, feeling the need to challenge him again. "Anxious to leave?"

"I have homework to do." He didn't meet my eyes.

Kootch stood, stacking all the cups on his tray. "Come on, then. Geneva's leaving the lot. Better take your potty break now Malcolm or you'll miss your ride."

I got out and stood off to the side, waiting for Malcolm to exit the booth. He slid to the edge and looked up at Kootch. "What? Are you my mother now?"

"No. But I know you have that bladder problem or whatever, so better hurry up."

Malcolm frowned as he stood. "I don't have a bladder problem. Who told you that?"

"No one told me, man. But you spend half your life in there, so I just figured it was something medical. Ain't no thang to me." He walked away with the tray, headed toward the garbage bin.

"I don't have a damn bladder problem," grumbled Malcolm, mostly to himself.

"Just ignore him," said Jasmine. "He doesn't understand that some people might choose to hide from him in a bathroom. He'd rather blame it on your bladder." She walked away to join Kootch at the garbage can. She must have immediately given him some crap because he started flapping his arms around and making her laugh.

"How does she know that?" asked Malcolm, staring after Jasmine.

"Know what?" I asked.

Malcolm jerked in fright, staring at me like he'd forgotten I was standing there.

"Nothing."

"That you hide in the bathroom to avoid people?"

He didn't respond.

My heart started beating furiously. I couldn't believe he was doing that - hiding from people. *Like me.* Maybe he's incredibly shy. Maybe he has a phobia about being around other people too much. Maybe he can't stand Kootch and doesn't want to be mean. Or maybe ...

"I do that too." I said it really fast and in a low voice so only he'd hear me.

He stared at me hard, searching my face and eyes. "Do what?" he finally asked, waiting for my answer, not moving and not looking away.

"Hide in the bathroom. Away from people."

"What people?" he asked, almost whispering.

"People who want to get too close," I whispered back. My face was flaming red, and my pulse was pounding hard. I'd never told anyone that before. The bathroom was my one sanctuary; the only place I could go and hide while also seeming normal to other people. No matter how badly someone wanted to be with me, they always stopped at the toilet stall door.

Now someone knew my secret. Malcolm. Would he follow me in one day, knowing it was a place he'd find me alone? Did I just sign my own death warrant? *No. I can't believe that about him. Not Malcolm. Please don't let Malcolm be a Rainbow.*

"Why would anyone want to do that? Get too close?" he whispered.

I could tell the answer meant a lot to him, knowing he had no idea how much it meant to me. I glanced down and noticed that his hand was shaking a little. My imagination was going a million miles an hour. *Maybe he's met someone like me before. Maybe he knows what my problem is. Could there be someone else out there like me? Would it be dangerous for us to be near each other? Could he be like me? If he is, why would he ask a question he already knows the answer to?*

I opened my mouth to answer, but I never got the chance to say anything.

"Come on," said Kootch, coming up behind Malcolm and grabbing his arm, pulling him back. "We're leaving. You can chat in the car."

Malcolm stumble-walked backwards, staring at me the whole time. I followed slowly in his tracks, never breaking eye contact. When he got near the front of the restaurant he finally snapped out of his trance or whatever had him so captivated and he turned around, speeding up to pass Kootch out the front door.

I felt empty at the loss of our locked gaze. It was so rare for me to have a connection like that, to allow one. Normally they were dangerous. With Malcolm, it just felt right.

I walked fast to catch up to the others. Jasmine was already outside, standing on the sidewalk, about to walk out into the parking lot. She was stubbing out a cigarette in the can next to her.

My phone beeped. I pulled it out of my purse while pushing through the doors. A text from my father flashed on the screen.

*Where are you? You should have been home by now.*

I sighed, knowing what this meant. If I didn't get home right away, my dad was going to call the police. It was beyond humiliating when he did that. I could feel myself getting angry at the thought of him messing up my first day of a new school like that. He had a tracker on my phone, and he could find me with it using the internet. I'd left my cell behind once to thwart his efforts and he'd nearly had a coronary. I decided that it wasn't worth the moment of freedom I'd enjoyed, and had never done that again. The last thing I needed to do was give him an excuse to cut me off from the world. I know it's what he really wanted to do.

I texted him back, copying my mom on the message. They didn't always talk to each other about what they were doing with me and sometimes they got jealous of each other if I paid more attention to one of them.

*On my way. See you in fifteen.*

He responded immediately.

*Fifteen minutes. No later.*

I looked at the time on my phone. It was almost five o'clock. I rushed from the sidewalk over to Kootch's car, waiting for him to open the door so I could get inside. I was just about to tell everyone that I needed to go home right away when Jasmine spoke up from outside the door.

"Uh-oh. Kootch. Did you see this?"

I walked around the vehicle to stand near her, just as Kootch started swearing.

"Goddamn it! What the hell?! A flat? Are you kidding me?"

I stared at the tiny tire whose rim was resting on the surface of the asphalt. "Oh, geez. That sucks." My heart skipped a beat as I realized how *much* it really sucked. I was going to be late. My dad would call the cops. He always managed to get them immediately mobilized, too. There was never any of that 'she has to be gone for twenty-four hours before we do anything' nonsense when my dad was in charge of the search party.

"Oh, no," I said, staring at the tire and then my phone, imagining the humiliation and awfulness of police cars zooming into the McDonald's parking lot. Maybe they'd even mess with my friends; it wouldn't be the first time.

"Sucks," said Jasmine, looking at it with me. "You going to get in trouble?"

"Uh, yeah. Like major trouble. My dad says I have to be home in fifteen minutes."

Kootch was at the trunk, banging around inside. "What the hell? How can I get a flat tire parked in the lot, huh? Someone tell me that? That's bullshit. I'll bet someone did this to me."

"What's wrong? Got a problem?" asked Brody, coming up behind Kootch and standing near the back of the Gremlin.

"Yeah, I got a fucking problem. Someone flattened my tire."

Brody frowned and walked around the car until he found the issue. "Oh, man." He bent down and touched the edges of it. "I don't see any holes. I don't think anyone slashed it or anything."

"Whatever. They're just a couple years old."

"Maybe you picked up a nail." Brody stood and grinned at me. "I guess you need a ride now, huh?"

I grimaced, not able to bring myself to completely smile. I felt like I was abandoning my friends, but I really couldn't make my dad wait. He'd see a request to stay out later as a trick. And if I stayed here, he's show up and make a scene. I didn't want him identifying any of my friends; he'd make it his personal business to keep me as far away from them as possible.

"I kind of do," I said. I looked at Jasmine. "I'm so sorry. I don't want to leave you guys here, but if I'm late I'll get seriously grounded."

"Sounds like your parents suck donkey kong," she said simply.

"Yes. They really do. Big donkey kong." I stepped over and gave her a hug.

She patted me on the back but not very enthusiastically.

"Thanks for inviting me along," I said, pulling away, wondering if I was losing the first friend I'd had in a long time for being a freak with messed up parents.

"I need a ride too," said Malcolm from behind us.

"No room," said Brody, pressing a button on his car and opening the locks. "Sorry, bud."

Derek stood off to the side, texting into his phone rapidly, his fingers flying over the keys.

"I can't go unless you give him a ride too," I said quickly, before I could talk myself out of it. I held my breath as I waited for Brody's answer.

Malcolm raised an eyebrow at me but didn't say anything.

"I don't have room," said Brody, sounding irritated. "The back is too small, and it's full of my football shit."

"What about me?" asked Derek, laughing in a confused way, his fingers frozen in mid-text.

"You stay here, and I'll come back and get you."

"No way, man. I'll ride in the front with her. We'll squeeze in."

"No," I said, letting my breath out in a rush. "I'll do that with Malcolm, but not Derek. We both have to get home or we'll get in trouble." I reached out and touched Brody's arm. "Please?"

The angry lines on his face smoothed out and he smiled lazily. "Yeah. Okay."

"No. Fuck that," said Derek. "Take the football shit out and put it in the POS." Derek was pointing at the Gremlin.

"Hey, watch what you're calling my car!" Kootch clenched his fists, flexing his arm muscles as they hung at his sides.

Jasmine walked over and stood in between Kootch and Brody, addressing Brody. "I'm going to stay here with Kootch. Put your crap in his car and come back and get it later. We'll put the spare on while you're gone. If you're not back by the time we're done, you'll either have to come get it at his house or at school Monday."

"I need it for tomorrow, so give me your address." Brody held out his phone, sounding defeated.

Kootch took Brody's cell and typed the information in. "Here. Don't come late," he grumbled, turning back to the hatch of the car so he could dig around some more. A few seconds later he was trying to pull out a tiny spare tire.

Malcolm and I stood off to the side as Derek and Brody made quick work of getting football pads, a beat-up helmet, a bag of balls, uniform parts, and some shoes into the other car. The smell that wafted over as the stuff went by was not pleasant. It reminded me of a combination of sweat, metal, and cat pee.

"Alright, climb in," said Brody.

Derek finished off a text and put his phone in his pocket, climbing into the back seat behind Brody's spot.

Malcolm and I exchanged a look. I was so glad he'd volunteered to go with me, but I couldn't figure out why he'd done it. Maybe he had parents like mine who were overprotective, or maybe he just didn't want to hang out with Kootch anymore.

"You okay with this?" he asked in a low tone as we walked over to the passenger side of the car.

I nodded. "Yeah. I just really need to get home."

I waited for Malcolm to get in and sit next to Derek. Once he was settled, I pushed the front seat back into position so I could get into the front passenger spot. As I eased myself down into the low seat, the scent of leather and men's cologne went up into my nose. It was nice, but I preferred how Malcolm smelled. The memory of it made me smile.

Brody was looking at me, grinning again with those perfectly straight white teeth of his. "So ... where am I going?"

"Highlands," I said.

"I live just past there," said Malcolm.

"I'll drop you off first," Brody said, looking into the mirror at Malcolm.

I glanced at my phone. *Five oh six.* The panic rose. "Um, I hate to be a big pain in the butt, but I need to be home no later than five fifteen. Can you drop me off first?"

Brody patted me on the leg. "Don't you worry. You'll be fine."

I didn't know what he meant by that, but he was in the driver's seat and I didn't want to come off as a freak in the middle of a demented panic attack. I looked down at my phone again, trying to calculate exactly how late I was going to be. Every minute mattered to my parents.

"Just drop us both at her house. I'll walk the rest of the way," said Malcolm.

"Fine," said Brody, not sounding very happy about the idea. His grin completely disappeared. "I gotta get back to my gear anyway."

We were several blocks away from the restaurant and in a residential district when Brody slowed down at a four-way stop, looking left and right. He was just pushing on the accelerator to move us into the intersection when a speeding car came out of nowhere and got there first.

A flash of red caught my eye and I screamed, bracing my hands against the dashboard for impact.

## Chapter Fifteen
# Malcolm

THE CAR CAME AT US from the left. Maybe I'm nuts, but I could have sworn it accelerated when we started moving forward past the stop sign. It should have been slowing down; that driver had a stop sign too, just like us.

"Gaaarrrben!" I yelled, throwing my arms out, my brain and mouth apparently once again unable to coordinate with each other and form an actual word in the middle of a panicked moment. One of my hands smacked Derek in the head and the other hit the side of the car.

The red car smashed into the front left quarter panel of the Porsche, sending us spinning. My body jerked sharply to the side and slammed into the door, and then the world turned into a blur.

Everyone was screaming, but the voice I heard above all the others was Rae's. I had a sudden, strong desire to stop time and pluck her out of the fray so I could set her gently down on the nearby sidewalk, like some kind of superhero in tights and a cape. It's possible I hit my head on the interior of the car during the accident.

ELLE CASEY

When the car finally came to rest, it was pointing a little to the left of where it had started. We had done a three-quarter turn, but it sure felt like more than that. I was queasy and had a headache. It felt like a tiny knife was stabbing me in the temple.

Just as I was thinking that and picturing a little man poking me in the side of my head with a tiny knife, Rae reached up and rubbed her left temple with her finger. I had the irrational thought that my pain was causing her to have it too. That would be a whole new layer of awful to add to my already eight-tier cake of a shit life.

"Headache?" I asked her. It was stupid, I know. Here we were just going through a car accident and that's the best I could come up with. This is what comes of avoiding girls for seventeen years - zero skills. None.

"Yeah," she whispered. It's like someone's sticking a needle in my brain.

"Me too," I said, rubbing mine now too, wondering if it would work to ease the pain. It didn't. I stopped five seconds after starting because it was making it worse.

Brody either finally realized what had happened or had just recovered his voice. He roared in anger. "Errrrraaawwww, what the fuuuuck?!" He pushed his door open and stumbled out of the car. "You are so dead, man! Dead!" He took off towards the red Toyota that had steam coming from under its hood, his gait a little off-kilter.

Derek shoved me in the shoulder. "Get out! Hurry up before he does something stupid!"

Rae beat us to it, jumping out of the car on her side. I watched her through the windshield, rushing over and putting her hand on Brody's arm.

Reaching forward and scrambling around with my hand, I finally found the lever that would release the seat-catch and let me out of the back. On my way out, Derek pushed me so hard I almost fell flat on my face on the street. Three stumbling steps got me to the grass so I could fall there instead. I rolled over onto my side. "What the hell, Derek?!"

He didn't even acknowledge me. He was already out and striding over to Brody, stopping on his left side, his hand on his friend's shoulder to stop him from going forward while he spoke. I couldn't hear what he was saying.

Rae lifted her hand from Brody's arm and stepped around behind him, running over on her toes toward me. Her hair was a mess, flying around her head in a tangle.

"Are you okay?" She dropped to her knees right next to my face as I was rolling over onto my back. She hurriedly tucked two clumps of hair behind her ears.

It was embarrassing to have her all worried over me when the only thing wrong was Derek's enthusiasm over getting to his friend. The headache was still there, but it wasn't a migraine or anything.

"I'm fine. Just fell getting out."

"Derek mowed you over, I saw it. I thought he was nicer than Brody, but I've changed my mind." She turned her head and looked at him for a second. When she was facing me again, she had a frown on her face.

"Don't hate on Derek for that. He just wanted to stop Brody from flying off the handle."

Rae stood and offered me her hand. "Come on. Let's go. I have to start walking or my parents are going to flip out completely."

"We'll never make it in time," I said, taking her hand.

I swear I felt something weird when our fingers touched. Gritting my teeth, I pulled on the hand she offered and stood, releasing her as soon as I had my balance. I wiped both palms off on my pants, trying to clear them of the weird tingling sensation that lingered.

Her mouth turned down at the corners as soon as our contact stopped. It gave me a weird thrill to see a person smile when they touched me and then frown when they stopped. That was a first for me.

The other driver got out and shouted at Brody as a brown sedan pulled up behind his disabled red car. "Shit, man! What the hell happened? Where'd you come from?" It was a kid from

ELLE CASEY

our school, Dan, known to his friends as Dan the Man. He plays
football with Brody and sells pot to anyone interested in buying,
including - it was rumored - certain teachers.

"Dan? What the ... dude, you fucked my car all up!" Brody
tried to walk in his direction again, but Derek's grip on his shirt
held him back.

"Let go, D!" Brody yanked his shirt with his opposite hand,
pulling it away and then trying to straighten it on his shoulders
as he stood there glaring at Dan.

"Don't do anything stupid. Holder's here." Derek pointed to
the person getting out of the brown sedan.

*Holder. What's he doing here?* The voices from the bathroom
came back to me - Holder in the restroom talking to another student about getting a girl alone. I got a seriously messed-up feeling
about it all over again.

What are the chances that I'd see this guy in a weird situation twice in one day when I almost never see him otherwise?
Probably not good. I tried to convince myself that it was totally
random, but it didn't work. In my experience, there was no such
thing. The only random event that had ever happened in my life
was me being born the way I was. That's it. Everything else followed a pattern and was totally predictable.

"What's going on here?" the teacher asked, walking up onto
the curb to reach the spot where Brody was standing, near the
front of the red car with its smashed-in front.

"I'll tell you what's going on here, Mr. Holder ... that *dick* ran
the stop sign and smashed into my Porsche. And the repairs are
going to cost a fortune. You better have a shitload of insurance,
Dan."

"That's not what happened!" Dan was waving his arms
around, a trickle of blood dripping down from a small cut near
his hairline. "You weren't even there! The intersection was totally clear, and then, BAM! There you were! You must have been
speeding. That's the only explanation. I hope *you* have good insurance, because you're going to have to pay for this shit." He
gestured to his car.

"Like hell! The only explanation is you're fucking blind and probably stoned, and now you're going to be *dead* too!"

Brody leaped for him, but was tackled from behind by Derek.

"No! Let it go, man!" Derek had gotten him by the waist and took him down in the grass. Brody was struggling to get away but Derek was on top of him, holding him down.

Rae spoke up. "Um, I'm really sorry this happened, Brody, and I'd love to stay and help you work it out, but I have to go." She was inching away from the scene and towards the sidewalk that would take her in the direction of her house.

"Where are you going?" asked Mr. Holder. "I can give you a lift."

"Highlands," she said, looking from him to me. She was worried, that much was clear. "Do you know him?" she asked me.

I nodded. "He teaches Chemistry at the high school."

She gave the teacher a tentative smile. "If it's not too much trouble. My parents are expecting me home any minute."

He smiled back at her, ignoring the students wrestling in the grass and acting like they weren't even there. "It's not a problem at all. Come on. Let's get you home." He held out his arm, gesturing towards his car. "Did you get hurt? Do you need to go to the hospital?"

I stood there frozen in place for a few seconds. Rae was smiling, tucking a piece of hair behind her ear and walking towards Mr. Holder. She looked so innocent with her hair a mess, that dimple in her cheek, and her JC Penney clothes. And he looked so ... not.

I forced my feet to start working. They were heavy and uncooperative. I almost fell as I shuffled and stumbled through the grass trying to get to her. "I need a ride too. You can drop me with Rae." It was a struggle to speak. It would have been so much easier to just stand there as an observer and do nothing. I'd trained myself so well to stay out of other people's business I didn't even know how to get involved now. My best skill is being alone, and up until now, I considered that a good thing. Now it just felt wrong.

Rae was almost to the door of Mr. Holder's car when I spoke. She looked up and smiled. It was like a light had gone on inside her and all her apprehension had melted away. "Yes! Malcolm can't be late. He needs to come with us."

Mr. Holder's expression went from agreeable and solicitous to dark and foreboding. Or maybe I just imagined it.

"Don't you think you should stay here and help with the police report? You're a witness." He frowned at me, giving me the stern look I know he used to intimidate students into doing their homework and not cheat on his tests.

It crossed my mind that I should stay and help Brody. That's what a real friend would do. That's what a responsible person would do. That's what *I* should do. I blinked a few times as the pain from that frigging headache kicked in again. It snapped me out of my good samaritan fog and woke me up to the creepy vibe I was getting from Mr. Holder again.

"Nah." I took four purposeful strides in their direction, my legs finally cooperating with my desire. "My parents will get really upset if I'm not home. I have to go now. With you guys." Hopefully this guy didn't know that I really don't have parents. At least not like I was pretending I do.

Mr. Holder continued to frown at me, his eyes following my progress all the way to the car.

Rae shut the front door she had just been about to go in and opened the back door instead. "I'll ride with you," she said, waiting for me to get in first.

My heart immediately felt lighter. I had this irrational sensation that I'd just avoided something bad in my life. And it was seriously weird that getting into Mr. Holder's car would do that for me; the brown Taurus was one of the ugliest vehicles I'd ever seen, especially with the paint's clear coat wearing off on the top and hood in patches, leaving mottled whitish splotches all over it. It looked like it had car leprosy. The interior wasn't much better, either. The stains on the upholstery made me wonder if this thing had been used as a taxi for drunks and drug addicts at some point.

I got into the car and slid over to the far side. The hard springs in the seat pressed into my butt through my jeans. Rae followed me in and immediately buckled her seatbelt. We sat there in silence as Mr. Holder walked over to the driver's side door. I buckled my seatbelt, trying not to look too hard at the stains on it as it lay across my chest.

Rae's nostrils flared. I noticed it out of the corner of my eye and turned in time to see the disgusted expression that crossed her face.

"Stinks, huh?" I asked, smiling ruefully.

She tried to hold in a grin, nodding. Then she whispered. "Like a rat's ass."

I coughed out a laugh as Mr. Holder got in, forcing my expression to go back to being bland. For some reason I didn't want him seeing me happy in his car.

He looked up at us, using the rearview mirror. "Seatbelts on? We don't want anyone getting hurt."

We both nodded.

"Good. Where am I going again?"

"Highlands."

"And step on it. Please. I mean, Rae's in a hurry." I tried to smile my apology at bossing him around.

I could see Mr. Holder's frown in the mirror as he started the engine and put his turn signal on. He pulled out into the road and went around the disabled Toyota to the stop sign.

"Maybe hurrying is what got you into trouble already. I think I should just drive the speed limit, don't you?" He looked up at me in the mirror, eyebrows raised.

Immediately cowed and worried I was going to get Brody in trouble, I nodded. Brody hadn't been speeding, and like him, I hadn't seen that damn red car until it was on us. The accident was totally Dan's fault, and I was going to make sure to call the police department and give them my statement when I got home.

"It wasn't Brody's fault," said Rae.

My hand flew out and tapped her on the thigh, almost of its own volition, telling her to shut up.

She looked at me with a question in her eyes.

I just stared at her, willing her to stop talking. Mr. Holder was a nice enough guy, but something about this whole scenario was bugging me. Here he was showing up on the scene at just the right time and getting a girl alone - or trying to. The chances that it was Rae he'd been talking about in the bathroom were pretty much zero. Mr. Holder and the student had been talking about someone they knew, someone with a history at the school. Today was Rae's first day, so it couldn't be her. But still...

"So, Rae, how do you like our school so far?" Mr. Holder squeezed the steering wheel over and over as he waited for her answer.

"It's nice." She glanced at me and then stared pointedly at the wheel.

I nodded very slightly. She'd noticed it too. I tried to give him the benefit of the doubt in my mind; maybe he was as creeped out at being with students in a car as we were about being with a teacher.

"And where did you come from?"

My face started a slow burn. The flush was moving up my neck. *Why does that sound like a loaded question?*

"South Carolina."

"How long were you there?"

"Um ...," I interrupted before Rae could answer, trying to think of something to say. "I think you have to turn left up here." His questions were bothering me, and I hoped to get him off track.

"I know where the Highlands are, Malcolm, thank you. Where do you live, son? I'll drop you first."

"Highlands. Drop me at the Highlands with Rae. That'll be fine."

He squeezed the steering wheel again, this time until his knuckles turned white.

Rae wrung her hands in her lap.

"So, Rae ...," he continued, "... how long were you in South Carolina?"

"I can't remember, really."

His reflection in the rearview mirror showed him drawing his eyebrows together in confusion. "How can you not remember? Was it a long time or a short time? Do you move around a lot?"

I had no idea why he was so desperate to know her answers, but it was obvious he was. He wasn't even watching the road anymore, he was so focused on looking at Rae in his mirror.

"Mr. Holder? There's a car coming," I warned, pointing over the front seat to the windshield. He'd veered a little into the wrong lane.

Mr. Holder jerked the wheel back.

Rae looked down at her phone. "I have about one more minute before I'm late. Are we close?" She looked up, desperation written all over her face.

I resisted the urge to reach over and squeeze her hand for support. It's not like someone was dying. Why was she so freaked out about being a minute late? Her parents must be serious jerks.

"We're almost there. I'll get you there on time. Your parents must be really strict. Are they possessive?"

I couldn't take it anymore. Rae opened her mouth to speak, but I cut her off again. "What kind of question is that?"

Mr. Holder hit the brakes. "Get out. Get out of my car right now." His voice was low, but the menacing tone left no question that he was serious.

I was taken aback by his change of tone and obvious anger. "What?"

"I said ... get out of my car. Right now, Malcolm. If you can't be polite, you can't ride. Goodbye. I'll see you in school Monday."

I looked at Rae and noticed tears in her eyes. She was shaking her head, pleading with me silently not to leave her there alone.

I grabbed her wrist with my right hand and the door handle with my left. "Fine. I'm going." I threw the door open and put my leg out, dropping my foot to the ground. "And I'm taking Rae with me." I shifted my weight and jumped out the rest of the way, yanking on her arm for all I was worth.

The car leaped forward a few feet before she was completely out.

She screamed, hanging halfway out of the car, held up from the road only by my kung fu grip. I used every muscle in my body to pull her the rest of the way out, my back straining with the effort.

"What the hell, Mr. Holder!" I grunted. "Jesus!" My headache pain ratcheted up to new levels of awful.

"I'm sorry! My foot slipped!" He leaned out of the front window, his whole arm out and gesturing as he threw the car into park. The car rocked to a stop. "Rae, please, my apologies. Please get back into the car and let me take you home. Your parents will be so worried." He gave her a weird playful kind of frown that only made him look more like a lunatic.

Rae had partially fallen against me with my last yank and her hurry to get out of the car. She had a grip on my forearms, and I kept them bent and stiff so she could use them as leverage to get up.

"Let's go," she whispered to me once she was on her feet, rubbing her temple again.

"Can you run?" I asked her in a low tone.

"Yes. Please."

"Gotta go, Mr. Holder. See you on Monday." I took off running, holding onto Rae's hand for dear life, ignoring the throbbing pain in my head. We raced down the sidewalk and around the nearest corner, trying to put as much distance between him and us as we could.

The farther away we got, the more my headache receded.

# Chapter Sixteen
# Rae

WHEN MR. HOLDER SHOWED UP at the scene of the accident, he was like a knight in shining armor. For about fifteen seconds. Then he just got ... weird. It started with his smile. I hated to be thinking this way, but it looked wrong on him. Fake. And then the car itself. Wow. I'm not a snob; I'm happy to ride in Gremlins and all kinds of other beaters. But this particular vehicle was just plain nasty inside, and it smelled like death or something equally bad. Maybe death was exaggerating, but it was pretty awful.

When Malcolm volunteered to go with me I felt like I'd been drowning and then someone had thrown me one of those orange rings to save me. I latched onto him so quickly, I must have looked like a desperate loser. But I didn't care. I had a monster headache and my parents were one minute away from calling out the National Guard.

As we drove away from the scene, I thought I'd feel better since I was finally heading towards home again. But then Mr. Holder's questions started. I like to avoid sharing personal stuff in general, but I especially don't like talking about anything related to where I've lived and how often I've moved around. If my dad or mom were in the military, it would explain our constant changes and wouldn't be any big deal. But neither of them were or ever had been involved with the government other than to pay taxes. We were just freaks, and the longer I could hide that fact from the world, the better it always was for me.

Mr. Holder wasn't taking my hints that I didn't want to answer him, though. He was persistent, annoying, and just plain weird. It made me really glad I didn't have him for Chemistry.

"We're almost there," he said. "I'll get you there on time. Your parents must be really strict. Are they possessive?"

I was getting ready to say something non-committal, but before I could get a single word out, Malcolm butted in.

"What kind of question is that?" He sounded offended on my behalf, and it warmed me to my toes. Rainbows defended me all the time, but they did it with a fanatical fervor that always rang false. Malcolm sounded more like a regular friend. I tried not to read too much into it, but it was hard. It could mean so many things. I wouldn't let myself think that he was interested in me, but maybe he was okay with being friends. I could definitely live with that; it's more than I could hope for, really.

I wanted to reach over and take Malcolm's hand and squeeze it, to thank him and let him know how much I appreciated him calling Mr. Holder out on his strange probing questions. I didn't, because I didn't want to creep him out, but even though I kept my hands to myself, I couldn't help but be thrilled over the fact that it was like he could read my mind or my emotions and wanted to help me. Rainbows always did everything for themselves, not for me. Malcolm was definitely not a Rainbow.

The car jerked to a stop. "Get out. Get out of my car right now." In two seconds flat, Mr. Holder went from being Mister Nice Guy to being Mister Evil Buttbag.

Malcolm sounded as confused as I was feeling. "What?"

"I said, get out of my car. Right now, Malcolm. If you can't be polite, you can't ride. Goodbye. I'll see you in school on Monday."

His tone was like he was discussing homework or something just as mundane and not ordering a kid out onto the street in mid-ride.

I got a terrible feeling in my gut. Tears leaped to my eyes as I thought about Malcolm leaving me alone in the car that smelled like something had died in it with the guy who asked too many personal questions.

Malcolm looked over at me, and I shook my head, begging him silently not to leave. I don't know why I didn't just say it out loud. Maybe because my parents had taught me manners, and I'd learned to never cause a fuss, I stayed silent when I wanted to yell. My lifelong training and adaptions were making it impossible for me to stick up for myself and tell Malcolm what I really wanted him to do.

But it didn't matter, because apparently, Malcolm can read minds. He grabbed my wrist. "Fine. I'm going. He pushed the door open and got out, pulling me as he went. "And I'm taking Rae with me."

As he pulled on my wrist, I pushed with my legs so I could get out with him, snatching my purse up on the way. I was hampered slightly by the fact that I didn't have both hands to push across the seat with. He was dragging me out as best he could, but the back seat was so long...

The car jumped forward a few feet before I was out of it completely. "Ahhh!" I screamed, now half out of the car and staring at the road rolling by very close to my face. I was quickly coming to the conclusion that a disgusting road rash was in my future, when Malcolm yanked me clear of the car. I tumbled out and landed against him in the grass on the side of the road.

"What the hell, Mr. Holder! Jesus!" Malcolm struggled to get me on my feet. I was trying to find him with my free hand so I could get the leverage I needed to stand. I finally grabbed a hold of his stiff arms and pulled myself up.

"I'm sorry! My foot slipped!" yelled Mr. Holder. "Rae, please, my apologies. Please get back into the car and let me take you home. Your parents will be so worried." I looked over my shoulder at him and stared for a moment, horrified at the weird expression on his face. I'm sure he just meant to be friendly, but he looked more desperate than anything else. He was like at Rainbow level ten and he'd only just met me. This was a bad sign. Now I felt the desperate urge to get the hell away from Mr. Holder that had nothing to do with upset parents and being late or a smelly car. "Let's go," I whispered to Malcolm. The headache that had started during the accident spiked again, and I reached up to rub my temple, trying to make it calm down. I hissed with the pain.

"Can you run?" Malcolm whispered.

"Yes. Please." I dropped my fingers from my head so I could hold his hand.

Malcolm and I took off running, holding hands as we went. I had no idea where we were going, so I just followed his lead. We flew down the sidewalk and around a corner, our feet slapping the pavement in a frantic rhythm. This was a day I wished I'd avoided boots and gone with sneakers. My heels were already seriously sore but I tried to disregard the pain and focus on putting distance between us and Mr. Holder.

At first my headache was pounding so bad I wanted to stop and just rub my temples, but I ignored it, worried about holding Malcolm back. And then when we made it around the corner and were out of Mr. Holder's sight, it got better. With every square of concrete that passed under our feet, the lighter the pain became.

Two blocks down, Malcolm dragged me off the sidewalk and through a sideyard of someone's house. We cut through their back yard diagonally and entered the yard of the house behind it. They were two of the few places that didn't have fences. I silently thanked Malcolm for not making me climb during our escape. I'd had about enough of beating my body up for one day, and I had never been one for gymnastics. We got over onto the street in front of this second house and ran another three blocks north before Malcolm finally stopped.

I bent over, trying to catch my breath, swaying on my feet a little. My stomach was burning from the exercise I wasn't used to. I had a cramp developing in my side, and I squeezed it to try and make it go away.

"Are you okay?" Malcolm asked, taking a step away from me.

"Yeah," I gasped out. "I just had a headache and ... I don't know." How could I explain all my irrational fears to him? That I thought the teacher was out to get me? That he was probably a Rainbow already, and I was going to have to work to avoid him for the rest of the year or I'd have to leave? I couldn't say any of that or Malcolm would never want to hang out with me again. I wasn't even sure he'd wanted to in the first place.

"Me too. Bad headache. But it's gone now."

I stood, reaching up to touch my temples, rubbing them in little circles to test it out. "Mine too. Like all the way gone." I dropped my arms to my sides, wondering what the hell was going on.

"Weird, right?" Malcolm was giving me one of those confused smiles again.

"Today has been a weird day all the way around." I sighed heavily, taking my phone out from my back pocket. A new text was there.

*You're late.* It was time-stamped two minutes earlier.

"How far are we from the Highlands?" I asked, resigned to the fact that my parents were going to freak and I was going to have to do some fancy footwork to keep names out of the discussion and lecture that would surely follow my arrival.

"Eight blocks. We could run it in about two minutes."

I texted my dad back. *8 blocks away. Running over. Battery dead. C u soon.*

I shut my phone off and put it in my back pocket, hoping my response would keep him from driving around to find me. "Let's go. Warn me when we're a block or two away."

Malcolm started jogging, and I ran fast for a couple seconds to get even with him. He kept up a steady pace and said nothing. On another day it might have been fun and even peaceful to run with him like this. A day when I didn't have my crazy parents breathing down my neck and an overly enthusiastic chemistry teacher trying to give me a lift. A day when I was wearing running shoes and breathable cotton clothes, not boots and my school outfit, my purse banging away on my hip.

"We're two blocks from the Highlands now." Malcolm kept going at the same pace, but I slowed. When he realized I wasn't next to him anymore, he stopped, turning around to face me. "What's wrong?"

"I can't show up with you." I felt ashamed saying that. I really didn't want him to think it was about him personally.

He frowned. "Okaaay..."

"It's not you. It's my parents." I walked fast so I could stand nearer to him. "They're really, really overprotective. If they see me with you, they'll think you're the reason I'm late and they'll make sure I never see you again."

"Seriously?"

"I know you don't believe me, I can tell by the look on your face. But I swear on everything holy that I'm not lying. And I'm not exaggerating either." I stared him in the eyes, begging him silently to believe me. My heart ached with it. *Please don't think I'm a freak.*

"What's going on, Rae?" He said it so calmly, like he really wanted to know. Like he wasn't judging. And he was no Rainbow, at least not yet. I'd never met anyone who was so determined to *not* be one.

I wanted nothing more than to tell him. Tell him everything. But I couldn't. He'd never understand, and he'd think I'm a mental patient. Then I'd never see him again, and I really, really wanted to see him again.

"Just parents." I rolled my eyes and shrugged, trying to act all casual. "You know how they are."

"Not really," he said, pulling out his cell. "Give me your number."

A secret thrill ran through me, overriding my sadness for a moment. Goosebumps actually rose up on my arms. This was the opposite of what I'd been expecting, the rejection that always came with the introduction to my crazy life. I had a feeling he didn't give out his number very often. Even Kootch didn't have it, and he appeared to be Malcolm's only friend.

I took Malcolm's phone from him and typed my number in, giving the cell back to him when I was done.

"This isn't a local number," he said, looking down at it and frowning.

"No. I got this one about three moves ago. I'll be getting a new one this weekend, but this one should work for a few more days." I tried to smile, but it wavered with the tears that threatened. *Don't cry, don't cry, whatever you do, don't cry!*

"Why did Mr. Holder ask you that question? About you moving around?"

My face flamed red. I so didn't want to get into the details of my sorry life right then when I knew my dad was itching to come out after me. I cleared my throat and stared at the ground. "I have to go. I'll see you Monday." I turned around, planning to run away. But then I realized I didn't even know where I was or where to find my house.

I turned back to Malcolm. "Which way do I go?" I sniffed and lifted my chin, determined to get control of my emotions and seem unaffected by everything.

Malcolm stared at me for a few precious seconds before finally answering. "Go to the end of the street and turn right. The entrance to the Highlands will be just a block down on your left."

Just as he finished with his directions, I heard the telltale sound of my father's engine. His BMW SUV was impossible to mistake with its high performance whine and occasional roar coming from under the hood.

"Hurry!" I said, desperation heating my voice, my hands flying up and waving around. "Hide!"

Malcolm looked at me in confusion. "What?"

The front end of my dad's car was just pulling up to the corner. He hadn't seen me yet, his head turned the other way.

I gestured to the bushes next to us with both hands. "Hide! Please!"

Malcolm jumped off the sidewalk without another word and ran behind the wall of bushes on the edge of the yard we were standing in front of. I quickly lost details of his form among the leaves, just barely make out some flashes of blue from his jeans and the darker green of his shirt. I prayed my father wouldn't notice him.

I turned to face the direction of my house and took my phone out, pretending to mess with it as I walked slowly down the side-walk away from the bushes. I didn't look up, even as I heard the car approaching a few seconds later.

*Stay calm. Do not look back at Malcolm. Act like you were wandering out here all by yourself in no hurry or panic.*

The car swerved over to the edge of the street, the driver's side window going down in a smooth electric motion.

"There you are. I was about to call the police, you know." My father was frowning at me. This was nothing new for him. Smiles were only doled out on special occasions, and almost as rare as the dodo bird. The saddest thing about my father is that being with me makes him overly happy, but he's too afraid about losing me to enjoy it.

I stopped walking and feigned surprise at seeing him there. "Oh! Hi, Dad! Sorry about that. You don't need to do that, you know. Come out or call the police. I was just down the street." I gestured with my thumb behind me, smiling as innocently as I know how. *I'm just a happy-go-lucky teenager without a care in the world. Nothing to see here. Move along, move along.*

He put the car in park. We were about ten feet away from where I'd left Malcolm, and I prayed he couldn't hear us.

"You know very well I do. What are you doing walking home? Your mother told you we'd pick you up. Come get in the car."

"I can walk. It's just a block away." I smiled, pointing up the street, pretending like we were a normal father and daughter and he'd say, *'Okay, Rae, go ahead and walk. The sun and exercise are good for you. I'll see you at home.'*

"Like hell you'll walk. Get in the car." He hit the electric door locks to open them and shifted his hand to put it on his door handle. It was his unspoken threat that if I resisted, he'd get out and *make* me accept the ride. He never had to get physical with me; he just had to act like he was going to and I'd run. Touching my parents was never a good idea.

I sighed. I don't know why I bothered offering to walk home from here. I knew better. Malcolm was probably listening to all of this and thinking we were the most messed up family he'd ever seen.

I could have fought my father on this, threatened him with denial of my presence to get my way, but my first priority needed to be getting him out of here - or at least getting him to put his window up so he wasn't blabbing his psychosis all over the place anymore. Fantasizing that we're normal and hoping he'd have a different answer than he always did was a waste of time.

I walked around the front of the SUV and got in the passenger side, making sure to keep my gaze on the windshield once I was seated. *Do not look at the bushes. Do not make eye contact with Dad. He'll read your expression and know you're lying.*

"I don't know what's gotten into you." He put the car into Drive. His window was still down.

"Can we go please?" I buckled my seatbelt, even though there were moments like this when I wondered if I might be better off leaving it off and dying in a car accident. The click of the locking mechanism reminded me that as tempting as it might be to end it all, I had a really strong will to live. Even though the life I was living pretty much sucked most of the time, I still ignored every suicidal thought that tried to sneak into my brain. At least today life had been a little different - until now, that is.

"We'll go when I'm ready to go. You *know* you can't be out wandering around, Rae. It's not safe. Did you walk all the way from school?"

"No. I got a ride." I tapped my fingers on my leg, trying to control my nervous energy by pretending to be singing in my head. I tried to whistle too, but gave up when it came out sounding like the wind blowing through a haunted forest.

"From whom?"

"Just a guy." I cringed inwardly. *Dammit, that was the wrong thing to say.* Guys were always trouble in my dad's eyes.

"A guy? Just a *guy?*" His tone became angry. "I want to know *who* this guy is and what business it is of his to be driving you home." His tone switched to one of disappointed scolding. "Rae, you know better than to do that. You can't let boys drive you home."

He was talking to me like I'm an idiot again, and I was sick and tired of it. Usually I had more patience with my parents, but knowing Malcolm could still be there by those bushes listening in to my father's ranting was making me sick to my stomach.

"Dad, just go, okay?! I'm not going to talk about this anymore until we're home."

"Rae..."

I turned the full force of my glare on him, speaking in a low, slightly menacing tone. "I will lock myself in my room and refuse to come out the entire weekend. Is that what you want?" I did it; I played the isolation card with him. I hated doing it, but he'd left me with no choice.

The shame I felt over using my power on him was almost over-whelming. I tortured myself when this happened with the idea that there's a special place in hell for kids who did that to their parents. Even when their parents were a pain in the butt. No one deserved to be manipulated, and I hated that I felt pushed into doing it. Maybe I should have been more patient, just tuned it out more. His response didn't help me feel any better.

His face fell and all the power from his anger disappeared, leaving a scared and lonely Rainbow behind in the driver's seat. "No, please don't. You know your mother and I don't like when you shut yourself away from us."

Tears burned my eyes and my throat felt too full, like I was choking. My words came out sounding strangled. "Then take me home and stop with the questions for just five minutes. That's all I'm asking." I turned away so I couldn't see his pitiful expression anymore.

He reached out and put his hand on my arm. I struggled not to flinch away from him. A smile lit his voice. "Sweetie, you know we just worry about you."

My chest ached with the pain I kept inside me. I stared out the side window. "Yeah. I know." My voice was rough with unexpressed emotion. "You can't help yourselves." To anyone listening it might have sounded like I was being a smart-ass teen, confident in her parents' love for her. But it was something much more sinister than that. They really were addicted, and like most addicts, in complete denial.

We pulled away from the curb and got over on the right side of the road. A block down the street my father did a u-turn to head back towards the Highlands.

The tears finally escaped and began to roll down my cheeks when I glanced out the side window and saw the solid dark green of Malcolm's shirt through the lighter leaves of the bush. He'd been there the whole time and had probably heard every word.

## Chapter Seventeen
# Malcolm

I STOOD THERE IN THE bushes, not moving a muscle, listening to bits and pieces of the conversation Rae was having with her father. She'd said the guy was overprotective, but that was a serious exaggeration as far as I could tell. The guy was a possessive freak. I was tempted to step out of my hiding place and pull Rae away from him, just like I had with Mr. Holder. But that was ridiculous. I pushed the urge and thought of it away right after it came into my head. This guy was her father, not some creepy teacher. He obviously loves her a lot and just wants her to be careful about who she hangs out with. Isn't that what all dads do? I wouldn't know. My dad left a long time ago, or that's what I hear, anyway. But if I were a dad, that's what I'd do.

When the car was out of sight, I left the bushes and jogged the rest of the way home, realizing for the first time I didn't have my backpack. I'd been in such a panic before, all I'd been able to think about was getting Rae safe. I must have left it in Brody's car. The only thing of value in it was my journal, which he'd probably read. I sighed, thinking about the shit he'd be giving me on

Monday. Guys like him weren't into poetry. They mocked what they didn't appreciate.

It took me twenty minutes to get home. I lied before when I said I live by the Highlands. My house is in a much more colorful part of town. And when I say colorful, I mean shitty.

I kicked an empty paper-bag-covered can out of the way as I mounted the stairs inside the concrete block apartment building where I live. There was trash along the edges of the stairway and in the hallways too, but I always left it where it was. I've seen the people who put that stuff there, and I strongly suspect they have infectious diseases I could catch. I shuddered at the thought of it as I passed by a used, twisted up condom just two doors down from my apartment at the end of the hall.

I pulled my key out of my shirt. I kept it on a chain around my neck. More than once I've had to abandon my backpack and then ended up locked out. I've learned to keep certain things close, and access to shelter was tops on my list.

I pushed open the door and shut it behind me, making sure to draw the two bolts and hook up the chain. Drug deals and angry domestic situations were normal around here, and I didn't like unexpected visitors wandering in. They were hard to get rid of and always made me feel sick, the way they stared at me and looked so needy, craving my darkness, wanting to consume it in great quantities. Just me being in this building was a problem for a lot of the tenants, but I had to live somewhere. Until the State was off my ass and out of my life, it had to be with other people, including people who were paid to foster orphans like me, even though they had zero qualifications or desire to be parents.

I picked up the phone to check for voicemails, but the line was dead. I slammed it back into the cradle. *Typical.* Bills only get paid when people are around to notice things aren't working anymore. I hadn't seen my current foster mother in weeks. It was better that way, though. She was one of the lucky ones. The foster parents who stuck around always ended up getting very messed up. Even though most of them were jerks, I still felt bad about that.

I sat down on the ratty couch on the far edge of the family room and thought about my day. Usually my days bled into weeks that bled into months; I hardly recognized one from the other. My life was an endless stream of regular patterns, nothing varying beyond me walking around trying to be invisible and ducking into bathrooms, avoiding contact with people as much as possible.

I laughed a little as I remembered Kootch being all magnanimous about my supposed bladder problem. I didn't have the heart to tell the guy I'd been in there hiding from him, but apparently Jasmine was perfectly happy with not candy-coating bad news. The look on Kootch's face was classic.

And then the world just kind of stopped. When Rae said she does the same thing. She hides in bathrooms too. I couldn't believe it when she said it; it was like my brain was refusing to compute the words.

I pulled my phone out and stared at her number.

*She hides in bathrooms too.*

I said it out loud, testing the sound of it, wondering if it meant anything at all. "She hides in bathrooms too."

I shook my head, disgusted with myself for wandering down that path. "Bullshit," I said out into the room. "She's no agent of darkness. No fucking way." I threw my phone down on the couch, watching it bounce off the opposite arm and land in a crack between the cushions. I was such a sad, sorry, fuck - sitting there thinking some girl who was so shy she sometimes took an extra bathroom break was an agent of evil like me. *Yeah. Right.*

I was still scowling when a knock came at the door, interrupting my next thought about where I was going to find some dinner. The cupboards had long been bare in this house, and I had almost no cash left.

"Hello? Malcolm?" came a lady's voice, slightly accented as if Spanish were her first language. "Malcolm McNamara? Mrs. Brown? Is anyone home?"

I sighed heavily. *Hello, Shitty Day? Meet Shittier Day.* I stood up from the couch, knowing that ignoring this problem would only make it worse. Walking to the door, I took those few seconds to smooth down my hair and shirt, trying to look less like a sweaty mess that had just escaped a weirded out teacher and jail keeper father and more like a studious teenager staying out of trouble, keeping his nose clean.

I opened the door and smiled as best I could. "Hello, Mrs. Gonzalez. What are you doing here?"

The rotund Hispanic woman in the brown and black polyester shirt and skirt outfit pursed her lips at me and nodded a few times before she answered. "Like you don't know. Is Mrs. Brown in?" She stood on her tiptoes to try and see over my shoulder. She needed another few inches to accomplish that goal. She wasn't much over five feet.

"No, she's not home. But if you come back tomorrow early, maybe you can catch her before work."

"No, that's okay. I'm here for you, too. Open up."

"Aren't you supposed to call and tell us you're coming first?" It was worth a shot. It only worked on the newbies, and Mrs. Gonzalez had been at the social worker thing for more years than I've been alive.

She pushed on the door and moved me back with the threat of a belly bump. "I would be happy to do that if you had a working phone. Did you get a cell phone yet?"

My face burned at the memory of my phone sitting on the couch. "Nope. Not yet. Soon, though. Soon." I walked backwards until I was near the couch. I sat down right on top of my phone, wiggling my butt a little to try and push it deeper into the crack between the cushions. "Have a seat," I said, gesturing to the rickety chair to the right of me.

She followed me over and sat down, the sound of panty hose and polyester swishing together reminding me strongly of every social worker who'd ever entered my life. There had been many. Why they were so attached to wearing those uncomfortable materials was a mystery to me. I had a polyester shirt once, a hand-me-down gift from a drunk foster father with seriously bad taste in clothes, and I'd sweated so bad in it I had to throw it in the garbage the next day. There isn't anything much more heinous in my book than a polyester sweat stink.

"So, you have no phone, Mrs. Brown is missing..."

"She's not missing. She's just at work." *That's right. Play stupid. Maybe she'll fall for it.*

"Sorry, but that game's already done played out. She's missing." She opened up a folder she'd brought with her and pulled out a form, dangling it between us. "See this? Missing person's report. Filed by her sister yesterday." She swung it back and forth a few times for emphasis.

"How'd you get a copy?" In my experience that part of the police department and social services didn't always work so well together. I'd had months of uninterrupted and unsupervised living as a result, which made me sad to see Mrs. Gonzalez was so damn on top of things. *Friggin computers.*

She frowned at me and put the paper away. "I know all. I see all. You're alone in this place, and you don't have a phone or probably any food either. Try and tell me I'm wrong." She challenged me with a raised eyebrow and a little bob-n-weave of her head.

I knew what was coming, so I tried to head it off. "I have plenty of food. I eat breakfast and lunch at school and dinner down the street. I'm fat." I pushed my stomach out and patted it, praying she'd buy it.

"Nice try, but you're not fat. You're puffing out your belly to look fat, but you are most definitely *not* fat. You're hungry. I can see it in your face." She leaned in, getting closer, studying me with her muddy brown eyes. The folder was in danger of being suffocated by her massive boobs.

I shrank back, putting as much distance between us as I could. I had to get her out of here ASAP. This woman was surrounded by misery on a daily basis. All she needed was a shot of darkness from me to push her over the edge and she'd be a goner. No retirement for her.

"I'm fine, I really am," I assured her. "I run all the time, so I have almost no body fat. I'm trying out for the track team. Really, I'm fine. And Mrs. Brown's sister checks in on me when she's gone, so it's no big deal."

She sighed, leaning back. "It's not good enough, Malcolm, and you know that. We have minimum standards."

I snorted. I couldn't help it. I tried to cover my expression with the back of my hand and faked a cough. She had to have seen the used condom in the hallway. *Minimum standards my butt.*

She frowned at me and then opened up her file again. "I'm putting you in emergency placement."

I jumped to my feet. "No!" I held out my hands in an apologetic way. "No. Seriously, it's not necessary. I can hang out at my friend's house. He offered to take me in just today." I was totally making shit up. Kootch's face was flashing across my mind, but there was no way I was going to even talk to him about this crap. No frigging way. He'd be dead in a week, living with me.

She pursed her lips. I could tell she was thinking about it. It was so much easier for her to just say yes and not do all the paperwork required to move a foster kid. She knew it. I knew it. The silence in the room was deafening. It was broken finally by the sound of the neighbors three doors down screaming at each other. I wondered briefly if an ambulance would be called this time. The thought crossed my mind that maybe I should just let Mrs. Gonzalez move me so I could give these people a break. But then there would be another group of people going dark on me at the new place, so I disregarded that idea. It was better to just ride it out here and then disappear when my birthday came.

"You know I only have three more months left in the system, Mrs. G. And I'm totally clean. No drugs, no crimes, nothing. I stay out of everyone's way and just mind my own business. My grades are good, too." Hopefully, she hadn't seen my latest report cards. I spend too much time trying not to stick out to do well in school, and teachers naturally felt like giving me crappy grades just because I bummed them out, anyway. I learned not to bother with homework and participation a long time ago. I only did the minimum to pass and that was it. I'm convinced teachers gave me Cs just so they wouldn't have to see me in class ever again. It worked for everyone, so I never said a word to anyone.

"But I wouldn't be doing my job if I just let you slide and live in this ... place." Mrs. Gonzalez was looking around the room, taking in the two pieces of furniture and the thick layer of grime on every surface, her lip curled in distaste.

"I'm fine ... *you're* doing fine. Don't you have about a hundred other kids who need you to take care of them? Kids with problems like drugs and pregnancy and stuff?"

"Try two hundred. But that doesn't mean I ignore kids, just because they'd rather I go away." She fixed me with a stare.

I've seen this expression before on lots of other faces. Faces of people who think they have my best interests at heart. People who think they know better than me how to keep me alive and healthy.

I decided to try and appeal to her overworked schedule, play the delay game. "How about we cut a deal ... you give Mrs. Brown another few days to show up, because you know she always does, and then if she doesn't, we'll talk about me moving in with my friend, okay? That way you can avoid all the paperwork if it's not necessary."

She stood and gathered her folders and purse. "Two days. The weekend. I'm back on Monday, and you'd better not hide from me. I'll call the police and get them involved, and then your clean record will go bye-bye." She stood there, gripping the folder to her chest and staring at me, making sure I knew she was serious.

"Yes, ma'am. I get you totally. I hear you. One hundred percent. See you Monday after school."

"Be here, or I show up at the school on Tuesday making a big stink." She walked herself out without another word, shutting the thin door behind her with a bang and leaving me with a sense of dread so heavy it felt like I was suffocating under a blanket of it.

My heart sank and I slumped over on the couch, arms dangling uselessly off to the side. I stared at the stained and sagging ceiling.

There was no way of getting out of this. I'd made it all the way to seventeen years and nine months, and yet despite doing everything right, doing everything I could to keep people safe, I was going to get fucked during the home run stretch. People were going to get hurt. People might even die.

Today was seriously not my day.

I felt something hard jabbing into my ribs. I reached around my side and dug the phone out of the cushions. Hitting the green button, I saw the last number dialed.

Rae's number.

# Chapter Eighteen
# Rae

AS SOON AS WE GOT home, I ran upstairs to my room. I ignored my mom standing in the front hall wringing her hands, knowing my father would fill her in on the details and keep her from freaking out too much.

His voice followed me into the upper hallway. "Be sure you're down soon to spend some time with us before dinner."

I didn't answer. I just went into my room and shut the door. I didn't bother locking it because they have a doo-hickey that would open it anyway, and they always got really upset when I locked them out. It made them kind of desperate, knowing I really didn't want to be with them.

I pulled my phone out of my purse and then hit the power button on the stereo that rested on my desk, filling my room with the sounds of Lana Del Rey's soulful, sad voice. I needed her music to take the edge off the Rainbow madness that I knew waited for me downstairs. Something about her songs always made me feel slightly anesthetized to all of it, making it easier to bear, making the thought of tomorrow seem not quite so terrible.

Kicking off my boots, I looked at my cell. The texts from my father were still showing on the screen. As I laid on my bed on my side, my hand tucked under the pillow that was beneath my head, I cleared them off, one-by-one.

I let my mind wander to the better part of my afternoon. The part when Malcolm asked for my number. I couldn't believe it had actually happened. Just seeing his name there on my phone made me grin like a fool. Butterflies flitted around in my stomach at the idea of hearing his voice over the line. I committed his number to memory, even though I knew I'd never call it, never press that green button on my phone when his number was on the screen. He'd probably never call me either, but that was okay. Just giving it to him at his request had been thrilling enough. For now, anyway.

Worried I was getting a little too nutty over a stupid phone number, I scrolled through the contacts until found Jasmine's. Two people in one day had given me their numbers or had asked for mine. It was some kind of miracle.

I laughed softly to myself when her number came up. I hadn't noticed before, but she'd put in *Jazzy Butts* as the name. I pressed the message button before I could second-guess myself and typed out a text.

*"Everything go ok with the tire?"*

My face burned a little as I pressed the Send key, my fear of losing my new friend making me think that maybe I should have waited for her to text me first. I didn't want to seem too eager to be her friend, scare her away. I was so out of my element talking to another teenager about mundane things. With me, everything meant so much, even what should have been meaningless stuff.

My phone beeped and a new message popped up, sending my heart racing with anticipation.

*"If by ok u mean I listened to K bitch 20 minutes straight then yeah. Stellar. U?"*

I answered back, forcing myself to wait ten full seconds before pressing the button to send it off. I'm cool. I don't have to speed-type at warp speed and send it before she takes another breath.

*"Got in an accident. Got a ride from mr holder. Chemistry? Home now."*

Two seconds later my phone rang.

"Are you frigging kidding me?" Jasmine said without preamble.

"Yeah. I mean, no. I'm not kidding." I rolled over onto my back, staring at my pristine white ceiling.

"An accident? In the *Porsche?*"

"Yes. The front side is a little smashed." I lifted my legs up and practiced pointing and flexing my toes. My feet were so sore from all the running around.

"Hoooly, shit. Brody must be furious. That car is his penis."

I barked out a laugh, my legs dropping. "What?" I was pretty sure I'd heard her wrong.

"His penis. The Porsche is his sorry-about-your-penis car. You know, overcompensating..."

"Okay, I get it." My hearing was just fine, apparently. I cringed. "I hate that word, though."

"Would you prefer I use dick?"

"Uh, no." I was still laughing.

"Schlong?"

"No. Not really."

"Trouser trout? Baloney Pony? Cock-a-doodle-doo?"

"Please, no! Stick with the first one."

"Penis? You want me to stick with penis? You're sure about the penis thing?"

I was holding my stomach with the giggling now, rolling back over onto my side. "Okay, stop. You have to stop or I'll pee, and I don't want to get up."

"Fine. How'd it happen?"

"We were going through a stop sign and some guy named Dan ran his sign on the other side and hit us."

"What kind of car was it?"

"The other one? Red. Something red."

"From our school?"

"Yeah."

"Dan the stoner. He was probably toasted. He always is."

"He didn't seem like it. He was freaked out, but not wasted-looking or acting."

"How'd you end up getting a ride with Holder? He's a freak."

"Yeah, he was a little freaky. He happened to be riding behind Dan, I guess. He just showed up, kind of."

"Did you check the comb-over? Wicked, right?"

"I didn't notice." I'd been too busy flipping out over his probing questions. Or maybe I'd been too gassed out by the stench in his car.

"How can you *not* notice it? It starts at his ass crack and ends at his upper lip."

My stomach was cramping with the laughter. I hadn't had this much fun on the phone in years. Maybe ever. "Malcolm rode with me."

I held my breath, realizing I might have said too much.

"That's cool. Kind of strange, but cool."

"Why strange?" My laughter faded quickly.

"He never goes anywhere with anyone. Then all of a sudden he's insisting he go in the Porsche today? I'm pretty sure he hates Brody. He must like you."

My heart skipped a beat. "Nooo ... he was just being nice. And he had to get home."

"If you say so. But I've seen more of him today than I have in the last year. The ghost has materialized ... and whaddya know, he's a real boy. Anyway, I gotta go. I need to go throw a rock over the fence at Kootch."

I half-laughed. "Are you serious?"

"A little. Talk to you tomorrow."

"Okay. Bye." I pressed the red button to end the call and tried to stop smiling. It was impossible. She said she'd talk to me tomorrow. Tomorrow is Saturday, which meant she wanted to hang out or at least connect on the weekend. I hugged the phone to my chest, my face lit up with the joy of friendship.

The door to my room opened and my mom's face was there in the crack. I erased my smile and any sign that it had even been there, letting my phone slide down to the bed.

"Hi, honey. How was your first day? Mind if I come in?" She waited patiently in the hallway, working hard at not pissing me off. But even with her restraint, I could tell from her eager expression that she wanted nothing more than to come into my room and sit right next to me, touch me and soak up the Rainbow vibe she craved. The poison she was addicted to. She was worse than Dan the stoner could ever be with his drug of choice.

My parents make me feel like I'm a monster teenager who throws tantrums and makes her parents jump through hoops just for the fun of it. No matter how many times I try to explain to them that they force me into putting up these ridiculous boundaries, they never understand. They can never see that the things they do aren't normal, that their obsessions over me are unhealthy and downright freaky. And even after almost eighteen years of it, I still could never get used to it, never be okay with being smothered. I had to put limits on our contact and break their hearts in the process, just to keep us alive.

I couldn't wait to be free of that guilt, be gone from this place that was nothing more than a gilded cage filled with bribes for touches and apologies for needs they could not and did not want to control.

"Yeah, you can come in for a minute. I was just about to come down." I sat up in the bed, drawing my legs up to my chest, tucking my phone under my pillow behind me.

She came in and shut the door, like she always does. I think she does it to keep my father out. They get jealous of each other sometimes, hoarding alone-time with me like it's gold.

She sat down on the edge of the bed next to me, her hand hovering just above my knee.

I gave her the look that said, *Don't do it.*

She pulled her hand away and rested it in her lap, a small sigh escaping before she smiled at me again. Nothing ever keeps a Rainbow down for long, not even a daughter's rejection.

"So, about your first day ..."

"It was fine. Pretty much like normal. Just went to my classes, kept to myself, and then had detention."

She frowned. "I don't understand. Detention?"

I couldn't help but smile. "I know, right? It was awesome."

"How can being punished be awesome? And who sent you there? I think we should have a talk with whoever it was or the principal."

"No, you don't need to talk to anyone. I was fine. I had to sit at a table and study for an hour. It was very ... peaceful."

"Did anyone bother you?"

"No."

"Get too close?"

"No."

"Act too interested?"

I sighed. "No, Mom. No, okay? Everyone was fine. Everything was fine. I got a ride partway back and walked the rest."

"Who did you get a ride with?"

The heat rose up in my neck as this friendly mother-daughter talk started feeling more like an interrogation. My annoyance found its way into my voice. "A guy. Just a random student who I barely talked to. It was no big deal. I got out of the car when I was close and walked. No story. The end."

My mother pressed her lips together, battling herself. She wanted to say something but was trying really hard not to.

I nudged her with my foot to distract her. "What'd you and Dad do all day?"

She gave me a watery smile and waved in the air with one of her hands near the side of her head. "Oh, you know. The usual. He was online most of the day with work, and I did some baking."

My mom's baking days were legendary. Sometimes she channeled her obsession over me and concerns about what I was doing into flour and sugar concoctions, and then we'd be up to our ears in cookies and cakes for weeks solid.

"Did you make eight batches of brownies this time?" I was teasing her, trying to get rid of the anger simmering inside me. This wasn't her fault. She was doing the best she could.

"No. But I made a tart. Or a couple tarts, actually."

I tilted my head down and looked up at her. "How many are a couple? Two?"

"Um ... no. More than two."

I smiled at her, she looked so embarrassed. "Tell me you didn't make twenty tarts."

"No, silly. Not that many." She stood. "Are you coming downstairs now? Your father wants to see you."

"I'll be down after I use the bathroom."

She wrung her hands. "Okay. Well, I'll be down in the kitchen. I have something in the oven."

"Tart number nineteen?"

She waved me off and left the room, leaving the door slightly open. Her evasiveness told me there would be tarts in my future for possibly the next week, maybe longer. Hopefully she managed to fit a blueberry one into her baking frenzy. No matter what she did with that fruit, I always liked it.

I was standing to go to the bathroom when I heard my phone beep again. Another text. I slid my hand under the pillow and pulled my phone out, fully expecting to see *Jazzy Butts* on the screen.

My heart nearly exploded when I saw Malcolm's name there instead.

"*R u ok?*" The text was blazing out at me. The words were so innocent, but they could have meant ever so much if he even had a clue about my life.

My hands were shaking so badly, I almost dropped the phone. I lifted up my thumb to type my response in on the keypad, and it remained poised over the buttons for several long seconds. My stomach was burning with nerves. *What should I say? Should I be cool? Just say one word and walk away? Act like I don't care?* Other people were way better at being cool than I am. I suck at cool. Cool and me, we're strangers.

*Just be honest. Speak from the heart. He's going to disappear out of your life anyway. Everyone always does.*

I typed out my response and hit send before I could talk myself out of it and flush my phone down the toilet.

"*Good. I guess. Sorry about my father. He's a pain.*"

I expected Malcolm to say it was okay or just blow it off. I wasn't expecting him to send the message that came across my screen next.

*"You hide in bathrooms."*

I felt like I couldn't breathe. My lungs were tightening up and my throat was closing, like I was having an allergic reaction. Total system shut down. I was flat-out a mess over a four-word question sent through my phone.

Maybe he was just making fun of me, but I didn't think so. This was something else. I was afraid to even wish for what it could be.

My thumb tried to respond quickly, but I kept hitting the wrong button, like one of the nightmares I have where I have to dial a number in an emergency and I cannot dial it at all, always hitting the key next to the one I really wanted. It took a full two minutes to finally finish my message, and even then, I waited to send it. This could be a big mistake. A huge one. Three simple words. They carried so much meaning.

*"So do you."*

I waited after sending it, holding my breath. My face turned red with the effort of denying my body what it needed. Pounding, pounding. My heart kept pounding, regardless, slower but still insisting I live. I finally let my breath out in a big gasp when his answer came.

*"Why? Why do u hide?"*

My finger was less shaky this time. I was doing this. I was telling him things I probably shouldn't, but I didn't care.

*"I told you already. Close. Ppl get 2 close."*

*"But why?"* he asked almost immediately.

I didn't know what to say. If I told him the truth, I'd sound like a freak. But if I lied, I'd never know why he was so interested in the answer. This was the second time he'd asked for it. If there was even one speck of a chance that he could know someone like me, or understand me even just a little, I had to take it ... *didn't I?* Would the chance of being able to be near him on a regular basis be worth the risk of losing it all? Or was I better off just letting it go, living my life, being friends with him as long as he could stand the Rainbows and then letting him go when he got sick of them?

Years of the same thing, of getting my hopes up and disappointment crashing down on top of not only my head but the heads of my parents too, told me that *No*, it wasn't worth the risk. I'm the only one of my kind in the entire world. I would never have a true friend, a boy who could love me for who I am. Any affection I ever received would be the kind given in exchange for the drugs I offered. Payment for the buzz my presence delivered.

I hit the red button to clear my screen. "Just let it go," I said out into the room, feeling sick to my stomach. I used the supreme strength of my well-practiced willpower to shove my phone under my pillow, leaving my room right after to join my parents downstairs. Every step I took away from my room tore my heart just a little farther in two, but I kept going until I was at the bottom of the stairs.

The television was on, and I could hear a football game being played, the commentators discussing the latest call made by the referees. Pots and pans banged around in the kitchen and the water splashed on.

Our house sounded like many of the other houses in America right now, with moms and dads doing what they do, and teens like me hovering on the outskirts of it, trying to fit in. But our house was like no other house anywhere. Of that, I was absolutely certain.

## Chapter Nineteen
# Malcolm

ISTARED AT MY PHONE for a full ten minutes before I finally accepted the fact that Rae wasn't going to answer my question. My words glowed out at me from the backlit screen, taunting me with their deeper meaning.

*"But why?"*

It was a great question, one I wish I had the answer to myself. I threw my phone down, disgusted with my ridiculous love-starved attitude. I've known this girl for less than a day and for some insane reason I was expecting her to have the answer to the question I've been haunted by my whole life. *Why do people want to get too close?*

I was halfway across the room when my phone beeped, signaling there was a text waiting for me. I ran and dove for the cell, dropping it in my hurry to read the message. *Answers, answers, answers.* My eyes scanned the screen, starving for the response I was hoping it held. It's the closest I've come to praying in a very long time.

Kootch's name came across the screen, dissolving my dream into a million unanswered pieces.

*"Dude. Party time. Meet me at the Mickey Ds. I'll get u at 9:45."*

I frowned. I was tempted to ignore it, but after the day I'd had today and the crap I'd been through, I realized I didn't want to blow him off. Not this time. So I at least had to be nice about turning him down.

*"Busy."*

*"Fuck that. B there at 9:45 or I kick ur ass."*

I laughed. All alone in my shitty apartment, I laughed at his attitude and boldness. Normally I'd write this persistence off as a Miserable's single-minded dedication to being unhappy, but today he'd sure seemed pretty un-Miserable.

I felt the tingle of excitement move out from my chest. Maybe I should take advantage of his good mood or temporary immunity to my effects and try to forget the fact that Rae was blowing me off - the one girl who I wanted to get to know better, the one person who I thought I might have a chance of getting to know better without death being involved.

*What the hell. Just say yes for once in your life. What's the worst that can happen in a single night at a stupid party?*

I punched in my response before I could be smart and run away again. I was tired of running. Just for tonight, I was going to stick.

*"C u there."*

# Chapter Twenty
# Rae

MY PARENTS INSISTED I STAY downstairs the entire night, greedily sucking up my last daylight and evening hours with veiled conversation and dinner. Every question was designed to seem innocent, but they all boiled down to finding out one thing: who was getting too close and acting like a threat to their total possession of me. They wanted names and contact information.

I did a pretty good job of throwing them off the scent of any new friends. I'd grown very adept at that over the years. The only person I did mention was Mr. Holder. As far as I was concerned, it couldn't hurt to have the principal watching that guy a little closer. I knew my parents would be on the phone with Mr. Tweeds over the weekend, now. Surely they would have his home number and cell too, just like they always did at every new school. Copies of police reports and restraining orders always gave them special privileges and an inside track to authority.

I didn't get back to my room until after eight. Glancing at my pillow, I walked over to my dresser and pulled out my pajamas.

I was determined to not look at my phone until tomorrow morning. Nothing would make me check my messages until then. If I did, I knew I'd answer them and then blow everything.

My phone rang as I was pulling my shirt over my head. Not wanting my parents to hear it, I raced over and grabbed it from under my pillow. Jazzy Butts was calling.

"Hello?" I pressed my phone to my ear and spoke in low tones, staring at the door while praying my parents wouldn't choose that moment to come in.

"Why aren't you answering my texts, woman? You think I've got nothing better to do than get eyeball cancer from staring at my damn cell screen all night?"

My smile came through in my voice. "Sorry. I was stuck downstairs with my parents and my phone was under my pillow in my room."

"What was it doing there?"

"Long story. What's up?"

"Party. Kootch broke his vow of silence and invited us. And by us, I'm pretty sure he meant you, but whatever. I'm going and so are you."

"Dammit, I wish I could." I stared harder at the door. "But my parents would never let me go in a million years."

"Lame. But you don't need to ask for their permission. Just go."

I laughed bitterly. "Yeah, right. I'll just walk out the front door and come back when I feel like it."

"You got it half right. Front door, no. Window? Yes."

"I live on the second floor."

"Fine. Front door it is. But you have to go. If you don't, then I can't, and if I don't get out of this empty house and intermingle with some other humans, I'm liable to do anything. Shaving cream might be involved. I might even go throw more stones at Kootch, and then where will we be?"

I laughed, wishing more than anything I could go.

"You don't want to be responsible for that, do you?" she asked. "He doesn't let shit go. I'll probably hit him right in the middle of his big-ass forehead, and then we'll have to call him Cyclops for the next five years. And as appealing as that sounds right now, I can easily think of eight other insults I'd like to use first."

"Oh, man, I wish I could go. I really do." My mind was turning and turning, trying to figure out how I might be able to sneak away. I'd never done that before, but it was mainly because my parents put our house on lock-down every night. They feared the eager Rainbows who had more than once come looking for me after school hours were long over.

"Listen, you need to just find a way and get your butt outside. Ten o'clock outside your gates, Kootch will be there with yours truly to pick you up."

I tapped my foot in agitation at my situation. I always hated being locked in, but this was worse, knowing there was something fun to go do on the outside.

"And, oh ... by the way? Malcolm will be there."

I squeezed the phone so hard I'm surprised it didn't break. "Fine. I'll be there." My heart slammed against my ribs like a bird crazy to be free from its cage.

"Good. Later, tater." Jasmine disconnected the phone before I could respond or ask her what she was wearing. I'd never been to a party before. I had no clue what to put on after school hours, at a place where no adults would be around to watch or scold or judge. Chances are nothing in my wardrobe would even be close to cool.

I threw my phone down on the bed, staring at the floor. I had to figure out an escape. The clothes were a minor issue compared to that little detail. I needed a way out that my parents wouldn't suspect or detect.

The first step would be letting them see me asleep, so I put on my pajamas and did all the things I normally do before bed. As I brushed my teeth in the bathroom, I thought of all the routes out of my house. The doors and windows were all alarmed, but I knew the code. And I knew the special system for shutting the alarm off of just one entry and leaving all the others connected. The back door was my best bet. It was farthest from the stairs and the least likely to be heard opening and closing by my parents whose door was near the top of the stairs. There was no way I could go out the front. They'd hear that too easily.

I rinsed my mouth out, and took my makeup off. I'd bring my eyeliner and mascara in my purse so I could put it back on fresh, outside when I was well away from the house. If my parents saw me before bed and noticed I still had it on, they'd get suspicious of the change in routine. I had to act as if this was like every other night in a string of typical nights, not a night like no other. A night when I'd run around in the dark, free of their web of protection.

My heart was racing with the excitement of seeing Malcolm again. I was also happy about hanging out with Jasmine, especially since she's a Neutral and I knew I wouldn't end up hurting her. But I would be lying if I said that my primary motivation for taking this big risk wasn't him, the boy who wanted to know why I couldn't let people get too close. Why I had to hide from them all the time in the bathroom.

I turned out the light and went out into the hallway, finding my father standing just past the bathroom door. I slid my hands behind my back, carefully tucking my makeup into my underwear so he wouldn't see me carrying it.

"Going to bed early?" he asked, his gaze taking in my pajamas and slippered feet.

"It's not early, really. It's almost nine."

"Yes, but it's not a school night. You usually stay up late on Fridays."

"I have a project to work on tomorrow, so I want to get an early start. I'm treating this like a school night." I'm pretty sure I'm the only seventeen-year-old in the entire Northern Hemisphere with a bedtime. I could have just told my parents to bite me over the whole thing, but I let them have their little victories whenever possible. This way, my threats had power when I did finally issue them. And there was no reason for me to stay up past nine normally, anyway. Until today, every evening had been the same, and nothing was a better escape from my life than sleep.

He came closer and stared into my eyes, smiling. "You're such a great kid. So responsible. How did we get so lucky?" He reached out a hand as if to brush the side of my head, but I shrank to the right, moving to go around him without making contact.

"I don't know, Dad. Just the luck of the draw, I guess." I made a beeline for my bedroom when I got past him.

"Sure you don't want to stay up and watch a movie with us?" He turned to face me.

I yawned for effect. "Nah. I'm tired. I jogged today in gym and now I'm more exhausted than usual. I'll see you at breakfast." Saturday I normally avoided my parents and ate alone out in the backyard, claiming a huge interest in morning bird activity just to get away from them. I knew this offer of a meal together would get him.

"Oh, we'll see you at breakfast? That's something new for a Saturday. What would you like? I'll make whatever you want. Pancakes, French toast, waffles ..."

A twinge of guilt over his easy accommodation and offer to spoil me slipped through my mind. "Just an egg is fine. And toast. Do we have raspberry jam?" Of course they had my favorite. They always did. But I asked so he could feel happy about getting it for me.

"I'll make sure we do." He stepped closer.

I backed into my room and shut the door almost all the way. "Night, Dad." I stood there, frozen in place, hoping he'd get the hint and not keep chatting about our breakfast. I didn't feel threatened by him at all, but I knew he'd stay and talk all night with little encouragement.

"Night, sweetie. See you at eight sharp. Your eggs will be ready."

My heart ached a little with the kindness he was showing. I'd give anything for his efforts to be coming from a different place in his mind.

"Okay. Eight sharp."

I walked away and laid down on the bed, leaving the door partway open. A closed door always made them a little freaky. With the door partway open I had a chance of throwing them off the scent of my deception.

When I was sure he'd gone down the hall, I got up and tiptoed over to my closet, pulling out a dark shirt to pair with the jeans I had over my chair from earlier today. I took the makeup out of my underwear and shoved it into my purse that was hanging from the corner of the chair. My shoes were already there on the floor, so I was ready to get dressed as soon as I was sure they were in their room.

I got back in bed and rolled over onto my side, facing the door, hoping one or both of them would check on me soon and see my fake-sleeping act. I quickly pulled my phone out from under my pillow and put it on silent before sliding it back under the soft material. I had just a little more than an hour to get into my party clothes and out the back door.

About fifteen minutes into my fake sleep, I heard my door opening. I kept my eyes closed, letting my lips fall apart in what I hoped was a perfect imitation of a totally relaxed teenager, exhausted from her first day of school.

My mother's whisper reached my ears. "Do you think she's really okay?"

"Yes, she's fine. She's a pro at this. Eight schools in five years ... she'll be fine."

"Maybe I should sleep in here tonight."

"Not tonight. We only do that when the danger signals come up, right? We agreed on this, and I haven't gotten any."

"But what about today? The walking home and the ride?" My mom sounded nervous, like she didn't trust my dad's all-clear evaluation.

"It's just Rae trying to spread her wings a little. I don't think we have anything to worry about."

My heart seized in my chest. This was the first time I'd heard anything about them sleeping in my room. I knew for a fact no one had ever been in my bed with me; it would have woken me up. *Did they sleep in my chair? On the floor? How weird is that?* My parents were creeping me out to a whole other level now. I battled to keep my breathing deep and even. My chest felt like it was going to explode with the restraint.

"Ready for bed?" My dad asked. I could tell he was pulling away from my door, his voice going softer.

"I suppose. If you're okay with it, I'm going to take a pill. I'm exhausted from all that baking, but I'm wound up from the worrying. I'm frazzled."

"Go ahead. I'll keep an ear out for anything out of the ordinary."

That was the last I heard as they got farther down the hall and went into their room. I climbed out of bed as quietly as I could, going over to my chair where I'd put out my clothes. Quickly dressing and putting on my sneakers, I kept an ear strained towards my door, listening for footsteps coming down the hallway or more whispering. But all I heard were the sounds of my parents getting ready for bed and the telltale sound of water going into a glass, signaling my mom's intent to sleep with Prince Valium tonight.

I walked softly over to my bed and shoved some stuffed animals under the covers, fluffing everything up to make it look like I was still there sleeping away. I grabbed my phone out from under my pillow and put it in my back pocket, but not before removing the battery from the back. If my parents woke up and found me gone, I didn't want them able to track where I was.

Standing in the doorway, I planned out my next moves in my mind, making sure I had every part of it figured out so I wouldn't give myself away. I had to get down the hallway and stairs, and over to the keypad by the back door without them hearing me. The alarm code was going to beep and echo all through the house. I took a pillow from my floor where I'd thrown it earlier and pushed the door open very slowly, planning to muffle the sounds of the beeping keypad by pushing the pillow over it while I pressed buttons. I waited a full minute before stepping out of my room and going down the hall.

My heart hammered in my chest and my breathing sounded way too loud to my ears. After five steps I stopped, listening for anything coming from my parents' room.

*Nothing.*

I continued down the stairs, stopping every few seconds to listen. It felt like it took forever, but I finally made it to the back door with no one following me or demanding to know where I was going. I breathed a deep sigh of relief as I stood in front of the alarm keypad. I raised the pillow up and smooshed it over the buttons, pressing the first key experimentally. A tiny, muffled beep came through, but not loud enough for anyone but me to hear it. My heart soared in triumph. *I'm going to a party!*

I quickly tapped out the rest of the complicated combination of digits that would take the alarm off the back door only, and then slid the deadbolt back on the door. Tossing the pillow over to the chair at our breakfast table, I turned the handle of the door, easing it open and thanking the gods above that it didn't squeak.

As soon as I was outside and the door was shut behind me, I took off running.

## Chapter Twenty-One
# Malcolm

I SAT IN KOOTCH'S GREMLIN, waiting in the backseat for Rae to appear out of the darkness. None of us knew if she was actually going to come, and there was no way in hell I was going to text her after getting dissed earlier. She obviously didn't want to talk to me. I wasn't even sure what I was doing here. I should be home packing for my disappearance. It was the only way out of my current dilemma. I'd just have to go into hiding until my birthday and say screw it to my diploma. The thought made me more depressed than usual.

"Where is she, man? She'd better come," whined Kootch, sounding put-out.

"She is. I talked to her a couple hours ago, and she said she'd come."

"If she's not here in ten, I'm leaving." Kootch was back to being his cranky, Miserable self. Even Jasmine's teasing wasn't helping, much as she was trying.

"Do you have cramps?" she asked.

"Cramps? What are you talking about?" He put his elbow up on the windowsill and glared at her.

"Well, you're so moody, I figured you were on your period."
She picked at her nail polish, acting like she wasn't trying to make
him nuts.

Kootch lifted his head off his fist. "Listen, Butts. Periods are off
limits, okay? We don't talk about that nasty girl shit in this car."

"Nasty girl shit? I take offense to that."

"Take whatever you want from it, but don't talk about it. I'm
serious. Say the word one more time and you're out."

"What word? Period?"

"I'm not kidding, Butts."

"I just want to be sure I know what word I'm not allowed to
say. Is it period? Is period the word? Is period what bothers you
or is it *cramps* that's a no-no?"

"Get out."

"Was it period or cramps that did it?" She was really good at
sounding totally serious when inside she had to be laughing hys-
terically. I know I was. The gloom over my new plan for avoiding
the State was lifting just a little.

"Both! Now get out!"

"No. Here's Rae, come on, open up."

My head snapped over to where Jasmine was pointing. A person was slipping around the gatehouse and heading our direction.

"Sweet," said Kootch, sounding excited. "You're safe from being voted off the island this time, Butts, but you'd better not say
that word when Rae's in here, or I'll kick you out anyway."

"What? You think she doesn't know what periods are?"

"Dammit, Butts!"

The rest of his admonishment disappeared as Rae showed up
at his window, grinning like a fool.

I tried to keep the smile off my face, but it was impossible after
seeing her that insanely happy about sneaking out. I couldn't blame
her in theory; I hadn't been to a party since I was six. For a few minutes anyway, this was going to be awesome, so long as I could keep
thoughts about my life out of the picture. Thirty minutes was all I
was giving it before I bailed and walked home, but it was going to be
a killer thirty minutes if I had anything to say about it.

"Hi, guys," Rae said as Kootch's door opened for her.

He held up his hand for a high five. "Skin me. And then you're in the back. Butts refuses to move from her seat."

"I called shotgun. I can't help it if she lives so far away." Jasmine leaned over and looked at Rae through Kootch's door. "I figured you'd want to sit with Malcolm anyway." She grinned very evilly, making me wonder what the heck she had in mind. Rae's expression looked anything but pleased at the idea.

Kootch pushed his seat forward and Rae climbed in. Maybe I was just imagining things, but it seemed like she was avoiding looking at me.

"How far do you live from here?" Rae asked, looking between the seats at Jasmine.

"Ten minutes, not far. Kootch is just whining again, as usual."

"Ha. Talk about whining. You're the queen of that shit." Kootch got in and turned the engine over. "Ready to go party hardy and kick that keg in the balls?"

"Do kegs have balls? I've never noticed that before," said Jasmine in a calm voice, staring out the front window.

"Shut up, Butts." Kootch pulled away from the curb. "Seriously, I hear they have three kegs of Heineken. I'm going to help waste at least one of them."

"You're not going to touch that stuff," said Jasmine, sounding serious for the first time. "You're the driver, therefore you remain sober. No debate."

"Aw, man. That sucks." Kootch's frown was lit up in the mirror for a moment as a car passed by coming from the other direction. "How about just one? One beer?" He sounded like he was appealing to his parents.

"No. Not even one," she responded, just like a real mother.

Rae reached up and lifted her hand to hover over Kootch's shoulder, but before she could touch him like I expected her to, she pulled it back and put her hand in her lap. "Don't worry. I'm not going to drink either, so you won't be alone."

Jasmine turned around. "You straight edge?"

"Uh, maybe?" Rae sounded lost.

"Either you are or you aren't."

"I don't really know what that is, actually." Rae shrank down a little in her seat.

Jasmine explained. "Straight edge is no drugs, no smoke, no drink, no nothing. But still cool, like me."

Kootch snorted.

"Yeah. I'm straight edge," said Rae, sounding more confident. "I think."

"Whatdya mean, you think?" asked Kootch, trying to see her in his rearview mirror. "How can you not know?"

"Well, I don't go to parties and my parents don't have alcohol at our house, so I guess I've never made a conscious choice about it."

"Holy crap. Are you a nun or what?" asked Kootch.

Jasmine punched him in the arm. "Shut up, Cyclops."

"Ow! Watch those pirate rings, lady! And what're you calling me Cyclops for?" He leaned closer to the mirror and rubbed the middle of his forehead with his index finger. "Do I have a zit? Fuck, don't tell me I have a zit in the middle of my forehead."

Rae and I laughed. She looked at me and then quickly turned away. For the brief moment that our eyes met, I noticed surprise. Like she was shocked to find me back there with her. I worked pretty hard at staying invisible, but it kind of burned my chest a little to know I was doing that well at it with her. I shrugged the feeling away, knowing it was for the best.

"No, you don't have a zit, idiot. But if you keep saying clueless shit like that I'm gonna nail you with a boulder like you did to me when I was just a baby and give you another eye socket."

"First of all, it wasn't a boulder for chrissake. And second, you weren't a baby, you were fully grown with the same big butt you have now. And third, you guys heard her. Threatening me with physical violence." He pointed a finger near her face. "That's assault."

"No, *this* is assault," Jasmine said, grabbing his finger and bending it backwards.

"Ahh! Back, you gnarly beast, back!" He yanked his hand away and ducked to the left, barely paying attention to his driving as he waved his elbow in her general direction.

"Eyes on the road," I reminded him.

"Yeah. Eyes on the road," Kootch said in a bratty voice to Jasmine. "Leave me be, wild woman."

"All three eyes," Jasmine mumbled.

Rae snorted.

"So where is this party?" I asked, sneaking a glance at Rae. She kept her eyes forward.

"Just a few blocks away," said Kootch. "Two minute countdown to party time." He started banging his hands on the steering wheel, keeping time to some music that must've been playing in his head.

"Are either of you guys sore from the accident?" Jasmine asked, twisting in her seat to look at us.

I shook my head.

"No, I'm fine," said Rae, looking at me for a second before facing Jasmine again. I hated that she was purposely not looking at me, and I hated even more that I cared.

"That's good," said Jasmine. "I wonder what Brody's doing right now. Probably crying in his sleep over his stupid penis car."

"Hey, what accident? What are you guys talking about?" Kootch slowed down, looking at Jasmine.

"Brody's car got smashed when they were in it," she explained.

Kootch stopped altogether, several feet before the upcoming stop sign. "What?! How do you know this and I don't?" He turned to face me. "Dude, what's your problem?"

"What? What'd I do?"

"You're supposed to tell me major shit like that. It's Dude-Code. Total fail, man. Total fail. Someone tell me why he's in my car."

Before I could respond, Jasmine butted in. "Dude-Code? Oh, God, please don't share. It doesn't matter anyway. They're fine, see? Let's just go to the party, and I'll drink some beers for you, okay?"

"No," said Kootch, putting the car in first and pulling up to the stop sign. "If I can't drink, neither can you, Butts. You're the co-pilot. Co-pilots can't drink."

"Eff that."

"No, not eff that. Drink and you find another ride home. My car, my rules. Besides, you're supposed to be Miss Cool Straight-Edge. You can't drink."

Kootch pulled into the intersection, going slow as he reached the other side, his eyes swinging left and right. "The place is here somewhere. Can you guys see the addresses?"

Jasmine pointed out the windshield. "Any chance it might be up there were the ten thousand cars are parked?"

Kootch frowned at her before downshifting and giving the car more gas. We went two blocks before he parked and responded.

"Arrive alive, that's my motto. Now everyone out so I can lock my baby up." He threw the door open and yelled, "Wooo hooo!! Party time!!"

"Shut up, asshole!" came a voice from across the lawn.

We all snickered as we got out of the car.

"What's his problem?" grumbled Kootch. "Just trying to have a little fun."

"Maybe they want the party to last a little longer. You know, not piss off the neighbors?" suggested Jasmine.

"Oh. Yeah." Kootch walked with his head down for a few paces after locking up the car.

"Don't worry about it, Kootch," said Rae, walking a step behind him and just in front of me. "A party's not a party until someone's whooping it up, right?"

Kootch smiled big at her. "Exactly what I was thinking, right? Fuck that guy." He opened his mouth to yell again, but Rae's hand on his arm stopped him. The shout came out as a burst of air followed by a weak whine at the end.

"What the hell was that?" asked Jasmine, laughing.

"Uhhh ... I don't know," said Kootch, staring at the place where Rae's hand had been.

I tried not to be jealous of the fact that she was making such an effort where he was concerned and was so obviously doing the opposite with me. Had my question freaked her out? Did I push too hard? *Probably.* I had zero experience with girls other than to run away from them far and fast. The one time I hadn't was more than enough to feed my nightmares for years to come. Why was I trying to start another nightmare? I slowed down to put more distance between us.

"Come on, Cy, let's go find some Coke." Jasmine grabbed Kootch's sleeve and pulled him down the sidewalk.

"Coke? I thought we were straight edge tonight. And don't call me Cyclops or I'll call you something worse."

"First of all you can't be straight edge just for a night. And second, I'm talking about the drink. Stop being a dumbass, would ya?"

Their voices faded as the distance between us grew. I didn't want to stay too close, preferring to hang back and watch. Rae seemed to be doing the same thing, although she was making sure to stay ahead of me.

Kootch's response to Jasmine's comment was lost in the sounds spilling out of the door that had just opened ahead of us. Apparently, we'd reached party central.

Kootch turned around and walked backwards, holding up his arms. "Party people in da houuuuse toniiiight!"

Rae stopped walking.

I came up next to her and stopped too. "You okay?" I asked, not looking at her. I didn't want to spook her like I had with my text. *Play it cool. Act like you really don't care.*

"I think so," she said, not sounding very sure at all.

"Just stick with me and you'll be fine." I wanted to take her hand so badly. My fingers tingled with the need. But I didn't. I stayed right where I was, not looking at her. Sweat broke out at my temples.

She laughed nervously. "I'm not so sure about that."

I turned my head to look at her. "I'm not going to bite you, you know. I'm not a vampire."

She looked at me, a grin creeping out. "That's too bad."

I raised an eyebrow. "You want someone to suck the life out of you?"

She shrugged, the humor disappearing from her face. "Sometimes it sounds like a really good idea, actually."

*Damn it all and everything she might be thinking. I am going to do this.* I sighed heavily, reaching down to grab her hand. "Believe me, it's a bad idea. Come on."

She didn't resist, but she didn't hold on to me either. "What do you know about vampires and death?" she asked, staying even with me as we walked up the front steps to the door.

"I know enough about darkness to know you don't want to go there." We stepped through the entrance behind Jasmine and Kootch, the blast of noise immediately pouring over us and shutting out any chance of a normal conversation.

I quickly lost Jasmine in the mix, but I could still see Kootch's head and arms lifted up to the sky. He was very determined to make sure everyone knew the party prince had finally arrived.

I pulled Rae through the throng of kids, most of whom I didn't know or even recognize. There were people here from another school district, competing colors all over the place.

"Come on," I shouted, "let's go out back." The pressing need of all these kids, some of them very unhappy people, was already making me nervous.

Rae offered zero resistance. She pressed into me when the crowd got too thick and moved behind me, putting her other hand on my back. I twisted my arm around so we could keep contact while we pushed our way through.

The thrill that buzzed every nerve ending in my body over touching her made me feel like a goofy jerk, but I didn't care. I hadn't been this close to a girl in a long time, and I'd never been close to someone like Rae before. Ever.

We finally made it to the back door and went outside, joining about fifty other people around a totally decked-out pool area. There was a built-in barbecue with accompanying outdoor kitchen, colorful awnings, a tiki hut bar, and several tables and chairs set up around in groups. No one was in the pool yet, but I could tell it wasn't going to stay empty for long. People just needed a little more alcohol, and clothes were either going to come off or get soaked.

I brought Rae over to the outskirts of a lighted area, near the back part of the yard and the fence that went around it. We could see everyone inside the house through the back windows and all the kids hanging around the pool with no obstructions. One of the famous kegs was off to our left near the grill with a huge group of guys around it and a few girls busy flirting for more beer and attention.

"Wow," said Rae, pulling her hand away from mine. "That was ... interesting."

I was sad that she'd broken contact, but it probably would have been weird to keep holding hands when it wasn't necessary anymore, especially since she'd been working so hard at not even looking at me earlier.

Questions burned in my brain. The one from before and now one about why she was suddenly so afraid of me or not interested. I didn't ask her though, because I wasn't sure I wanted to know the answers. Not yet. There was plenty of time for hurt feelings later. For now I'd pretend we were friends who might be considering something else. The fantasy shouldn't be too hard to keep going for an hour. That's how long I was planning to stay. An hour tops.

"So ... you okay?" she asked me, looking at the pool.

"Yeah. I'm fine. You?" I had no idea what she was talking about, so I just rolled with it.

"I'm fine. No problem. The accident wasn't that bad." Her eyes were roaming around the backyard. She was doing such a good job of acting like she could care less about our conversation that I was starting to believe I'd imagined any kind of connection before. It made me sick to my stomach.

"Nah," I agreed. "Not bad for anyone but Dan and Brody, I guess."

She dropped her gaze to the ground. "Yeah. Sucked for them."

"Lucky for us Mr. Holder was there, right?" It was a loaded question. It didn't feel lucky by the end of it. More like really unlucky.

"Yeah. Lucky."

I held my breath for a few seconds, wondering if I should risk it. "And weird, too, right?"

She stopped looking anywhere but her feet. She just stared at them for a long time. After a while it started to freak me out.

I let the breath out that I'd been holding in a big gust. "I'm going to get a beer. You want one?" I had to get away from her so I could stop making a fool of myself.

"Yes. Please. Make it a double." She finally looked up and gave me a lopsided grin. It made her dimple appear, and I felt like punching myself in the face when I saw it.

"Be right back." I took off. I couldn't bear to be near her for a single second longer. She was a nice girl, and she didn't want to acknowledge the darkness I brought with me. She was just feeling sorry for me or something. Why was I trying to force it on her? Was I trying to turn her into some kind of fantasy savior? It was the most ridiculous idea I've had in a long, long time. Almost as ridiculous as the bullshit story I told the social worker about moving in with a friend.

I shoved that out of my mind as quickly as it appeared to taunt me. I had a day and a half to figure something out that didn't involve running away. Right now, I was just going to spend the next forty-five minutes being confused by a girl who I had no hope of figuring out in the short time I'd be around her. Maybe she'd already be gone by the time I was done getting our drinks.

I grabbed two big plastic cups as soon as my turn came up, shoving them under the spigot held by a football player.

"You pay yet?" he asked.

"Uh, no. How much?"

"Five each, unlimited refills. Give it to him." He pointed with the black nozzle at the skinny kid next to him holding a wad of cash.

I reached into my pocket and pulled out the last ten bucks to my name. *I guess I'll be drinking my next few meals tonight.* "Fill them to the top, man. I gotta drown my sorrows."

He laughed, pressing the trigger and letting the yellow liquid flow into the cup. "Any guy standing over there with that girl and drowning sorrows has gotta be gay." His head bobbed up and down slowly as the foam rose to the top.

I shook my head. "Not me, man." I took several long pulls off the first glass, putting it down to join the second after I'd drained half of it.

He filled the second cup and then topped off the first. I walked away, taking another huge gulp of my drink, thinking maybe if I got a buzz on I wouldn't feel so shitty about what a complete loser I am.

"Thanks," Rae said when I handed her the second cup. She took several long swallows, wincing when she finally pulled it away from her mouth. "Ew. I hate beer, I think."

I laughed a little. "I can tell by the look on your face. Why are you drinking it if you don't like it?"

She shrugged, holding the cup with both hands at chest-level. "I've never tried it before. But I hear it's an acquired taste, so I'm going to finish this before I make my decision." She lifted it to her lips and chugged a few more times.

"Better slow down or you'll find your decision tainted by your buzz."

She glanced up at me for a second before looking back at the beer. "That's what I'm hoping."

We stood there and drank in silence for a few more minutes. When she was done, I took her cup and went back to the keg, filling both of them up again. I took the time to chug a full glass down while hers was being refilled, so I got two more instead of just one for myself.

I finished that third beer next to her before speaking again. The buzz from the alcohol was warming me up and loosening my tongue, making it easier for me to think about what I wanted to say. None of the worries that normally plagued me were getting in the way and clouding my decision-making.

"So, you didn't answer my text today. Did I piss you off? Do you totally hate me now?" *Did I just say that? Did I just fucking say that?!*

Her glass stopped in mid-tilt. For a few seconds it just stayed there. She pulled it away and looked down at it, biting her lip.

"You can just say it." I was encouraging her, feeling really bold and sure of myself, now. I'd already blown it; I had nothing left to lose. "I'm used to rejection. Just say, 'Malcolm, you're a dick. Stop texting me,' and I'll stop, I swear. I was just curious, you know?" I had diarrhea of the mouth, apparently. I couldn't shut up because she was just standing there, saying nothing, not even looking at me. It made me brave and foolish at the same time - a dangerous combination. "In fact, you don't have to say anything. That's weird, right? That I'm telling you to reject me? Doesn't matter. Just do what you did. Don't answer. I can take a hint. I'll never text you again. Promise." I threw my cup up to my lips and tipped it back as far as I could, leaning back a little to get every last drop. "I need to get another beer. You ready for another one?" I held out my hand to take her cup.

"Please don't," she said, finally looking at me. Her eyes were shiny.

I burped a little, unable to stop the carbonation from coming up. "'Scuse me. What'd you say? Please don't what? Sorry, I'm confused." I scratched my head with my cup-holding hand, managing to spill a little liquid down my ear in the process.

"Don't." She reached up and wiped under her eye. It kind of deflated my energy a little, and the idea of another beer quickly lost its appeal. I wasn't sure if she was crying or if I'd splashed her.

"Don't what, Rae? Don't get another beer?"

"No. Not that."

I sighed. "Okaaay. Don't what, then? Don't keep talking about stupid shit? I can do that." I turned to leave her there. I had made enough of a fool of myself. *Time to go home.*

She grabbed my arm and pulled me back. I stumbled a little, bumping into her and making her fall back. She caught herself but swayed a bit. "No, that's not what I meant. Don't go."

"Oh." I got my feet back under me and shrugged her off. I didn't want her to think she had to hold me up. I was buzzed but not drunk. "Okay, I won't go. What do you want to talk about?"

"I didn't mean don't go."

I rolled my eyes up to the sky, searching for guidance. Either I was buzzing harder than I thought or she was talking in circles. When I looked back down at her I felt my heart spasm painfully in my chest. Her expression slayed me. She was getting ready to cry, big time. There were huge pools of tears just balanced at the edge of her eyes.

"Why are you going to cry?"

"Because. I don't want you to stop texting me."

I jerked my chin back towards my chest, totally confused now. "But ... you just ... you said ..." I ran my fingers through my hair, my cup bouncing off my head and falling to the ground. "Shit, Rae. You're confusing the crap out of me right now." I bent down and snatched my cup off the ground.

She smiled weakly, a giant tear slipping out to track down her cheek. "Sorry about that."

I reached up without thinking, using a bent forefinger to start at her jaw and draw it upwards, taking the tear away. I wiped it on my pant leg. "No crying allowed." I pointed at her face playfully. "This is a party, you know, not a funeral."

She looked over her shoulder. "It could be, you know. It could easily go from something really happy to something really sad."

My hand froze in mid tear-squeegeeing. "Don't I fucking know it." I stood there, staring at her, trying to read her mind. What I wouldn't give to know it was the same thing that was going through mine...

She reached up and took my hand. We slowly let them fall together until they were there between us, down by my waist. I reached out with my other hand and took her free one, letting our fingers tangle together. We stood face to face, staring each other in the eye, holding hands.

"You wanted to know why I hide in bathrooms," she said, her gaze never leaving my face. She took a deep breath, her chest expanding with it and then collapsing again as she let it out slowly. Her breasts pressed against her shirt, making my pants suddenly tighter.

"Yes. I want to know why you hide in bathrooms, just like me. That's what I want to know. Please tell me you don't have a bladder problem."

She giggled, the movement forcing another tear to fall and then her chin to quiver. I reached up with her hand still in mine and used my finger to wipe it off.

"No, I don't have a bladder problem."

"Then why do you do it? Tell me." I leaned in, my voice getting lower. "Your secret is safe with me."

"It *is* a secret," she said in almost a whisper.

"I know it is. We both have secrets." Our foreheads were almost touching.

"I hide in bathrooms because ... because people try to get too close." She bit her lip. There was fear in her expression, but I couldn't tell if it was fear of the secret, fear of me, or fear of the people she ran from.

"And what happens when they get too close?" I was just inches from her face, looking down into her beautiful eyes, her soft-looking skin glowing as it reflected the terrace lights.

Mad prayers were rushing through my brain, as I begged any higher power that might be listening to make her reason not what I thought it was. Before I came here, before this exact moment, I'd wanted Rae to be just like me. But now that I was touching her, feeling her warmth and seeing her beautiful face and eyes up close, those windows to her soul so deep and full of wounds, I didn't want her to be like me. I wanted her to have a bladder problem or a failing kidney or another medical condition that could be cured with prescription drugs and hospital stays. I didn't want her to be an agent of darkness. I didn't want her to be like me at all.

"When they get too close, they get hooked," she said, oblivious to my prayers. "And then they won't go away. They get obsessed. Dangerous."

I swallowed hard, feeling the burning sickness in my belly rising up into my throat. I wanted to say something, but I didn't know how to react other than to want to run, run, run away. This was awful, terrible. *She's cursed, just like me.*

But something kept me there. Something kept my grip soft and relaxed, my eyes staring into hers. The desire to protect her was overriding my sense of self-preservation or my hero complex or whatever it was that always forced me to keep people at a distance.

I opened my mouth to speak, weighing my words carefully. I looked her deeply in the eyes and finally said, "I know *exactly* what you mean."

"But how?" she asked, squeezing my hands for all she was worth. Her skin had gone clammy against mine all of sudden and she was trembling. The malt from the beer was on her breath, and it washed over me, making me want to kiss her and see if it was on her tongue too.

I had to say it. Get it out there, front and center. It was the last bit, the last piece of the puzzle between us. With these words, I'd bind her to me forever. We'd either be two of the same, two in a billion people like no one else, or we just wouldn't. She'd be a regular girl and I'd be me. The guy who makes people want to die.

"Cops are here!" yelled someone from the back door.

My head jerked right, looking for the source of the warning, trying to decide if it was credible or not.

Rae squeezed my hands, her nails digging into my skin. "Tell me!" The desperation in her voice yanked me out of the world of parties and cops and getting busted for underage drinking right before I was out of the foster system with a clean record.

"Tell you what?" I was stalling for time, afraid to say the words.

She spoke through gritted teeth. "Tell me how you know about the people. About the hiding. About *all* of it!" She yanked on me hard, pulling me even closer.

We were pressed up together from knees to stomach, and by the expression on her face, I could tell she hadn't meant for that to happen. Fear turned to acceptance though, as she stared me down, daring me to answer her.

Something like anger and frustration and desire to feel more of her got all wrapped up together into a giant tangle of emotion I didn't understand. "Fine. You want to know? I'll tell you how I know." I hesitated only a fraction of a second. "I'm like you. I have the same problem. I am ... an agent of darkness."

"What?" she said weakly, moving back half a step.

Desire and hope turned quickly to something else. But I was too overwhelmed with the idea that I'd just spilled my guts to her, told her my biggest secret, the thing that I could never tell another living soul before this moment, to really care about why she was moving away.

I pulled her hands and put them around my back, bringing her closer. Taking her by the shoulders, I drew her body up against mine. I could feel almost every inch of her, and even though we were both fully clothed and her in the most conservative outfit of any girl in the whole damn state, pure desire shot through me. I swear just touching her made bolts of energy fly out of my body and out into the night.

I couldn't tear my eyes away from her as I dipped my head down closer and closer. She didn't move a muscle as I quickly pressed my lips to hers, before I could change my mind.

## Chapter Twenty-Two
# Rae

THE BEER WAS DEFINITELY HAVING an effect. Crazy ideas were swirling through my head. I actually told Malcolm my intent was to get drunk or tipsy or whatever. I was practically flirting with him. My grand idea to ignore him and let him live his life was completely out the window. All I wanted to do now was see him without his shirt on.

I shook my head and then stared at the ground, only able to collect my thoughts when he was gone and getting us more beer. When he returned, I drank it greedily, looking for the bravery I felt just behind the next cup of bubbly amber liquid.

The alcohol was going to make things happen, for better or for worse, and I wanted that. Good or bad, I wanted to just *make* something happen instead of running from things that were always happening to me. This was probably a really bad way of going about it, but I couldn't think of anything else to do at the moment, and just straight up going for it without a crutch wasn't going to work. I was too afraid. Liquid bravery, that's what I needed.

Malcolm started crazy-talking about not texting me anymore and being a dick and I just lost it. I could picture him shunning me for real - not going in Kootch's car with me anymore, him sitting at a different table in detention - and all it did was make me want to cry. Stupid tears came rushing up, and I had to focus every bit of willpower I had over my emotions to make them not fall.

"Why are you going to cry?" Malcolm asked, his face full of concern.

*Busted.* It crossed my mind that lying would be the best plan right now, but the beer had other ideas. "Because. I don't want you to stop texting me."

He was totally confused over my mixed messages, making me feel guilty as hell. It caused another tear to join the other ones already swimming in my eyes, and that was one tear too many. I was mortified as I felt the moisture break loose and slide down my cheek.

I stopped breathing for a few seconds when he reached up and wiped it away. His touch was so tender, and his eyes were so full of concern for me, I'm pretty sure I lost a piece of my heart permanently to him in that moment.

"Sorry about that," I said, feeling like I was manipulating him with my tears. But I wasn't. These emotions were one-hundred-percent real and I couldn't control them, much as I might have liked to.

And then he asked me. He asked me about my secret. I wanted to keep it from him, to pretend for just a little while longer that I'm normal, just some girl who thinks he's cute and sits next to him in Art class, put him off. But he wouldn't let it go. And he kept hinting, like he knew. *Like he knew!*

So I did it. I told him my deepest darkest secret. The one my parents wouldn't acknowledge, and the one I had never dared hope to share with anyone else. "I hide in bathrooms because ... because people try to get too close." I was scared to death he was going to look at me funny, tell me I'm crazy. Or just walk away shaking his head. End of story.

But he didn't. "And what happens when they get too close?" he asked. He was so close I could feel his breath on my face. It was sweet, like the beer. I could smell his boy-scent too, something uniquely Malcolm. The shadow of a small beard on his chin gave him a slightly rough look, maybe a little sinister. My blood heated up at the idea of it and I got goosebumps all over. My palms went sweaty.

I had to answer. To walk away now would be the end of it all, and I so wasn't ready for it to be over. "When they get too close, they get hooked. And then they won't go away. They get obsessed. Dangerous." Jerry the Rainbow came to mind. Big. Hulking. Desperate. Determined. I shivered at the memory of his face, his hands, his too-strong arms pulling and pressing...

"I know *exactly* what you mean." Malcolm stood there, acting totally cool. Like I hadn't just told him I'm a freak of the highest degree.

"But how?" There was no way he could know. I didn't see a single Rainbow hanging around him in school, and he'd been there a long time. He couldn't possibly know what I was going through. He couldn't understand what it's like to be me. *Could he?*

Someone yelled something from the house, distracting Malcolm from answering. I almost had a nervous breakdown as I saw our conversation disintegrating because of some loud partying idiot.

"Tell me!" I yelled, yanking on his hands, pulling him back into the conversation. I couldn't let it go this far and then fall apart. I had to know.

"Tell you what?" He stood there, acting like he wasn't breaking my heart in two with his casual attitude about the whole thing.

I barely controlled my anger, near-insanity bubbling beneath the surface as I waited for the answer to the one question I'd been asking the heavens all my life. *Is there someone else out there like me or am I all alone in the world?* "Tell me how you know about the people! About the hiding! About *all* of it!" I jerked his hands again without thinking, accidentally pulling him against me.

At first I was freaked out. If he attached himself to me and attacked me now, it would be my fault. He'd done nothing to make this happen, it was all me. But as I stared up into his eyes and saw the concern there and the confusion, yet none of the fervor that usually came from Rainbows, fear turned to something else. I wanted him to touch me again. But more than that, I wanted him to answer my question.

His jaw muscle tightened and his voice came out strained. "Fine. You want to know? I'll tell you how I know. I'm like you. I have the same problem. I am an agent of darkness."

I pulled back slightly, confused. I had been expecting about three possible answers to my question: 'I'm just like you' or 'You're a nut job' or 'I don't understand'. But at no point did I expect to hear *that*. "What?" His words banked the heat that had been building up between us. I suddenly felt threatened, but I wasn't sure why.

He pulled on my hands, drawing me near, and put them behind him, placing them on his lower back. I left them there, gripping onto his belt, part of me wanting to run but a bigger part wanting to feel him against me again. *Screw the risk. Screw the weird answer. Screw everything. Just touch me, please...*

He put his hands on my shoulders and leaned down. His hard body pressed into mine.

I could smell him again. The heat was back and stronger than ever. I let it wash over me, welcoming the shiver it brought to my bones.

His eyes were dark pools of sadness mixed with a tiny spark of hope that I knew mirrored my own emotions. Just coming into contact with him made bolts of energy fly out of my body and out into the night. Something wild was happening, uncontrollable, destined maybe.

We didn't break eye contact until his lips met mine. My lids fluttered closed on their own as the last bit of distance between us disappeared into oneness.

His mouth was soft at first, almost questioning as he kissed me in little bits. The tentative touches continued in longer and longer stretches, the sounds of our more frantic breathing making the whole experience more sensual, hot. His touch became more insistent, and his lips were wet now, sliding along mine and causing tickling sensations to build deep in my belly.

He pulled away just the tiniest bit, making me think he was done kissing me, but then his tongue came out to stroke my bottom lip, causing me to gasp in surprise. I know about kissing, I'd done it once before, but the results hadn't been anything like this.

I pulled him closer to me, tilting my head to reach more of his mouth with mine. I wanted to consume him, feel him everywhere, go deeper.

My fingers roamed across his muscled back as his hands slid up to my neck and then to the sides of my face to hold me there tenderly, deepening our kisses and moaning when I tangled my tongue with his.

"Hey, what are you guys doing over here?" said an annoyed Kootch. "You want to get arrested for underage drinking? Come on!"

I jerked away from Malcolm, my face flaming red with embarrassment over being caught. The cool night air doused the fire that had grown way too hot, and the presence of our friend woke me up to our reality. We were getting all hot and bothered in the middle of a party and the cops were here to arrest people. *Holy crap, what is my problem?!*

"Shit are they here?" asked Malcolm, looking a little lost as he ran his hands through his hair. He was as flustered as I was.

"Hey, love birds, what's this all about?" Jasmine had walked up behind Kootch and was pointing to both of us in turn with a huge grin on her face. "Geez, we leave you alone for ten minutes and you're over here making babies already."

"Shut up, Butts," growled Kootch. "Come on, we have to get out of here. Geneva does *not* like being towed. She hates not sleeping in my driveway."

I said nothing, too embarrassed at being caught climbing down Malcolm's throat to find my voice. I followed Kootch with Jasmine next to me. Malcolm brought up the rear.

"You are going to spill every last bean you have, girl, or there will be blood." Jasmine was trying to give me a tough look, but I was too flustered to play along.

"Just get me out of here," was all I could manage.

"Cops!" yelled a guy, running past us. "Go out back! Over the fence!"

Kootch spun around and shoved Jasmine and me in a half-circle. "Go, go, go!" he yelled.

I didn't question him, I just turned and ran. Malcolm was there, taking me by the hand and running with me. I was glad for his touch and the sense of security he brought, rational or not.

We got to the fence, and I panicked. There was no way I was going to make it over; it was way too high.

Malcolm laced his hands together and held them down by his knees for me. "Step here. Go!"

I grabbed the edge of the fence and put the bottom of my shoe on his hands. He launched me up at the same time as I stood straight, and in a rush of air I found myself at the top of the fence, screaming in fright.

Jasmine popped up next to me, using Kootch as her launching pad. "Climb over, dork!" she shouted in my face, just before throwing her leg over. She lowered herself down and dropped to her feet on the other side. "Now!" she yelled, gesturing for me to follow.

I lifted my leg up and straddled the fence. Looking back, I nearly had a stroke. Several police officers were coming out the back door and into the backyard.

Kootch climbed up the fence like a monkey and flopped over onto the other side, falling on the ground and just barely missing landing on Jasmine.

She kicked him once in the side as he tried to get up. "You almost squashed me, dummy!"

"Stop right there, young lady!" one of the officers yelled, pointing a flashlight beam in my face as I turned around.

I froze.

"Jump down!" yelled Jasmine, her voice getting harder to hear as she ran away. "Come on!"

"Go, Rae!" said Malcolm.

"No! I can't leave you here!" I probably could have jumped down and escaped to the Gremlin with Jazzy Butts and the

Cyclops, but I really didn't want to leave Malcolm to the cops. We were connected now, for better or for worse. My only hope was to work some Rainbow magic on these guys to help us get out of this mess before either of our parents found out what we'd been doing.

I flipped my leg back over to the house-side of the fence and climbed down with Malcolm's help. We stood next to each other holding hands as the officers descended.

# Chapter Twenty-Three
# Malcolm

I HELD ONTO RAE'S HAND and stepped a little in front of her. Normally when I interact with cops, I keep my distance. They're around negativity and violence all day long, and the last thing they need is a dose of darkness to add to the mix. But this time, I had more than them to think about. I had Rae, and I didn't want any guy with a gun getting near her.

"Is this your residence?" asked the officer who was the first to approach. Two more of them wandered around the yard, checking behind trees and in corners. I could have saved them the trouble and told them that Rae and I were the only people left back there, the only ones not smart enough to jump the fence in time, but I didn't bother. They wouldn't have listened anyway.

I blamed myself for us being there. Kissing her, I'd been in some kind of weird trance that blocked out all sense of reality. Now we were going to pay for it, me especially. I had some very dark days ahead of me for sure. Mrs. Gonzalez would never let this slide.

"No, sir, we don't live here," I said, gently squeezing Rae's hand, trying to let her know that I'd take care of her.

"What are you doing here?"

"Just hanging out," I answered, trying to sound respectful and non-threatening.

"Do you know the residents of this house?" He rested his hands on his belt, one near his nightstick and one near his handcuffs.

I swallowed hard. "No, sir. I was just here visiting."

"You're visiting a place where you don't know the residents, huh? How old are you?"

"Seventeen. Almost eighteen."

"Did you have any alcohol tonight?" His gaze slid to the keg across the yard.

"Uhh, no, sir." Of course he'd smell it on me if he got any closer, and any breathalyzer test would totally take me down, but I figured admitting it would be even worse. At least I had from now until he tested me to be presumed innocent.

"You sure about that?" The cop took a step closer.

Rae spoke up, stepping from around me to stand at my side. "He hasn't. But I have, and I'm only seventeen. I want to turn myself in. Come on." She walked forward like she was just going to hug the guy or something.

He backed up, pulling his nightstick partway out of his belt. "Stop right there. Don't come any closer."

"Rae, what are you doing?" I said, instantly freaking out, thinking she was going to get clubbed or something. That beer must have gone straight to her head and made her completely lose her grip on reality. It made me sick to think that I'd taken advantage of her and kissed her when she was that far gone. She probably never would have touched me if it hadn't been for the beer.

She stepped around him and began walking towards the house. "Come on, officer. Let's go to the station."

He tried to grab her arm, but she danced to the side and he missed. The other cops were too busy looking for kids inside now to do anything with Rae. Our interrogator stood there looking from me to her, total confusion written all over his face. She was already halfway to the door by the time he made his decision about how to handle the weird situation. "Stay put," he ordered, before turning to go after her.

I did as he said, but not because he told me to. I didn't want to abandon Rae. She was off the rails and someone needed to be there for her. No way was I going anywhere.

She reached the doorway and turned around, a huge grin on her face. She waved. "Bye, Malcolm! See you on Monday!" And then she spun around and ran inside.

"Hey!" yelled the cop. "Chuck! Banks! We've got a runner! In the house, coming from the back!"

I stood there not knowing what to do for a second or two. None of this made any sense. Who goes to a party, drinks a beer, and then surrenders to cops? That's just ... weird.

But then Rae's voice came from somewhere I couldn't see and solved my dilemma for me. "Run, Malcolm! Over the fence, run!"

I battled with my conscience for a few more precious seconds, wanting to follow her into the house so we could go down in flames together. But then I decided I might be able to do more to help her with some distance and time on my side. Maybe I could get around to the front of the house without being seen and aid in her escape from there.

I turned and ran. The fence loomed large, and I visualized myself leaping from three feet away, grabbing the top, and climbing up like Kootch had.

"Hey! Where do you think you're going?!"

I ignored the voice and grabbed the fence, the leap from three feet in my imagination much more graceful than it turned out in reality. My sneakers slipped on the smooth surface of the wood, looking for something to grip onto. I finally found the cross-bar of wood holding the upright parts together and used my toe to lift me to the top. I was almost all the way over when someone grabbed my pant leg.

"Oh, no you don't," said the voice, grunting with the effort of keeping me on his side.

I kicked the police officer hard, catching him in the chin.

"Sorry!" I yelled, as his hand fell away.

I threw myself off the fence to the ground below. I was on my knees when another officer came down the alley that separated the yard I had just left from the next section of neighborhood. I took off running in the opposite direction, down the narrow road, planning to loop back around when I got to the end. I easily outpaced the overweight officer behind me, and the one on the other side of the fence didn't follow me over. I was home free in under a minute.

At the end of the alley I turned left, acting like I was heading farther away from the house so they'd look on the wrong street if they were really dead set on arresting me. After only taking a couple steps in the wrong direction, I crept back and peeked up the path I'd just come from to see if the cop was still pursuing me. I was relieved to find him faced the other way, walking back to the other end of the alley. I quickly crossed over to the other side, looping around to the front of the house that was about ten down from the party place.

Going from house to house, staying close to the front porches and bushes, I made my way back. As I went, my gaze scanned the road lit by streetlamps, expecting to see nothing but a few remaining student cars and the officers' vehicles. This neighborhood is the kind where people tuck their SUVs away in garages, out of sight, so normally the street would be clear.

I almost looked away, certain I was seeing what I'd expect after a party raid, but then something caught my eye.

I froze, my body tingling all over.

My legs wouldn't move as I took in the brown sedan with leprosy that stood out and so obviously didn't belong. It gave me the weirdest sense of foreboding; I could almost feel it rushing over me like a wave of awfulness. *What the hell is he doing here? He couldn't possibly live in this neighborhood and drive that POS.*

I snuck over to stand behind a half-wall of manicured bushes that sat at the edge of the party-house yard, trying to see what was going on at the front of the house. The sedan was parked just behind me on the street.

Rae was standing on the front porch, her form illuminated by the lights that glowed brightly from lamps above her head and behind her on the front of the house. She had her hand on the arm of a police officer and he was nodding, looking at her intently. His other arm hung limply at his side. I've never seen a law enforcement person look less alert, like he was ready to take a nap standing up. Even his head was drooping down lazily.

Mr. Holder was walking across the grass, having just left his horrible, piece-of-crap car. I could see him aiming right for Rae with the single-minded determination of a frigging molester or something.

*No fucking way is that happening.* I had no idea what he was doing there or what his intentions were, but I couldn't see anything good coming of him being involved.

I came out from behind the bushes, no plan in mind, ready to go nuts with my darkness and bring everyone down in tears if I had to. I didn't even know if I could make that happen, but I sure as hell was going to try.

Rae looked to her left when Holder was halfway across the lawn and her jaw dropped open. She shifted to move behind the police officer, who was still acting like he was in a stand-up coma.

I ran, full out, taking in all the details of the situation as I drew near. *Holder. One cop near Rae. Two more inside probably. End of the porch is open, drop not too far. Good escape spot.* I arrived at the bottom step as my next thought burst out of me with as much force as I could manage, while trying to breathe through my panic: *Bring on the darkness.*

## Chapter Twenty-Four
# Rae

EVERYTHING WAS GOING PERFECTLY UNTIL Malcolm decided to go all knight in shining armor on me. One second I had the cop convinced that this was all just a silly misunderstanding and that he should let me go for a walk down the street by myself, and the next, Mr. Holder is walking up with a seriously creepy look on his face and Malcolm's there, standing at the bottom step, ready to do battle.

"Stay back!" Malcolm yelled at Mr. Holder, his back to me and the officer. Apparently he was as weirded out by the teacher being here as I was.

The cop snapped out of the happy trance I'd put him in. "Hey. What's ... what are you doing?" He looked at me like he'd just realized I was standing there in front of him. "What's going on?"

I smiled, reaching out to touch his arm again. "What's going on is you're letting me go."

He yanked his arm away. "Like hell I am. You're a minor and you're drunk. We're going to call your parents first, and if you give me any trouble we'll go down to the station, too."

I jerked my hand back, shocked that he was being so rude to me. "What happened to you?" I asked, before I could stop myself. I knew I sounded like a spoiled Hollywood starlet pulled over for drunk driving, but I couldn't help it. People never talked to me like this.

He rested his fingers on the handcuffs at his belt as he back-stepped towards the door. He yelled over his shoulder without taking his eyes off me. "Banks! Get out here on the front porch!"

Mr. Holder moved closer to Malcolm, pulling my attention away from the police officer. "Step aside, son," the teacher said, "I need to speak to Rae."

"Like hell. I'm not going anywhere. You stay away from her." Malcolm took a step up to the next stair closer to me, gaining a few inches on the teacher. He clenched his fists in front of him like he was going to fight.

"Malcolm what are you doing?" I asked, panicked he was going to get arrested for assault or something. I'd given him the perfect chance to get away. Why was he here screwing it all up? I could have gotten away on my own if he hadn't interfered and distracted the police officer.

Not only was I cranky that he'd gotten both of us in trouble, but I was also confused about how he'd actually done it so thoroughly. Usually people stayed in Rainbowland no matter what happened around them, so long as I stayed close and turned on the charm. But the cop had snapped out of it like someone had thrown a bucket of cold water on his head.

I had no time to figure it out now, though. Mr. Holder was in too much of a hurry to come rescue me, apparently. He waved a finger in my direction, like he was drawing squiggly lines in the air. "Officer, I'm taking charge of that minor up there. She's in my care." His comb-over chose that moment to flop off the side of his head. It waved around like a palm frond in a storm before settling into a limp position over his ear. All I could think about was grabbing a pair of scissors and hacking it off. He seriously needed to be de-comb-overed.

"And who are you?" asked the officer, detaching his handcuffs from his belt.

I swallowed hard, no longer worrying about Mr. Holder's terrible hairdo, but wondering if the restraints were for me or Malcolm. I looked around as casually as possible, trying to find a way out of this mess, now that my plan to entrance my captor wasn't going to work out. My eyes locked on the other end of the house.

There was only one option that I could see: through the officer who stood between me and the far end of the porch.

"I'm Edward Holder, and these are my students." Mr. Holder tried to come up the stairs, but Malcolm moved to block him, forcing him back down onto the front walk just by getting in the way.

"You're not going near her," Malcolm said. He turned his head to explain to the cop. "This guy tried to kidnap her earlier."

"Kidnap? What are you ... are you *crazy?!*"

Mr. Holder was acting all offended, but to me it sounded like someone protesting a little bit too much, especially because what Malcolm was saying was kind of true. Maybe. I hadn't considered it kidnapping before, but now I wasn't sure what to think.

"I would never ... have never ... that's the most ridiculous thing I've ever heard. You need to go home, Malcolm McNamara, before you get yourself into some serious trouble not only with the law but with *me*. I could sue you for defamation!"

"Go ahead. And I'll tell anyone who will listen that you tried to drive away with her when she was trying to get out of your car."

"I never ..."

"Hey! That's enough!" yelled the cop. He moved towards the stairs. "Malcolm, is that your name?"

"Yes."

"Come up here on the porch. Mr. Holder, you stay where you are until we sort this out."

I breathed out a sigh of relief as Malcolm quickly joined me by the front door. He stood next to me and took my clammy hand in his, squeezing it gently several times in a row. He was probably trying to signal me about something, but I had no idea what. I hoped it was his plan to escape, because if my parents found out what I was doing right now, they'd move us to another state tomorrow. No way would they let this event slide by as just a little blip on the radar. Busted by the police at a party, drinking beer with a guy, sneaking out ... this would be a cataclysmic event in my world, but only if my parents found out.

Mr. Holder scowled, speaking to the officer like he was barely restraining his anger. "I told you, *officer*, I'm taking charge of Rae. She's coming with *me*." He took a step closer to the porch again.

My earlier ideas of Mr. Holder being kind of strange amplified about ten times. He was like a Rainbow, only angry at the same time. Desperate. Determined. Needy, but in a twisted kind of way. I hadn't even gotten close to the guy, and he wanted to take me with him in his nasty stink mobile for I don't know what. When he put a foot on the first step, goosebumps broke out on my skin - the bad kind - and my hair stood up on the back of my neck. He was going to ignore the police officer's order to stay away.

The officer bristled. "Sir, I'm going to tell you *one* more time to stay back. Do *not* come up those stairs." He kept his eyes on Mr. Holder as he yelled for his buddies. "Banks! Chuck! Get out here!" His hand moved to a taser in a holster at his back.

Malcolm squeezed my hand hard, and I looked up at him, wondering what he was trying to say. He lifted his chin towards the end of the porch, the place I'd already decided would be my jumping off point if I decided to run, and then he stared at me pointedly, nodding slightly.

Before I could agree on his plan, the front door opened and another police officer came out partway. "We have a little problem inside. Found a girl upstairs in a bedroom. She's been drugged and possibly other things. Ambulance is on the way."

"Leave that to Charlie for now and call for backup. We have a situation out here." The first officer looked pointedly at Mr. Holder as the second officer drew up next to him, walking past us with barely a glance in our direction.

The second officer spoke to Mr. Holder. "What's the problem, sir?"

"As I've already explained ... I am taking charge of that young woman there." He pointed at me. "I'm her teacher and responsible for her."

"No, he's not," I said, sick over the idea of this guy making claims on me that he had no right to. No Rainbow in my past had ever been this obsessed this quickly. Normally it took months of constant nearness for them to lose their grip so thoroughly, and I'd never even touched him, not once. I'd remember that. "He's not my teacher, and he's definitely not taking charge of me or anything else. Keep him away from me."

Mr. Holder took another step, now with both feet on the bottom stair.

"Sir, move one more inch towards the girl and I'm going to arrest you. Back. Up!"

The posture of both officers went rigid with preparedness. They were so ready to take Mr. Holder down, it was scary to witness. They were planning to use tasers, but their big heavy-looking guns were enough threat just sitting there at their sides for any sane person to just back the hell off. Mr. Holder was obviously insane.

Unfortunately, Mr. Holder was so over the edge, he either didn't notice they were ready to kick butt or he didn't care that they both had tasers out and plenty of other weapons at their disposal. He was giving them every signal in the book that he didn't give a flying hoot about being electrified. He stared at me, narrowing his eyes. "Tell them to let you come with me, Rae." He lifted a foot to go up to the next stair.

I frowned at him. The guy was totally bonkers, and his fixation couldn't be explained by normal Rainbow problems. "No, I don't want to go with you. Stay away from me."

He lunged up the stairs with zero warning or sign that he was going to do it, taking the officers by surprise. They rushed to block him from getting through. I heard a heavy clatter and watched a taser fall down the stairs and into the grass near the front walk.

As the officers converged on Mr. Holder, wrestling around to get him under control, Malcolm yanked me closer to his side and then forward. We took off running down the porch, towards the open end where there was no railing.

I heard the cops yell. I turned, poised to leap off the porch, staring at the nightmare behind me. Somehow Mr. Holder, the skinny geeky chemistry teacher with his hair still flopping around, had managed to break through their wall of uniforms and weapons and was coming our way.

"Jump!" yelled Malcolm, springing from the porch while still holding my hand.

I screamed as I was jerked along with him, flying towards the ground completely out of control. I landed on top of Malcolm, taking him down in a crazy tackle, both of us rolling into the bushes and flowers nearby.

Mr. Holder stood on the edge of the porch above us, looking down. "Rae!" he yelled, "you're coming with me!" And then he arched backwards, a shocked expression coming over his face and staying there, like he was frozen. Then his body convulsed over and over, and I heard a clicking sound coming from behind him.

*Taser!* I wanted to cheer with joy but I stayed silent and yelled in my head instead. *You got tazed, you crazy Rainbow bastard!*

"Come on!" yelled Malcolm, scrambling to his feet. "We have to go!"

I joined him, finally untangled from his legs and the stupid shrub that had wrapped itself around my shoelaces. We ran across the side yard and then into the neighbor's front yard. Two people were standing by their door, staring at us as we sprinted by. I ignored them, too focused on running as fast as I possibly could to worry about witnesses or anything else. My family was too new in town for anyone to know me or my parents anyway.

"Come on," said Malcolm through his heavy breathing, "let's get as far away as we can before we stop."

I didn't bother answering. I had to conserve my oxygen for the running. I was so not in shape for escape on foot.

Our shoes pounded on the concrete sidewalk and over the deep lawns that slowed me down way more than I would have liked. My thighs burned, and I got a stitch in my side after four blocks. The beer sloshed around in my stomach, reminding me of my stupid decision to try and drink some bravery into my system.

We rounded the end of the street and took several turns onto other side roads before Malcolm took a sharp left across someone's lawn to go in between two dark houses. I followed a few feet behind, no longer able to keep up. He turned when he realized I wasn't there and waited for me to catch up. Taking me by the hand, he drew me up to the side of a house where we would be sheltered from the view of anyone on the street behind a large, oval-shaped and very dense bush.

He pulled something out of his back pocket, his chest heaving as he tried to catch his breath. When the thing in his hand lit up, I realized it was his phone.

"Who are you calling? The police?" I had no idea why he'd want to do that since we'd just spent so much time trying to run away from three of them.

"No. I'm calling us a ride." He put the phone to his ear.

"To where? I have to go home."

He shook his head. "I don't think you should."

"Why? My parents will freak if they find me gone."

"They really don't know you're out?"

"No. Do yours?"

He looked at me funny. "Not exactly."

"Well ... then ... I guess we both just have to go home and hope they haven't figured out we were gone." I felt so weird right now. Less than thirty minutes ago we were making out all hot and heavy in someone's backyard with people standing all around us. Now we were in a quiet side yard, totally alone, and it felt awkward. Nothing was making sense tonight. Nothing.

"I'm calling Kootch to see if he can come get us. He's probably still around here somewhere. We'll both go home. I doubt Mr. Holder will follow us. He has to know parents would call the cops on him the way he's acting."

"Good. Tell Kootch to hurry."

Malcolm walked out from behind the bush. "Stay here. I just need to see the house number."

I could hear him talking in a soft voice as he disappeared into the darkness, but I couldn't make out the words. I was just happy Kootch had answered. We were way too far from my house to walk.

Malcolm came back a few seconds later, still talking to Kootch. "Dude, just do it. You just got home, and we have no way to get back." He waited a few seconds and then said, "Fine. Come as fast as you can." He put his phone in his back pocket. "Kootch is coming. He and Jasmine texted you a bunch of times to see if we still needed a ride, but you never answered, so they left. He's acting like he's been home forever, but I know it's only been ten minutes tops."

"My battery died. Is Jasmine still with him?" I considered putting my battery back in, but since it would pinpoint my location to my father if he was looking for me, I decided to wait. I'd do it when I was closer to home. I didn't want to be caught out with Malcolm or in this neighborhood. My Plan B of pretending to be out for a walk would never work if my father found me this far from home.

"I don't think she is. I don't know. He was whining about having Geneva out too late." He shook his head in disbelief. "He needs to get a life."

"Or at least a clue," I said, trying to joke around and lighten the mood, suddenly feeling much better about my situation. I had a ride home now, I wasn't running from the police anymore, and my parents would hopefully never know I'd been out. That was the last thing I had to worry about. I put my hands behind my back and crossed my fingers. *Please let them be sleeping when I get home.*

"Speaking of getting a clue, what in the hell was going on with Mr. Holder tonight? And that cop?" Malcolm stood there in front of me, his expression full of confusion. "He was standing there in a frigging coma or something when I came over. What did you say to him?"

My face and neck heated up with embarrassment, caught having used my influence over someone in a very manipulative way. I was ashamed about it, even though I knew I'd done it only because I was in a desperate situation. Somewhere deep inside of me, I'd always had the feeling that using the influence I had over people's emotions was cheating. Unfair. Just not right. And I'd avoided doing it deliberately and this strongly until now. Tonight was a first on so many levels. My head was spinning with it. Before the spinning had been a good thing, but now it was making me a little ill.

Part of me wanted to just spill my guts and get it over with, let him look at me like I'm a freak and leave me there on the side of this house to find my own way home. The other part of me wanted to live in the fantasy for a little while longer, where I pretend I'm a normal girl who happens to find this normal, totally sweet and chivalrous guy very attractive. So attractive that she'd be bold and make a move towards him, tempting him to kiss her again. It was the more dangerous course in some ways, but the safer one in others. And I wanted Malcolm to stay with me for just a little while longer. Kissing him had been so nice.

I took a step towards him, looking up into his eyes as I went. I reached for him, intending to put my hands on his waist, but he grabbed my wrists and halted my movements.

"No. You stay right where you are and tell me what the hell is going on." His voice was sharp. Angry. Cruel.

I felt my heart cracking as he shoved my hands away and stared at me with a granite-hard expression. He wasn't messing around anymore, and apparently the kissing I'd nearly drowned in before hadn't meant anything to him at all.

I stepped away and stared at the ground, my heart aching, willing the tears that rushed to my eyes not to fall. For a few minutes I'd been allowed to live in a fantasy realm, but now the trip was over. I was back to the real world where people either loved me or hated me but none of them could ever truly know me.

And now I knew I could never tell him the truth. He was already done with me.

## Chapter Twenty-Five
# Malcolm

WE RAN, ME GOING A lot slower than I would have liked, to make sure Rae could keep up. In my imagination there were hungry wolves after us, ready to take us down and devour us whole. I knew in reality it was just a couple of overweight cops and a lunatic chemistry teacher, but my instincts were on high alert, telling me that things were not exactly what they seemed tonight in so many ways.

After finally convincing a whiney Kootch to come and get us, I had to face Rae and get everything out in the open. I'd pushed too far and taken advantage of her being buzzed back at the party, and it was making me sick. When I'd showed up at the porch to try and help she'd made it clear she didn't want me there. Her angry words still stung - *"Malcolm, what are you doing?!"* The truth is, I had no idea what I was doing, besides just trying to rescue her like a lovesick idiot with zero plan and even less finesse.

*Love? No frigging way. I don't even know her.*

But despite her trying to blow me off, I still *wanted* to know her. I wanted to know why when I was with her, she still smiled and talked about happy things, why she hides in bathrooms like me, why people can't get too close, and why that cop was standing there like a zombie until I showed up. And I also wanted to know why she kissed me, hoping beyond hope that maybe it wasn't just because of the alcohol.

Kootch was complaining over the phone that he'd already parked the Gremlin and taken off his shoes, even though I knew he was still going to come. He just wanted to hear me beg or something. This was my punishment for having hid from him so many times.

"Dude, just do it. We have no way to get home."

"You're gonna have to wait for me to get my shoes on again. And I have to warm the car up, too."

I knew he was full of crap, but he needed to complain so I let him. "Fine. Come as fast as you can." I put my phone in my pocket, turning my attention to Rae. "Kootch is coming," I said in a low voice, trying not to let my hurt show through. I'd blown it with this girl, but that was to be expected. Guys like me can't have girlfriends. They can't have dates and they can't fall in love.

"Is Jasmine still with him?" She looked hopeful, like having more people between her and me would make things better. The heartache was settling in deep now. I could feel it burrowing into the muscle, making itself comfortable. I welcomed the pain. It would make leaving so much easier.

"I don't think so. I don't know. He was whining about having Geneva out too late." I shook my head over his weird connection to his crappy car. It was like a real person to him, a best friend or something. "He needs to get a life." *Just like me. Three more months and I'm going to go get one. Kind of.*

"Or at least a clue." Rae gave me a strange half-smile.

I couldn't help but think that she really meant that comment for me. It was like a knife piercing my chest. I was a stupid frigging jerk thinking she'd want to be with me. Get a clue was right.

"Speaking of getting a clue, what in the hell was going on with Mr. Holder tonight? And that cop?" My curiosity wasn't going to be content with just ignoring the mystery that is Rae. Even if she didn't want to be with me, I had to know. When I'd said she was an agent of darkness like me, she'd looked at me like I'd suddenly sprouted a horn in the middle of my forehead. It probably wasn't the smartest move in the world to use the stupid nickname I had for it, but it was the only way I'd come up with of expressing what it was like to be me. And no matter what, I knew she wasn't like other people. Maybe she wasn't like me, but she was something.

She didn't answer me right away, so I kept talking. "He was standing there in a frigging coma when I came over or something. What did you say to him?" I wondered if maybe I was completely wrong about her being strange like me. Maybe her parents had some kind of power in this town already, even though they'd just gotten here. Maybe her father was a senator or something. Maybe that's why people got too close and she had to hide in bathrooms.

I felt like a royal asshole now. I smiled bitterly, thinking how I'd tried to assign the agent of darkness label to her when all she was guilty of is being the child of someone powerful.

She suddenly seemed unsure of herself or like she was trying to figure out a way to tell me what she had to say.

I braced myself for the grand *fuck you* I was certain I was going to hear.

She looked down at the ground for a few seconds before raising her head again. She took a step towards me, staring me down as she came.

I waited in silence, ready to hear what she had to say. I could take it. I'd been burned and hurt before. This is my life. This is who I am.

Her arms came out and moved towards my hips.

I took her by the wrists and stopped her. She was drunk and didn't know what she was doing, and I wasn't going to take advantage of her ever again. It wasn't right, even though there was nothing in the world I'd rather do than kiss her and hold her close. Those few stolen moments in the back yard of that stupid party were seared into my brain. I'd be reliving that heaven, that once in a lifetime chance, over and over in my mind forever. I had no doubt of that at all. Stolen moments. Stolen kisses. Things I had no right to take. I was a thief.

I was angry at myself, so my words came out harsher than I meant for them to. "No. You stay right where you are and tell me what the hell is going on." I pushed her hands back to her sides firmly, letting her know that I intended to do the right thing this time and keep her safe - not just from that lunatic teacher but from me, too. I looked her in the eye, trying to show her how much it meant to me to do the right thing like this, even though it was the hardest, least selfish thing I'd ever done. I really wanted to do some more stealing tonight.

She immediately reacted like I'd crushed her heart. She moved back and stared at the ground, saying nothing in response.

"I'm sorry. I sound angry, but I'm not. I know you're mad at me and you have every right to be. But please just tell me. You can tell me to go to hell and I'll go, but before you do that, tell me why. Tell me why people can't get close to you. Is it because your father's important? Is he going to be the president or something?" I guess I needed some closure. This little spark of hope that I was keeping alive - that there was someone out there like me - needed to die. I needed it to be really over.

Words were tumbling out of my mouth. Seeing her standing there with her head down made me want to punch myself in the head. I'd put her in this situation. It was my fault we were standing here like this in the middle of the night, running from the cops.

She laughed, but it wasn't the happy kind of laugh. It was more bitter than anything. "No, my father isn't like that. He tries to keep a low profile. He'd never be in a public office ... be around people like that."

"Oh." *There goes that theory.* "Well, what is it, then? Is it your mother? Is she a senator?"

She finally looked up at me, tears falling from her eyes. I could see their glistening wetness in the moonlight shining bright above our heads. Just witnessing the evidence of her sadness or anger or whatever it was making her cry made my heart constrict painfully in my chest. I wanted to wipe the tears away, like I had earlier. Seeing them at all was just wrong, wrong, wrong. But I had no right to touch her. I watched them track down her cheeks, waiting for her to say something.

"You called yourself the agent of darkness."

"Yes. Any chance you can just pretend you didn't hear that? Pretend I never said it? I'm not crazy if that's what you're wondering. I promise I'm not."

She gave me a bitter smile. "Crazy people don't admit they're crazy."

I dropped my gaze, no longer able to handle the pain of seeing her like this. "I know. But I'm not. I wish I was. It would make life much easier if I could live in another reality."

"I know exactly what you mean."

The sound of a car going very slowly down the street caught my attention. I turned, trying to look over the bush we were hiding behind. It was too tall, so I left its shelter and walked around the side of it. A small car was moving very slowly down the street. I could already tell it wasn't Mr. Holder's car; his was longer and wider than this one.

"It's Kootch. Come on."

"Are you sure?" she asked, walking behind me, whispering.

"Yeah. Who else would be driving slow and trying to read addresses?" I ran towards the curb and stood at the street, waving my arms so he'd see us.

The car stopped for a second and then lurched forward, speeding up.

Rae reached my elbow. "What a relief," she said, breathing heavy again.

As the car drew nearer, my heart sank. It wasn't Kootch.

"Oh my god," said Rae, "that's not a Gremlin is it?"

"No. It's not."

The car pulled up next to us and the window rolled down. "Hey, guys. What are you doing out here standing on the side of the road?"

Before I could answer, Rae walked up to his window. "Hi, Derek. We were just leaving that party, running away so we didn't get busted."

"Oh, man. You guys were there? I was too, but I didn't see you. I just dropped Brody off. Want a lift?"

"Yes," said Rae without hesitation.

"Uh, no. That's okay," I said. "We have Kootch coming."

"I can take you right now," said Derek, his attention on Rae. "Do your parents know you're out?"

"No, they don't." She walked over to the passenger side of the car. "Can you take me home? I'm not sure how far it is."

"Sure, get in. Just tell me where to go and I'll find it."

"Highlands," she said, climbing into the passenger seat.

"I know it. It'll take us ten minutes max. Just put your seatbelt on."

Rae leaned over towards Derek, looking out his window at me. "Are you coming with us?"

I froze for a second, everything about this feeling wrong. "Uh ... no. I'm going to wait for Kootch. He's already on his way." Letting her go without me was making me physically ill. "Why don't you wait for Kootch to show up? I got him out of bed."

Derek put the car in Drive and took the liberty of answering for Rae. "He could take forever in that crap car. She's got to get home if her parents don't know she's out. What if they check her room?"

"I need to go, Malcolm," said Rae, sounding apologetic. "Tell Kootch thanks for me, would you? I'll see you on Monday."

I lifted my hand to say goodbye as they drove off, words not coming to my brain or my lips. She was leaving. She was eager to get away from me. This was better.

Derek's taillights went up the street. The right one was broken. The left one got smaller and dimmer as the distance between us grew.

I didn't even know Kootch had arrived until he pulled even with me and honked the horn. I nearly jumped out of my skin, my heart beating like a runaway train.

"Shit, Kootch. What the hell?"

I looked back at Derek's car. He was just turning the corner.

"Get in, loser. I'm tired."

"Hey, lover boy!" came Jasmine's voice from the passenger seat. "Where's your date?"

"She just took off." I got in pushing Jasmine's seat forward while she stayed in it.

"Took off? What do you mean, took off?" she asked as she slammed the creaky door shut, angry now. "Did you let her run away or something?"

I scowled as I put on my seatbelt. "Hell no, I didn't let her run away. She got in Derek's car and left. Just now. You just missed her."

"Derek's car?" asked Kootch. "What's Derek doing out here? Did she call him?"

"No, of course not. She doesn't even know the guy."

"Then what'd she get in his car for?" asked Jasmine, turning around to glare at me. Then she looked at Kootch. "I don't like this."

"He wouldn't do anything. He's a douche, but he ain't no rapist," said Kootch, slamming the gear into first and moving the car forward.

"Which way did they go?" asked Jasmine. "You said they just left. Let's catch up to them, make sure he brings her home."

"Oh, come on!" yelled Kootch. "Geneva's tired. I'm tired!"

"Shut up, you big whiner baby. Just drive. Which way, Malcolm?" She was staring me down again.

I didn't know what to say. I didn't want to be a stalker. Rae already worried about people doing that for whatever reason. But her getting into Derek's car had literally made me sick with apprehension. Following her without her knowing couldn't hurt anyone.

"Turn right up there."

Kootch sighed loudly, but did as Jasmine asked. We turned the corner, and way up ahead there was a single tail light glowing weakly in the darkness.

"Step on it, Pokey, we need to catch up to them before we lose them." Jasmine was looking out the windshield, pointing to the car that was turning left. "Hurry up! They're going to take a couple turns and we'll never find them!"

Kootch sped up, but he didn't stop complaining. "But they're going to the Highlands! I know how to get there, woman!"

"You assume that's where they're going. Let's hope that's where they're going. But until they *go* there, we don't know, now do we? Now stop back-talking me and drive."

"Bossy cow," he muttered under his breath, but he did press on the gas pedal a little harder. Geneva's engine whined loudly, moving us closer and closer to the turn we needed to take.

"So what the heck was going on back there at the party with you guys, huh, Malcolm?" asked Jasmine, her tone going all sneaky. "I'm pretty sure I caught you giving her mouth-to-mouth. Was she not breathing or something?"

"Shut up." The memory of it burned. My stomach ached with regret.

"Seriously, Butts, shut up," agreed Kootch, taking the turn. He was getting crankier by the second.

I shouldn't be in this car with him. The darkness being enclosed in this small space was going to overwhelm him too quickly. Jasmine didn't seem bothered by it, but I could tell Kootch was. I opened the tiny window, hoping some of it would escape. I wasn't even sure it even worked like that, but anything was worth trying. The poor guy was doing me a favor, and here I was bringing him back down into his depression.

And the guilt piled on.

The car ahead of us turned right. We were just two blocks behind it now.

"Hey. What the hell?" asked Kootch, speeding up and leaning closer toward the windshield.

"What's wrong?" asked Jasmine, fear in her voice.

"He's going the wrong way." Kootch down-shifted as he got to the stop sign. "Highlands is that way." He pointed to the left and then looked at the back of Derek's car. "So why is he going *that* way?"

We all watched the red tail light getting smaller in the distance.

Jasmine punched Kootch in the arm. "Don't just sit there! Go after her!"

"What if it's not her?!" he yelled back.

"It is," I said in a hurry, the panic rising up to choke me. "Broken tail light on the right side. Go!" I shoved the back of his seat, forcing him forward a little.

"Stop pushing on my seat! I'm going!" He revved the engine and popped the clutch, stalling the car. We all jerked forward and then back.

"Jesus, Kootch, can't you drive?!" screamed Jasmine, her hands on the dash.

"Shut up, you're making me nervous, Butts!" He cranked the engine and shoved the shifter into first. Slamming down on the accelerator, he turned the corner at a high rate of speed, swerving out into the other lane. Thankfully, no one else was on the road, so he had time to straighten out and get back in the right lane without killing us. He ran through all four gears quickly, going fifty miles an hour through the residential area so we could catch up. We lost the tail light as Derek took another right turn.

"Maybe he's just taking another route," I said, leaning forward and holding onto Kootch's seat.

"Well that'd mean he's taking the seriously long way, since he's now headed in the opposite direction of where he should be," said Kootch.

"I don't like this at all," said Jasmine. "Hurry, Kootch. I'm not bossing you around, I'm just scared."

I was too. But this made no sense. "Why would Derek take her away from her house?"

"To rape her!" yelled Jasmine. "Why else do guys do stuff like that? Maybe murder her, too!"

"Rape and murder?!" yelled Kootch, looking from her to the windshield and back again. "Are you completely nuts? He's not a criminal. He's a douche, but he's not a murderer! Butts, you are totally crazy, you know that? You and your parents ... conspiracy nuts."

"It sounds crazy," I agreed, "but tonight has been nothing but crazy. Frigging Holder tried to take her away too. Back at the party."

"What are you talking about?" asked Jasmine, her eyes wide in her face. "He wasn't at the party. Is this the beer now? Is that whose in the driver's seat, with your brain riding shotgun?"

"I'm not drunk. I was buzzing before, but after all the running I did tonight, I'm not anymore." I stared at the broken tail light as I explained. "After the accident this afternoon in Brody's car, Holder tried to give us a ride home. He got all weird, so we decided to get out. But when we tried to leave the car, he started to take off while Rae was still in it. Then tonight when the cops were questioning Rae, he showed up and tried to take her away." It sounded stranger being said out loud than it had in my head.

"You're lying," said Jasmine.

"No, I swear on this Gremlin I'm not." I was desperate for them to believe me. If they thought I was lying maybe they'd stop following Rae and then she'd be lost.

"Hey! Watch it!" yelled Kootch, turning left to follow Derek. We were only one block behind him now. "No one swears on Geneva, no one."

"Tell us everything," said Jasmine. "All the details, like a girl would tell the story."

"He just showed up at the party after everyone left. The cops were questioning Rae on the front porch, and he kept saying he was there to take responsibility for her. And when he tried to break through the cops to get to us, they tazed his ass. The last time I saw him, he was having seizures on some guy's porch."

"That is the weirdest fucking thing you've ever said, dude," said Kootch. "You musta taken some X or something."

"X doesn't do this," said Jasmine. "This is either the truth or extreme paranoia. Did you smoke anything?"

I was disgusted with the fact that I was telling a totally true story and all they could think about was me doing drugs. "I'm not messing around and I'm not messed up, okay?! That's exactly what happened! That's the gist of it, anyway." I couldn't tell the story like a girl, like Jasmine wanted me to. Too many unnecessary details and we didn't have time.

"Uh. Yeah. So. Ah-hem..." Kootch sounded very nervous all of a sudden.

"What, Kootch. Spit it out," ordered Jasmine.

"Not that I totally believe that ridiculously stupid story, but ... you know ... Derek *is* the SA for Holder. That's kind of weird, right? Like a weird coincidence? That they'd both be there and trying to take Rae home?"

"Oh, shit. He *is*," said Jasmine. "When student aid spots came open, Holder requested him. I was there. I totally remember thinking that's how Derek's grade went from a D to an A in one semester, like maybe he bribed Holder or something."

I threw myself back against the seat, my hands splayed out on the bench-seat next to me. "What the hell? What the *hell* does that mean?"

"Probably nothing," said Kootch, speeding up even more to put us about three car lengths behind Rae. "She's hot and they want to date her, maybe. But just in case, I'm going to stay close and make sure he brings her home and doesn't rape and murder her in the meantime."

I ran my fingers through my hair, all kinds of crazy shit zipping around in my head. *Rape? Murder? Kidnapping? What the hell kind of bullshit is this?* It might be something innocent like wanting to date her, but I found that highly unlikely. Mr. Holder wasn't the student dating type. He was too old, too gross, and too ... weird.

"This is nowhere near Highlands, is it?" asked Jasmine, her voice full of concern. "Where are we going, can you tell?"

"Highlands is east of here. He's going northwest. No way is he taking her home," said Kootch.

"What are they doing?" I asked. We were on a main road now, and Derek's turn signal had come on. They were turning into a gas station.

"Getting gas or something," said Kootch. "Should I go in?"

"No drive by, drive by!" squeaked Jasmine. "Park nextdoor behind that other car there." She was pointing to a big sedan left overnight in a tire shop's parking lot.

Kootch passed the gas station, and I stared out the window as we went by, trying to see what was going on. "Derek's not at the pumps," I said. He'd parked off to the side of the building and a little in front, not using a parking space. The clerk in the store wouldn't see him there, making me wonder if that was intentional.

Jasmine had spun around, trying to see what was happening too. "She's getting out. Hurry up, Kootch."

"I am! Stop bossing me around!" He pulled into the nearby parking lot.

"She's going inside," said Jasmine, unbuckling her seatbelt. "I'm going in too."

I reached through the front seats and touched her shoulder. "Wait. What if Derek's just getting gas or letting her take a pit stop before bringing her home?"

"Yeah," agreed Kootch. "We could be making a big deal out of nothing."

"Look at her face," said Jasmine. "Does she look happy?"

All of us stared out the window, barely able to see the gas station around the car we'd just pulled in next to.

"She looks miserable. I'm going." Jasmine opened her door.

"Wait," I whispered. "Get back in. Let's get a plan together."

"Plan? You're not James Bond, dude, just go walk up to her and say we came to take you home. Simple," said Kootch.

"He's right," said Jasmine, referring to me. "We need a plan. If Derek is doing something wrong, he's not going to just let her go."

"He's a linebacker on the varsity football team," said Kootch. "If he wants to take her, I doubt we'll have much say in the matter."

"So we sneak her away," I said. "Jasmine, you go in the store. Derek's hanging in his car. Maybe he won't notice you. I'll hang back with Kootch, and if we see him getting out to follow you, we'll stall him."

"Awesome. I'll bring her here by going through a back door. Don't let Derek see you if you don't need to."

"We won't," I assured her.

Maybe Derek was just taking her home the only way he knew how. And maybe she needed to go to the bathroom, so he stopped for her because he's a nice guy. We could be acting like total freaks following them and rescuing her from nothing, but I decided that

I'd rather be safe than sorry. And if anything bad happened to Rae, I knew I'd be sorry for the rest of my life.

Jasmine walked quickly across the front of the store and went inside. Derek didn't get out of his car. I couldn't see what he was doing, but his door stayed shut and his engine remained running.

# Chapter Twenty-Six
# Rae

AS I RODE AWAY FROM the curb in Derek's car, the heart-ache settled in deep. I had a feeling this was the last I'd be seeing of Malcolm. Sure I'd sit next to him in art class or pass by in the hallways, but I'd probably never see him up close and personal, touching me, smiling at me again. It was over before it had really begun. Story of my life.

"So, you live in the Highlands. Do you know how to get there?"

I was suddenly nervous. He didn't have a GPS in his car that I could see. "Um, no. I just moved there. I don't know where anything is."

"Okay, no problem. I know the general area. I'm sure we'll find it no problem."

I smiled weakly, not feeling very confident in his navigating abilities. "Okay." I probably should have waited for Kootch. He knows where my neighborhood is, and Malcolm had gotten him out of bed to take us home.

But I didn't want to force Malcolm to be around me any longer, and Derek's comment about my parents had reminded me that every second counts. Getting back before my parents woke up and checked on me was a priority. They did that sometimes, probably more than I cared to know, and with the way things had gone so far tonight, I felt like I had a really big streak of bad luck following me around. Tonight would be the night they checked more than normal, probably.

"So, how do you like school so far?" Derek asked.

"Pretty good. It's only been one day." The boring conversation was keeping my mind off my parents catching me, so I went with it.

"Yeah, well, it's pretty decent. Who do you have for Chemistry?"

"Um, I can't remember. Some really long name that ends in ski." Thank God it wasn't Holder. I didn't know how I could face that guy on Monday. Hopefully I'd be able to avoid him in the hallways. I still wasn't sure what to do about him. If I reported him to my parents, the police, or the school administration, my parents would use it as an excuse to move. I really wasn't ready to move away yet. Even though Malcolm was acting cold, I still had a potential friend in Jasmine. I couldn't just walk away from something so precious. Friends might be a dime a dozen for other people, but for me, they're gold.

"Ah, you've got Chomanovsky. She's decent. But Holder's better. That's who I have. I'm his SA too."

"SA?"

"Student aid. I have a free period, and I go to his class and help him out and get credit for it. I stock materials in the labs, run errands, put in orders at supply for him."

"Oh." I had a lot to say on the Holder subject, but since Derek was a fan, I kept it to myself. I wondered if he knew his teacher was into crashing teen parties and engaging in the attempted kidnapping of girls. It made me nervous to be in Derek's car, knowing they were so close.

"Have you met him yet?" Derek asked.

"Yes. I have. Remember? At the accident? He kind of gave me a ride home."

"Oh, yeah, that's right. How could I forget? What did you think? Nice guy, right? A little weird, but nice."

I breathed out a sigh of relief that he at least noticed Mr. Holder's craziness. "Yeah, he's weird."

"Don't let that bother you. He's just this scientist guy, you know? Like, he doesn't know how to relate to people who aren't as smart as him, I think."

It seemed like a heck of a lot more than just social awkwardness going on, but I wasn't going to burst Derek's bubble and get him all worked up. I could already see him getting a little too happy about being around me. I had a potential Rainbow on my hands getting this close to him, being in this car alone with him. Better to keep my thoughts to myself.

Derek made a few turns in silence. I didn't recognize anything around us. Everything looked different at night.

"It's too bad you came at the end of the year," said Derek, glancing over at me and smiling. "That must be hard, moving so close to the end."

"Yeah. My dad got transferred." *Lie, lie, lie.*

"Oh, yeah? Where does he work?"

I hated these questions. I never knew how to answer them and always ended up looking clueless. "He works from home. On his computer."

"What's the company?"

"I'm not sure." I was fairly certain my dad owned his own company, but I couldn't very well say that now. I had to stick with the transfer story. I hated telling lies; they were so hard to keep track of.

"My parents work for Glacier Banks." He sounded proud.

"Oh. That's nice." I had no idea what that was. It could be a water bottling company or a law firm as far as I was concerned. All I could think about was my parents getting up to check on me and finding all my pillows stuffed under my covers. The police would be parked in my driveway if that had happened. I prayed I wouldn't find a cruiser at my house when we finally got there.

It was taking us too long to get to my house. I pulled my phone out of my tiny purse that was still slung across my shoulders and pushed the battery back in, powering it up as fast as I could.

When it finally came on, I looked at the time, wishing I'd checked it before I'd left Malcolm. This trip seemed like it was taking forever, but I wasn't sure how much time had passed.

Derek grabbed the phone out of my hand.

"Hey!" I was so shocked he'd done it, I sat there with my hand frozen out in front of me, my mouth hanging open.

"What model is this baby?" he asked, smiling and glancing down at it.

I grabbed for it. "Give it back, Derek!" Now I was pissed. Talk about rude!

He fumbled the phone trying to keep it away from me and dropped it on the floor by his feet. His left foot jerked back and kicked my cell under his seat. "Oh, shit. Sorry about that. Don't worry, I'll get it." He reached down and fished around, yanking the wheel left and right in his efforts.

"Don't! Just ... get it later. You're swerving all over the place. The cops are going to pull you over for drunk driving." The last think I needed was to be delivered home by a cop, assuming they weren't already there.

*Why did I do this at all? Why did I agree to sneak out?* I had never so spectacularly destroyed a first day ever in my life. I figured I had about a five percent chance of getting out of this with my life and heart still intact.

"Sorry about that. That was stupid," he said, back to driving like a sober person again. He looked sorry, but it didn't make me any less mad.

"Are we going the right way? I don't recognize any of this and it's taking a really long time. It didn't take that long to get to the party."

He looked at me, no longer smiling. "What? You think I'm trying to kidnap you or something?"

My heart stopped beating for three full seconds. A huge thump from it got it going again, but now it was racing like I'd just run a mile. "Um, no. I hope not. I'm just ... I want to get home is all." I felt bad for making him think that. I dropped my gaze to my lap. "I'm just freaked out from talking to the cops earlier."

"Oh, I see. You had the cops after you. Well that explains why you were hiding in the bushes with McNamara." He snorted, looking out the windshield again.

I didn't like his tone at all. "I was hiding with him because we were running together. Away from the cops *and* Mr. Holder if you must know." I regretted the words as soon as they were out of my mouth.

He clenched his teeth together, making the side of his jaw bounce out a few times. When he finally spoke it was in a low, almost dead tone. "Mr. Holder is a genius. No one appreciates him like they should."

I smiled weakly, trying to placate Derek and just inspire him to drive me home without yelling at me. "I'm sure he is. He seems very ... smart." *Not! He seems very nuts is the truth, but I'm not going to say that to you because you're blind, apparently!*

"You just need to get to know him better. Then you'll see. He has all our best interests at heart."

Now I felt like I was being inducted into a cult or something. I had to get out of this car. Anyone who thought Mr. Holder was some kind of savior or whatever was no friend of mine. "I really have to pee," I said, suddenly inspired to try and escape. Screw worrying about cops and parents. I had to get away from this crazy Rainbow. "Can you pull into that gas station? I'm afraid I'm going to go in my pants. I had a bunch of beer." I grinned at him, turning on the happy as hard as I could. That's twice tonight I'd used my charms to get my way. I reached out to touch his arm and seal the deal.

"Don't touch me!" he yelled, pulling his arm across his chest to get it away from me.

"Sorry," I said, acting offended. Either he had a touching phobia or he was worried about what I'd do to him. I prayed it was the former because if it was the latter, that meant he knew something he shouldn't.

"Here," he said, putting on his turn signal as a gas station came into view. "I'll bring you in here and wait. But hurry up. Your parents are going to figure out you're gone and then the shit's gonna hit the fan. I have to get home too."

I forced my features to remain normal and not show how horrified I was. I was getting the distinct suspicion that he knew about the effects of my touch *and* that the fear I had of my parents finding out was more than just a normal teenage reaction to being out past curfew. But that was nuts. No one knew. And he wasn't like me, so how could he know anything? I just needed to be alone for a little while so I could think and sort this all out.

"Don't take a long time," he said, shifting the car into park.

"Aren't you going to take a parking spot?" I asked, unbuckling my seatbelt, slowly, trying to pretend I didn't want to run out of there and never come back. I was afraid he'd pull away before I could get out the door, so I had to be cool.

"No. I'll wait over here." He stared out the front windshield, not looking at me.

I really, really wanted my phone. "Can I have my cell back?"

"I'll get it while you're in there. It's under my seat. Hurry up, would you? I have parents too, you know."

I felt guilty, scared, and confused, all at the same time. My head was ready to explode with all the conflict swimming around in it.

"Sorry. I'll be right back," I said, getting out. I ran to the front of the store like a girl barely controlling her bladder and threw the door open. "Where's your bathroom?" I asked the seriously bored-looking clerk.

"In the back. But you have to buy something."

"I'll do it on my way out," I said, not even sure I had any money in my purse.

I raced to the bathroom and locked myself in. Pulling my pants down, I took advantage of my current situation while I figured out what to do.

My thoughts were interrupted before they could even start by someone banging on the door. My bladder froze up, cutting off its stream.

*Oh my god! He followed me in!*

"Rae, open up!" came a girl's voice. "It's me! Jasmine!"

I froze, hovering in mid-squat over the toilet. "Jasmine?"

"Yes! Jazzy Butts, remember? Open the door! I think you're in trouble!"

I pulled my pants up and ran to the door, sliding the lock free and pulling on the handle. Jasmine chose that moment to push on the door at the same time and the thing flew in, hitting me in the knee.

"Ow!" I yelled, bending over to rub it. "Oh, crapski, that hurt!"

"Sorry! Sorry!" she whisper shrieked, pushing the door shut behind her and locking it. "I'm so sorry! Are you okay?" She bent over with me and put her hand on my back, her face full of concern.

I was looking up at her, totally confused. "I'm fine, but what are you doing here?" I stood straight and hobbled back to the toilet.

She took a deep breath and let it out. "I'm here to rescue you. With Kootch and Malcolm."

"What?" I paused, ready to pull my pants down again.

"We're here to *rescue* you. We think Derek's up to something."

"Can we talk about this while I pee?" I asked. All that beer and the panic and now the stinky toilet reminding me where I was all added up to a serious urge.

"Fine. Pee and then let's go." She stood in front of the mirror, checking her lipstick.

I talked as I went. "He's not bringing me to the Highlands is he?"

"No. He's going the opposite way."

My stomach clenched. "That's what I thought. It was taking so long."

"Why didn't you text me or something?" she asked, walking over to take some toilet paper off the roll for me. For some reason the dispenser was across the room, totally out of my reach. She handed me a wad of scratchy, thin paper and stepped back.

"He took my phone."

"What?! That's ... he's a frigging *kidnapper!*"

"It was an accident. I think. I don't know. I'm so confused right now I have no idea what's going on."

I finished my business and pulled up my pants, moving to the sink so I could wash up. I zipped up when I was done.

"Neither do I. All I know is we need to get you out of here without him seeing. We're going out the back door. Kootch and Mal are waiting next door."

I shut off the water and flicked my fingers at the sink. "Okay, I'm ready." I wiped my wet hands on the sides of my jeans.

Jasmine stood at the door and looked back at me. "Just stay close, and if Derek sees you, run to the tire store that's to the right of this place and find the Gremlin."

"But what about you?"

"Don't worry about me. I'll be right on your ass the whole way."

I smiled, knowing I had a true friend standing in front of me. I couldn't help it; I grabbed her in a hug and squeezed her hard. "Thank you for rescuing me, Jazzy Butts."

"Don't thank me yet," she said, hugging me back. "We're not in Geneva yet."

I grinned as we parted. "That sounds so wrong."

"Tell me about it." She slid the lock to the side and opened the door slowly.

Two male voices were conversing in the main part of the store. One of them sounded a lot like Derek.

## Chapter Twenty-Seven
# Malcolm

JASMINE DISAPPEARED INTO THE STORE, and about two minutes later, Derek got out of his car and went inside too.

"Dammit!" yelled Kootch, hitting the steering wheel. "He went in. Now what?" He frowned and smoothed the spot on the wheel where he'd punched it.

"I'm going to get out and see if I can find out what's going on inside. I don't want him to know we're here, though. Keep the car running and maybe point it out of the lot so we can take off in a hurry."

"What, you think he's just going to let them go?" Kootch sounded skeptical.

"Jasmine said they'd go out the back, so maybe he won't see them."

"Fine. You go, but not too close."

I got out and shut the door. Kootch slowly pulled out of the spot he'd taken, doing a couple moves forward and back until he was facing the exit.

I walked a few feet down the lot bordering the store's property.

From my new position, I could see Derek standing at the counter, talking to the clerk. The clerk was pointing to something in the store, towards the back. Derek nodded and started walking in that direction.

A noise on the side of the building caught my attention. I heard whispering voices and running footsteps. Movement near a dumpster told me Jasmine and Rae were on their way.

"Over here!" I yelled as loud as I dared. "He's going to the back of the store from inside!"

The two girls came into view as the light from the store reached them. They scrambled up the small incline separating the two properties. I waited at the top, grabbing each of their hands and pulling them towards me. "Come on, Kootch is waiting!"

We ran to the Gremlin, our feet slapping on the blacktop.

"Rae!" came Derek's voice. He sounded angry.

I looked over my shoulder as I waited for the girls to get into the back seat. They were shouting in their panic, easy to hear from anywhere around.

"Rae, where are you?!" Derek was standing outside the front of the store, searching the parking lot desperately. He looked panicked and mad at the same time.

I didn't waste anymore time looking at him or wondering what the hell he was doing. I threw the seat back into position, knocking Jasmine on her butt, and jumped in, slamming the door shut. "Go! Go! Go! Step on it, Kootch!"

Kootch revved the engine and it roared, its weak little motor doing the best it could to follow Kootch's commands. But the car didn't go anywhere. Kootch still had his foot on the clutch.

"Come on, Kootch, go!" screamed Jasmine, banging on the side of his seat.

Rae started to cry, moaning with fear.

"Stop yelling at me!" he yelled as his foot left the clutch. The car jumped forward, just as Derek had reached my window, putting a small bit of distance between us.

"Rae!" Derek yelled, his face contorted into a mask of fury.

The car stopped and stalled.

Derek ran to catch up to us again and pointed to the window, speaking in a deadly calm voice. "Rae ... get out of the car." His chest was heaving and his nostrils flared, making him look crazy.

Both girls were screaming bloody murder.

"What the hell! What the hell! What the hell!" chanted Kootch, turning the engine over, shoving the shifter into gear, and revving the engine. The car jerked forward and then stopped, jerked forward and stopped. Our heads were snapping back and forth with the stuttering movements.

Derek banged on my window and grabbed the handle.

The door came open partway before I was finally able to grab the arm rest from inside and pull it closed again. I held onto it for dear life, knowing if he got in, people were going to get hurt, starting with me.

Jasmine's hand flew up from the back and slammed the lock down on my door. "Fuck off!" she screamed at Derek.

The car surged forward, this time leaving Derek behind. But then it stalled once more. I could hear him running to catch us again.

"Jesus, Kootch!" I yelled. "Drive the damn car, would ya?!"

Before we could get rolling again, Derek showed up at Kootch's door and pulled it open, grabbing Kootch by the shoulder. The Gremlin inched forward as Kootch hung out of the car.

"Assbag! Get off me!" Kootch swung out with his right fist and hit Derek, punching him in the arm hard enough that Derek lost his grip.

I pulled Kootch back in from my side, and he took the door with him, slamming it shut. Jasmine leaned over and smacked her hand on top of the lock, pushing it down just as Derek tried to open the door again.

I thought we were home free as Kootch threw the shifter into gear, but then Derek drew back and punched the glass near Kootch's face for all he was worth, shattering it.

"What the hell are you doing to my car?!" roared Kootch, finally getting his feet on the pedals and getting the car to go. We moved slowly, rolling along gradually, but not fast enough to get away.

Derek ran alongside the car and reached inside, trying to grab

Kootch's shirt through the broken window.

Derek screamed in agony a second later and yanked his hand out. I saw something black sticking out of the back of his fist before it disappeared.

Kootch slammed the gearshift into second and tore out of the lot, not even slowing down at the exit. The car jumped out onto the main road and quickly moved into third gear, picking up speed on the way.

The girls were crying in the back and Kootch was wild-eyed with fear and anger. "What in the holy fuck was that all about?" he finally asked when we were a couple blocks away, glancing over at me and then in the mirror at the girls. "Can someone please explain to me why that lunatic smashed my car and tried to kill me, please?!"

"What did you do to him?" I asked, looking back at the girls.

"She stabbed him with a frigging pen," said Jasmine, sounding proud. "That's gotta hurt."

"Just get me home, just get me home," cried Rae. She was shaking her head back and forth, lost in her misery.

"No! No one goes home until I say so!" Kootch was practically growling he was so mad.

"Come on, Kootch, you can't kidnap us. We're done with that shit," I said, suddenly very tired. Nothing had gone right tonight. Even the few moments that I had thought were amazing had turned to utter shit. I just wanted to leave town now. Screw the three months until my eighteenth birthday. Screw my diploma. I didn't need it that bad. It's not like I could get a regular job anyway.

Kootch calmed down, but now it was like a crazy kind of serenity that was coloring his tone. "Listen. All my life I've been going to school with that shit basket, and in all that time, the most fucked up thing he's ever done is slap another football player on the ass. Now he's kidnapping girls, punching windows, and trying to pull me out of a moving vehicle? No. No, no, no, no, NO. I do *not* accept that. Someone tell me, what. The fuck. Is going. *On!*" He turned around and glared at Jasmine for a few seconds before looking back at the road.

"What are you looking at me for? I didn't do anything!" she yelled.

"It's my fault," said Rae, sounding defeated. "Just take me home, and you won't ever have to worry about it happening again. I promise."

Jasmine took her hand. "Don't say that. We're not just going to dump you off at your house and say goodbye. Let us help you. We need to call the cops and report him. Derek's a nutbag."

"No!" Rae argued, her tears stopping in the wake of her obvious fear. "No cops. No cops ever."

Jasmine frowned. "Cops are there to protect you from douche bags like him. Seriously, you can't just let him get away with it."

"You don't understand," Rae said, dropping her face into her hands. "No one does. Just bring me home."

Kootch turned in the direction I knew would grant Rae her wish. I wasn't so sure it was the best choice, but it was hers to make, not mine. I pushed aside the guilty feelings and the ones of regret too.

"Come on, Rae, tell us what's going on. We won't judge, I promise," said Jasmine.

"Oh, yes we will," said Kootch, sounding absolutely sure of himself. "I already am. I've judged you guys nuts and crazy and anything else related to that."

Jasmine leaned forward and flicked him on the back of the ear.

"Ow! Butts! Cut it out!"

"Stop being an ass and just drive." She turned her attention back to Rae. "I'm serious. Kootch is not. He will understand whatever it is you have to say."

"No, I will not," he mumbled. Everyone ignored him.

Rae looked up, her face streaked with tears. "I can't tell you what's wrong. I just can't. I need to just go home and try to get in without my parents finding out I was gone, and hopefully Monday everything will be okay."

Nothing was ever going to be okay again. But I wasn't going

to destroy her fantasy with my reality and tell her that. Besides ...
maybe she'd be just fine on Monday, even though my world had
just imploded.

We drove the rest of the way in silence. As we approached the
Highlands community, the light in the sky grew brighter.

"What the hell is *this* now?" asked Kootch as we pulled near.
"Cops? Holy shit ... and fucking swat teams? What the hell? Did
someone rob a bank? Take hostages?"

Cops were coming out of the back of a van parked outside the
gates of the Highland neighborhood, dressed in military gear, including flak jackets and helmets. There had to be at least ten cop
cars in and around the entrance, too.

"Don't go in," shrieked Rae. Then in a calmer voice she said,
"Just drive. Pass by, please. Please don't go in." She was begging,
sounding more desperate than she had all night, and that was
saying a lot.

"Fine, I'm going, I'm going." Kootch sped up and passed the
entrance.

I watched the scene as we drove by, unable to look away. It
was surreal, like a movie about a bank robbery hostage scene.
They looked ready to take down an army of bad guys.

"What in the hell happened in there do you think?" asked
Jasmine.

"It's me," Rae said, staring out the opposite side of the car. It
was like she was deliberately not looking at the circus outside her
neighborhood.

Jasmine turned to Rae. "You can't be serious."

"Where am I supposed to go?" asked Kootch, looking into his
rearview mirror at Rae. "If I can't take you home, where can I take
you?"

"Take her to my house," said Jasmine without hesitation.
"Right now."

"What? Are you serious?" He turned into a nearby neighborhood and stopped at the side of the road. Pulling the emergency
brake, he twisted in his seat to look at all of us. "Someone who's
not insane, please tell me what's going on, where to go, and why

the world has fallen off its axis." He paused waiting for only a second before continuing. "Ha. I'm asking for the one not insane person to speak up, and I just realized that's me!" He turned to face the windshield, hissing out a big sigh of frustration. "Butts, you always get me in trouble. *Always*. Why did I listen to you? Why did I agree to go to that stupid party?"

"Because you wanted to go, you putz. No one twisted your arm. And everyone in here is perfectly sane, you least of all of us, so shut your pie hole and let me think."

"I don't want any fires in my car, so maybe you shouldn't," he said.

She flicked his ear again.

"Do that one more time and you're gonna be sorry."

He ducked as she reached forward to do it again.

"What ... you gonna throw another rock at my face?" she asked. She sat back, a look of concentration coming over her face. "Seriously, I need a cigarette, so take me home." She looked over at Rae, patting her on the leg. "You're coming with me. Don't argue. I have a bunk bed."

"But your parents..."

"My parents aren't home."

"Her parents are never home," said Kootch. "Lucky for her." He pulled away from the curb and made a u-turn.

As we turned onto the main road again, several cop cars sped past us heading in the other direction.

I turned to watch them go before looking at Rae. She was watching them fly by too.

"Those were for you, weren't they?" I asked.

She nodded, not looking at me.

"I'm not going to ask any more questions until we're at my house. My nicotine level is too low for me to talk sense right now."

"I think you'd better smoke more often, then," said Kootch, "cause you never make sense."

"Wet willy punishment," Jasmine said simply, just before sticking a slobbery finger into Kootch's ear.

He jerked the wheel and yelled, trying to smack her hand away before giving up and using his shirt to wipe his ear out. "You are so dead when we get to your house."

"Touch me and you get corn-holioed next," she threatened.

"What's that?" asked Rae, sounding slightly less pitiful than she had before.

"You don't want to know," said Kootch. "Just trust that I will not be touching her in the next million years."

Jasmine smiled at me and Rae. "A girl's gotta do what a girl's gotta do to defend herself."

We pulled into a neighborhood I didn't know, and three streets down stopped at a driveway between two single-story houses. It wasn't an overly affluent place, but it didn't suck like my area of town either.

"Everyone out. I have to tuck Geneva in for the night. I'll be over when I'm done."

We got out of the car and followed Jasmine up the front walk to her door as Kootch backed up and pulled into the driveway nextdoor. Jasmine took a key from her pocket and unlocked the door. Once we were inside, she shut the door and turned off the beeping alarm.

"Welcome to Casa Butts. Make yourselves at home." She gestured to a room on the right, grabbing a pack of cigarettes off the front hall table.

I stared at the living room, visible through the foyer. A streetlight just outside on the road lit up the entire room with a weird bluish glow. The walls of the space were covered in American flags, pictures of people in uniform, and mementoes of a military life.

"Wow. Is your dad a general or something?" I asked, moving into the room, taking in the case of ribbons affixed to the wall.

"Nah. He's a veteran, but he was enlisted. He's a little nutsos about the Air Force still, though. I broke his heart when I told him I wasn't going to enlist after high school."

Rae sniffed, sounding very stuffed up when she spoke. "Can I use your bathroom?"

"Sure. It's just down that hall and on the right." Jasmine

pointed to a dark recess in the wall that could only lead to another part of the house.

"Can we turn on a light?" Rae asked.

"Better not," said Jasmine. "Just in case." She walked over to a sliding glass door near the dining area and cracked it open, lighting a cigarette and blowing the smoke out into the backyard.

Rae and I nodded at each other and she walked away. I wasn't even sure what I was agreeing with exactly, but not calling attention to ourselves felt like a good idea right now.

When Rae was gone from the room, Jasmine turned to me. "So what the hell, dude ...? Quick, before she gets back, tell me what's going on."

"What do you mean?"

"You know what I mean. Don't play coy with me. How is it that you're a ghost for years, invisible to pretty much everyone but me, and the day Rae walks into the school suddenly you're mister social bee and then the shit hits the fan with everyone trying to kidnap you two and Derek going all Jack's-a-dull-boy on us?"

I raised an eyebrow. I had no idea how to respond to that, other than to try and convince her she was the crazy one. "Paranoid much?"

She pointed her lit cigarette at me. "Don't fucking talk to me about paranoid. I live with people who worked for the government, in a department you don't even know exists. You're standing over a panic room filled with supplies and guns like you've never seen before. My parents travel around the country meeting people you don't want to know." She swirled her cigarette around in a circle in my direction. "I know crazy shit when I see it, and *this* is it."

I stood there not knowing what to do or say. I couldn't believe she'd been onto me all these years. Why hadn't she said anything? And why hadn't she killed herself yet being that close to me?

Kootch came in the back door, pushing it open farther and waving the smoke away from his face as he walked past Jasmine. "I can't stay long," he said. "My dad's gonna get up and come looking for me."

Jasmine glared at me before flicking her butt out into the yard, shutting the sliding glass door and going back to the front foyer. The beeping sound of her turning on the alarm reached my ears.

"She's putting on the alarm while we're inside?" I asked.

Kootch rolled his eyes. "You have no idea. Her whole family's looney."

"Just like yours," Jasmine said, joining us again.

"No argument from me there." Kootch dropped down onto the couch, putting his feet up on the coffee table. "So ... what'd I miss?"

Rae came out of the hallway and stood at the entrance to the room, just in time to hear Jasmine's response.

"Malcolm was just about to tell us his secrets." She grinned at me with determination.

I knew there was no way I was getting out of this, short of jumping through the window. I glanced over to check it out. The glass looked really thick.

"What secrets? You been holding out on me, man?" asked Kootch, acting totally unconcerned, joking around again.

"I'd like to hear his secrets too," said Rae, moving into the room.

Jasmine walked over and sat down next to Kootch pointing to two armchairs across from them. "Tell you what, Rae... Why don't you sit there, and Malcolm, you sit there, and *both* of you can tell us your secrets. How's that sound?"

Rae looked panicked. "What?"

Jasmine waved to the chairs and leaned back, putting her feet up next to Kootch's. "Go ahead, don't be shy. Nothing will leave this room, I promise. Your secrets are safe with us. I think I already know them anyway, but let's just see."

"What? Are they doing it? Like *together?*" asked Kootch, sounding cranky again. "I don't need to know that crap. Whatever they do behind closed doors or in the bushes is none of my beeswax." He looked up at me. "But can I just say, *respect*, man. You're a fast mover."

"Oh, no. This is waaaay better than teen sex. Trust me." Jasmine sat up a little and stared at Rae first and then me. "Sit! Don't make me go get one of my guns."

"Is she serious?" Rae asked me. She didn't sound scared, but she did sound unsure. I knew exactly how she felt. My secrets had been mine alone for a very long time. Letting them out felt like I was opening Pandora's box.

"She is," I answered, sighing. Telling my big secret would be a mistake, but not telling it no longer felt like an option either. I'm weak. I admit that. I've wanted to unload this burden my whole life, and here I had a girl begging me to tell her, and another who had her own secrets I wanted to know. And I couldn't very well ask Rae to share hers if I wasn't willing to share mine.

"Fine," I said, taking the seat to the left of Jasmine. "I'll tell if she will." I looked over at Rae, staring at her now instead of avoiding her gaze.

Rae held my stare for several seconds before lifting her chin and walking over, sitting down next to me. "Challenge accepted," she said, glancing at me quickly before turning back to face Jasmine and Kootch. "I'll start." She cleared her throat and sat up straight in her chair, staring at the wall opposite her. "It all began when I was a little girl..."

# Chapter Twenty-Eight
# Rae

I SAT VERY STILL IN my chair, taking turns staring at Malcolm and then at Kootch and Jasmine, trying to gauge their reactions. Jasmine just nodded, looking like she was concentrating very hard on everything I was saying. Kootch alternately looked disbelieving and confused. Malcolm's face was a mask of no expression. He stared out into space, letting none of his feelings show.

"I noticed it when I was really little. Other kids had totally different lives than me. Their parents talked to other people when they were out in public, they talked to their kids about normal stuff or yelled at them or punished them. Mine stayed together, always watching me, watching other people watch me, not saying anything unless we were alone. They discouraged kids from coming near me. I've only been to a playground during the daytime twice. Both times I remember my parents making me leave when kids tried to talk to me or play with me. They only took me at night, after that. I played alone in the dark on playgrounds until I decided I didn't want to do that anymore and made them stop bringing me. It was lonely. I remember it being very, very lonely."

ELLE CASEY

"That's weird," said Kootch. "Your parents sound like they have mental problems."

"Save all questions and insults for the end, dumbass," said Jasmine, frowning at him. She looked back at me, giving me an encouraging smile. "Ignore the boy on the short bus. Just keep telling your story."

"How about the nutshell version?" I asked, sighing. No one wanted to hear the sad sorry story of my lame life. "I have a problem. Every time I go somewhere, people get attached to me and then get dangerous. They want to be with me all the time. I can't help it. It just happens. That's why I move around a lot. To get away from them."

"Wow. A little full of yourself, aren't you?" asked Kootch.

Jasmine grabbed a decorative pillow off the couch and jumped on him, pushing it into his face. "I will *smother* you, dickcheese! I will put you right out of your misery with my bare hands!"

"Ow, ow, okay!" came Kootch's muffled voice from under her. "I'll stop, I'll stop!" He didn't fight back at all. He just laid there until Jasmine decided to quit, which was only after she pushed the pillow harder a few times into his face while grunting with the effort.

Jasmine settled back down into her seat, acting like she hadn't just threatened to murder her next door neighbor. "Sorry for the interruption. I know you're not conceited. You're anything but." She turned a glare in Kootch's direction.

He put his hands up in surrender, saying nothing but rolling his eyes when she looked away.

"It's okay," I said. "I know how it looks and sounds. Believe me, I've lived this way my whole life." I didn't want to look at Malcolm, but I couldn't help it.

He was on the edge of his seat, mesmerized or something. He stared at me, a strange expression on his face.

I had to look away. I couldn't bear the idea that he'd find me repulsive or freakish. Not yet, anyway. I needed some time to get over the events of tonight and build up my walls again.

"So, how do you know this happens?" asked Jasmine.

I shrugged. "It just always has. People get all happy when I'm around. My parents are the worst. They're totally addicted to me or whatever it is that makes them happy when I'm around. They hate having me leave the house to be at school all day. They never let me out on weekends. I'm not allowed to have friends."

"Why don't they home school you, then?" asked Kootch. He sounded skeptical, but I didn't blame him or hold it against him either. It *is* nuts. My life is a freak show.

"They want to. They've begged me. But I told them no."

Kootch snorted. "Ha. Like they'd let you decide. *They're* the parents. *You're* the kid. The parents are in charge, not the kids."

I looked him straight in the eye. "I force them to let me go to school. That's how it works in *my* house." I was angry, but not at him. I really wished the parents could be in charge in my life.

Jasmine looked uneasy. "And how do you do that? Force them, I mean. Do you Spock-pinch them or something? Give 'em the old laser-eye?"

I laughed bitterly. "Nothing that sexy. I just threaten to leave and never come back."

"They love you," said Malcolm. He sounded wistful.

"No. They're addicted to me. There's a difference, a very *big* difference. They're Rainbows."

"You have gay parents?" asked Kootch. "What's that got to do with anything?"

"No. I call them Rainbows ... anyone who gets addicted and needs to feel the Happy ... they're Rainbows to me. They see me as bringing light and color and joy into their lives. Or they feel that way when they're around me." I shrugged, not able to describe it any better than that. I'd made the name up when I was a little kid, and it stuck. I never considered coming up with a more grown-up term for them. What would be the point when I only ever said it in my own head?

"Sorry to burst your multi-colored bubble or whatever, but I don't feel that way around you," said Kootch. "You're pretty and all, but you're just a regular girl." He looked over at Jasmine. "Can I go home now? I'm tired."

"Go whenever you want, I don't care," she said. "But first, a little experiment ... *if* you're not afraid." She grinned evilly at him.

"What kind of experiment?" Kootch asked, sounding suspicious.

Her tone made me uneasy. She sounded and looked like she was being sneaky. I had a feeling Kootch wasn't going to like the outcome.

Jasmine got up and came over to me, kneeling down by my chair. Leaning over, she whispered in my ear, putting her hand up next to her mouth so Kootch and Malcolm wouldn't hear. "I'm going to take Malcolm out of the room. I want you to kiss Kootch, right on the mouth."

"Ew, no," I whispered, leaning away from her.

She grabbed my shirt sleeve and pulled me back. "Yes. No tongue, just a smooch. Wait 'til we're gone, out of the room completely. Just consider it a science experiment." She stood before I could argue.

"Malcolm, come with me," she ordered, walking behind my chair to stand next to his.

Malcolm stood. "Where are we going?"

"Just follow me. Kootch, you stay here with Rae. She's got something to show you."

She walked out before I could tell her not to, pushing Malcolm in front of her. He tried to look at me over his shoulder, but she got him out of the room before he could do anything but listen to her boss him around. Her voice faded as they walked down a hallway until we couldn't hear it anymore.

Kootch stared at me across the open space, over the short coffee table. "What are you going to show me?" he asked, his suspicion slowly sliding away.

Seconds ticked by, the sound coming from a clock on the wall behind my head. The longer we were in here together alone, the smoother Kootch's face became. After forty-five seconds, all his anger or frustration slipped away. The colors of his Rainbow were showing through, glowing until they shined out from his face. Even though it was a term I came up with when I was little, it still described the effect I had on people perfectly.

I stood up, ignoring my fear and the strong sense of misgiving that nearly overwhelmed me at the idea of being alone with him and encouraging more closeness.

"Come over here," I said.

He stood and walked around the coffee table, stopping when he was in front of Malcolm's chair. He was smiling, no longer cranky. And I was sure he wasn't thinking about wanting to leave anymore either.

"Closer," I urged, getting seriously nervous about having him this near and tempting him to come even nearer. He had already been attaching to me before all this happened, in detention and before. Once a Rainbow got to a certain point with me, it was easy to push them beyond the safe zone. I've done it without trying, and right now I was going to do it on purpose. I was playing with fire and ignoring all the alarm bells ringing in my head.

He took two more steps around the coffee table until he was standing right next to me. I turned to face him, trying not to tremble. He was so much taller than me and very muscular. Bigger than Malcolm and broader in the shoulders. He needed a shave. I could smell his cologne. It was different than how Malcolm smelled. Sweeter. More spicy or something. I could tell he'd had some beer tonight as the odor of it wafted down towards me.

"What are you going to show me?" he asked, his voice going soft and smooth as he stared into my eyes. His were green and flecked with gold.

"I'm not going to show you anything. You're going to feel it."

The right side of his mouth went up in a charming half-grin. "Am I going to like it? It's not a wet willy is it?"

"No," I said, grinning a little too. He was pretty cute when he was relaxed. "It's definitely not a wet willy." I swallowed hard, feeling guilty already. "Put your hands behind your back and keep them there. Promise you won't move them."

He did as he was told, smiling bigger now. "Ooo, this is getting interesting. Maybe you should tie me up."

"Good idea," I said, yanking my purse over my head. "Turn around."

He didn't hesitate.

I tied his wrists together with my thin purse strap, knotting the leather as best I could. I didn't have the strength to make it as tight as I wanted to. "Turn back around."

He did as he was told, his breathing rate slightly elevated, either in anticipation of what was to come or because of the fact that he was standing so close to me.

"Close your eyes."

His lids dropped and so did his smile. He stood there waiting for something he didn't even know was coming, but he didn't care. At this point he would have let me do anything.

"You're happy to be standing here in front of me with your hands tied, aren't you?"

"Yes." He said it simply, with no emotion.

"Before you said I was conceited."

"I didn't mean it. I think you're amazing. You're not conceited, you're perfect. Beautiful in every way."

"You think that because you're close to me. Not because it's real."

"It's real. It's totally real. I can feel it. I can see it."

"No, it's not real. You just think it is." I desperately wanted him to understand.

"Whatever you say. All I know is, I'm a good looking guy and you're a cute girl. That's it. That's just chemistry, baby. No need to fight it."

"I'm going to kiss you."

A grin spread quickly. "Awesome. Let's do it." He puckered up his lips and leaned forward.

"You think you'll be able to handle it?"

He snorted, the pucker disappearing. "Please. I've kissed a hundred girls. Lay it on me. It's no big deal."

I closed the space between us. "Bend down a little."

He leaned over until his lips were just inches from mine.

"Here goes nothing," I said, placing my lips against his, pressing in just a little as I gave him a kiss.

He instantly moved forward, trying to deepen our connection. I wasn't expecting such a quick reaction, so he succeeded in getting more of me than I'd intended. Our lips smashed together, and then his parted. His tongue came out and licked my lips slightly before he moved his mouth over mine again. I leaned back to get away, but he leaned forward more, keeping our faces together.

He moaned, breaking free of the purse strings with little effort and wrapping his arms around me, dipping his head down to deepen our kiss and pressing his body into me tightly.

"Oh, Rae," he gasped, shoving his tongue into my mouth.

I jerked my head back and to the side to get away, pushing on his chest with both hands. "No, Kootch, no! You promised you wouldn't move your hands!" Panic swelled my heart and made it feel like it was going to explode. "Get off!"

"Please, just kiss me, Rae, we're so good together!" He kept leaning and leaning, straining his lips towards mine. Eventually his weight was too much for me to hold up anymore, and he pushed us both over until I fell back into the armchair.

He fell too, landing on top of me, and his face ended up near my chest. He started kissing it, at first trying to get back to my lips but then changing his mind, going for my left breast instead.

I screamed, struggling to get out from under him, hitting him on the head. He was going to keep going and going and going until he raped me. And he'd never even realize he was doing it, too. That's how it is with Rainbows; they were always oblivious to the things they did to themselves and me.

Kootch yelled in surprised anger when a giant pillow came down and brained him, knocking his mouth from the nipple he'd been trying to grab through my shirt and bra. His grip around my back slackened.

I wanted to kick him off, but at the same time I didn't want to hurt him. He hadn't been at fault here. I was the one who'd agreed to this stupid idea. The humiliation was complete when I heard Malcolm's angry, disgusted voice above me.

"What the hell, Kootch?!" yelled Malcolm, pulling him off me.

A cool rush of air washed over my body once Kootch's hot chest was no longer smothering it. I felt naked. Ashamed.

"You're such a dick! What the hell is wrong with you?!" Malcolm pulled his fist back and punched Kootch in the face, slamming him onto his back on the floor.

Kootch banged into the coffee table on the way down and cried out with pain as the corner of the wood jabbed him in the ribs. He laid on the floor writhing around, yelling in pain. "Gah! What the hell, man!"

"Hey! Time out! No fighting in the living room!" yelled Jasmine, standing in the middle of everything with the pillow under her arm, gesturing like a referee. I wouldn't have been surprised to see her bust out a whistle.

"He was forcing himself on her!" yelled Malcolm, not yet ready to let Kootch up off the floor. He stood over him with his legs spread and fist cocked.

"I don't know what happened!" yelled Kootch, sounding like he wanted to cry, ducking away from Malcolm's threat. "I was just sitting there, and then all of a sudden she was under me. It's not my fault! She put a spell on me or something!" He lifted his head and glared at me. "What'd you do? What are you, a witch or something?" He sat up partway and crawled backwards, trying to get away from me or Malcolm, it was hard to tell which. Maybe both of us.

It made my heart ache with regret. Why couldn't I have just left it alone? Why did I tell them anything? Why did I agree to something I knew would be a disaster? I looked at the front door. I had to leave. I had to get out of here and disappear.

"Don't even think about it," said Jasmine, looking down at me. "You aren't leaving, and neither are you, Kootch." She turned her attention to him. "Get up and sit on the couch and shut up."

"You're not the boss of me, Butts." He glared at her once before getting onto his hands and knees and crawling over to the couch. He climbed up into a sitting position and sat there, gingerly touching his cheekbone where Malcolm had hit him, moving his jaw around in several directions as if he was trying to see if it still worked properly.

"Malcolm, sit," ordered Jasmine. "Here across from Kootch. I don't want you getting too close to him."

Malcolm sat down. "Why?" he asked.

"You know why. Don't play games," she said. She sounded like an adult admonishing a child.

Malcolm looked down at his hands in his lap but didn't respond. It's possible he looked guilty, but I wasn't sure. Maybe I was just reflecting my own emotions onto him to try and make myself feel better about what I'd done.

"Okay, people." Jasmine stood at the end of the coffee table. "My experiment was successful. Maybe a little too successful."

"Your experiment was a *trick*," said Kootch. "Somebody roofied me."

"Don't be a baby. That was no trick and no one roofied you, cheese doodle. You claimed to have no interest in Rae and said you could resist her, but as soon as we left the room, you were all over her like white on rice. Of course now you regret it since Malcolm is back and punching you in the face over it, but that doesn't change anything that happened. Just call a spade a spade and admit it. She mind-fucked you."

"I've got nothing to feel guilty about," said Kootch, not sounding like he believed it much.

"No, you don't," I said, really feeling sorry for him. "I put you in that position, it's my fault."

He just frowned at me.

"I think to make this clearer, we need to hear from Malcolm. Then we'll have all the pieces and we can put this puzzle together." Jasmine was actually smiling. She looked so proud of herself, like she was the only one in the room who knew what the heck was going on.

I turned my head to look at Malcolm. He was sitting there staring at his feet, leaning over partway in his chair with his forearms resting on his thighs near his knees.

"You ready for this?" Jasmine asked him.

He sighed heavily and sat back, a defeated look on his face. His arms rested limply in his lap. "No, not really."

"Good. Tell us anyway," she said, taking her seat on the couch next to Kootch. "Nutshell version. Go."

Malcolm looked once at me and then at the ceiling before he began reciting his story.

"It all started when I was really young. Before my own memories even began, really. First it was my mom..."

# Chapter Twenty-Nine
# Malcolm

I TRAVELED DOWN MEMORY LANE, trying to picture my mom's face. It wouldn't come to me now, just like always. I'm not sure if I ever had a picture of her in my mind or if I'd just made one up. Dark brown hair like mine. Brown eyes. Pale skin.

"I was only two when she died. When she killed herself, actually. Dead by suicide, they said. She cut her wrists in the bathtub. My dad found me crying in my bedroom and her dead, floating in the water. Maybe I saw her too, I don't know. I don't remember the details."

"That's awful," said Rae, her voice so sad and raw with emotion, I was tempted to look at her. But I didn't. I couldn't.

I shrugged, acting like it didn't bother me too much. "Like I said, I don't remember it. This is just stuff in my records. My father was an alcoholic. I don't know if he drank before my mom died, but he sure did after. I only lived with him another two years before he left. I don't know if he's still alive or not. A neighbor found me eating out of her garbage can when I was four, and that was the beginning of my life as number 55548323142."

"You're a prisoner?" asked Kootch.

I laughed without really finding anything funny. "Kind of. It's my number in the foster system. They mean something, I don't know what. I don't care." I shrugged, as if it was no big deal to be a number on a piece of paper, one of thousands of other kids just like me but at the same time, not like me at all.

"So you live with a foster family?" asked Jasmine.

"I have lived with *many* foster families," I corrected. "See, I have a problem too." I finally looked over at Rae, wondering how she was going to take the news. Hearing her story had pretty much blown me away. I stayed calm on the outside, but inside I was running around in circles and getting dizzy, yelling, shouting out crazy nonsense. It was all too much to comprehend. How could I get so close to something and then have it yanked away? What kind of cruel world is this? What had I ever done to deserve this level of horrible karma?

All this time I'd been thinking she's like me, when it turns out she's the exact opposite. I'd come so close to finding someone I could be around, and then ... she was gone. She never existed though, not really - not like I'd imagined her to be. It was stupid to be upset about something that never existed. But my heart wasn't ready to let her go yet, the fantasy I'd cooked up where she and I could be together without me killing her was struggling to stay alive; so I was going to pretend for just a little while longer that I wasn't going to disappear tonight and never look back.

"What's your problem? You a Rainbow freak too?" asked Kootch, his arms folded over his chest.

Jasmine put up her hands in a T-sign. "Time out." She sat forward on the couch and twisted her upper body to face Kootch, her back to Rae. "Okay, Kootch. You've got two seconds to get your head out of your colon before I twist your scrotum off and make earrings out of your beanbags." She leaned in closer to him. "Do you feel me, dog?"

He uncrossed his arms and cupped his hands over his crotch. "I definitely feel you, Butts. I feel you too much, in fact. If you could just slide over a little, away from my jewels, that would be great."

"Try not to be a dicklick for ten minutes, and I'll give you a Scooby snack, okay?"

He held up a finger, leaving one hand still over his crotch. "First of all, I never have nor will I ever, lick a dick. I'm all about the tacos, know what I'm sayin'? And second, I'm just expressing my opinion that this is all a bunch of hooey, but if you want to give me a Ho-Ho or a Ding Dong, then I'll shut up for ten minutes."

Jasmine snorted, turning around to face Malcolm. "And he says he doesn't lick dicks."

"Hey!" protested Kootch. "Licking a Ding Dong is not the same as licking a dick!"

"If you say so. 'Course, you haven't actually seen yourself go to town on a Ding Dong like I have, so maybe you should withhold judgment on that."

He pushed his lips together and shook his head a few times back and forth. "One of these days, Butts ... I swear to God..." He wrinkled his mouth all up and acted like he was barely holding back his anger. I could tell it was all an act, though. I was pretty sure Jasmine could stab a pen through his hand right now and he'd just ask her what the hell she was doing. At some point in their next-door-neighbor relationship, he'd given her a free pass to abuse him however she saw fit, and she was taking full advantage of it. It made me being a freak seem a little less awful for some reason.

"What?" She looked at him again. "You threatenin' me? You gonna throw a rock at my face? Pssshhhh. Been there, done that." She turned to me again. "Please continue. Kootch will do anything for a Ding Dong, including shutting his pie hole for an entire ten minutes."

I was smiling at Jasmine and Kootch as they argued, even though my story was worse than depressing and something that should have been bringing me to tears. *So this is what it's like to have friends.* I was going to be sad to say goodbye to them. I would never forget them either. Our time together might have been short - really only part of a day - but it didn't matter. When you're like me, you take these small things that mean a lot and you give them the importance in your memory that they deserve. Everything counts in large amounts, especially when you're an agent of darkness.

"Where was I?" I said, trying to get my bearings while waiting for the sappy feelings to pass by. I was afraid a tear might leak out and then I'd just get pissed.

Rae's soft voice came to me, making me look over. I couldn't ignore her anymore.

"You were saying that you have a problem too. Like me."

"I do have a problem, but it's not like you. Actually, it's the opposite of you." I searched her face for recognition of our dilemma, the fact that we could not possibly be together, but there was nothing there. Just an openness. A desire to hear what I had to say. Something that felt like a shard of glass twisted in my heart, making it painful to breathe. I pushed past it with effort and continued my story. "Certain people are drawn to me. People who are sad or depressed. And when they get around me, they get worse. Way worse."

"What do you mean?" asked Jasmine.

"I mean, they get ... dark. My mom was the first one. Then my dad."

"Aw, come on, man! You can't blame your two-year-old self for your mother's suicide! That's just mental." Kootch had made it a whole minute not talking.

Jasmine slapped him in the face with a pillow. He closed his eyes and said nothing.

"My father was next," I explained. "And then foster parents, foster siblings, and neighbors ... anyone who spent too much time with me and got too close either died or made themselves very sick or hurt themselves. After I finally figured out it was me causing all the pain, I made sure they moved me around a lot."

"How'd you do that?" asked Rae, her eyes full of pity.

I don't know why, but her sympathy made me feel better. No one had ever felt sorry for me that I could remember. "I just made sure to suggest to people who were getting ... dark ... that they could call the social worker on my file and get me moved. The ones who didn't want to be depressed would jump on the idea.

The ones who were more attracted to the idea of darkness, well, I had to report things myself. It was easy. Drugs in the house, abuse, weapons, things the system frowns on."

"Dude, that is so messed up, I don't even know where to begin." Kootch didn't look quite as skeptical now.

I hadn't even told them the worst of it, and I wasn't going to. Not now and not ever. No one would ever know that stuff but me. I carried the memories around, refusing to let myself forget, so that at least *someone* would remember those who'd suffered because of me. If not me, then who? No one deserves to be forgotten forever.

"So anyone who comes near you wants to die, is that it?" asked Jasmine.

"No, not everyone."

"Not Jasmine," said Rae, sounding less sad and more confident. "She's a Neutral."

We all looked at Rae. I had no idea what she was talking about.

"Neutral? What's a neutral?" asked Jasmine. She looked happy about the idea.

"A Neutral is a person who isn't affected by me. I've met only a few in my life. They just kind of seem oblivious to it all."

"So, you've had some friends," I said, unable to keep the envy out of my voice.

"No," she said, sad again. "They'll hang around for a few days or weeks at the most. One made it a whole month and a half. But then the Rainbows descend and the Neutrals start getting mad at all the attention I get, and they start blaming me, saying I flirt or ask for it or whatever. It's jealousy or frustration, I don't know. They always leave, though. It's the Rainbows I can't get rid of."

"And you hide in the bathroom," I said, so quiet I wasn't sure she'd heard me.

"Yes. I hide in the bathroom." She smiled at me tenderly, and I swear I felt my heart melt a little as it warmed under her blue-eyed gaze.

And then I remembered her story. She makes people love her. She can't help it. It's just a power she has, and people can't control how they feel when they're around her.

I wanted to be sick, right there on the floor. *This isn't real. What I'm feeling for her isn't really me. It's her!* I broke my gaze away from her achingly beautiful face and stared at my shoes. It felt like someone had punched me in the gut, making it hard for me to breathe. This was like the worst joke the universe had ever played on me. All this time I'd thought being an agent of darkness was bad, awful, terrible; but this ... this was worse. Much worse. I finally found a girl I like, who I thought I could hang with ... and it turns out I probably don't even really like her at all. She's hypnotized me. I'm just another prick, hot after her ass because she's literally irresistible. I laughed bitterly at myself. I'd been so stupid.

"What's wrong?" Jasmine asked. "You have an ugly look on your face."

"Dude's got gas," said Kootch. "Bathroom's down that hall, on the right." He gestured to the place where Rae had gone earlier.

"Shut up, Kootch," I said, sounding tired. I was exhausted. Not just from the running from cops and Derek, but from the emotional upheaval too. Being a shadow was much easier; interacting with people and trying to fit in was completely draining.

"I know why he looks like that," said Jasmine, looking way too smug.

"Oh, yeah? Why don't you fill us in on your theory, Sherlock," said Kootch. "But before you do, why don't you run along to the kitchen and get me a Ding Dong."

She stood, talking as she walked to the other room. "What we have here is a yin and a yang, people. This is nature doing a delicate balancing act." The sound of a cupboard slamming shut came out into the room. "See, Malcolm, he's the yin. He's the darkness, the shadows, the void. And Rae? She's the yang. She's the light, the thing that uncovers the shadows and fills the void. Get it?" She came out of the kitchen a box of vintage Hostess cakes in it. She put it down on the table, gesturing to it. "Help yourselves before Kootch gets his grubby paws all over them."

I shook my head, sure I'd be even sicker if I ate that much sugar right now. Rae also declined, but Kootch leaned over and pulled out two packages, resting one in his lap while he opened the other noisily.

I wanted to pay attention to what Jasmine was saying, I knew it was important, but watching Kootch eat a Ding Dong was like seeing a train wreck in slow motion. I couldn't look away. I cringed at the horrific scene before me.

Jasmine could tell I was distracted. "Did you hear what I said? Malcolm?" She looked over at Kootch. "Oh, for chrissake, Kootch." She turned to me. "See what I mean? He is totally licking dick right now, is he not?"

Kootch froze with his tongue sticking out, on its second trip up the side of the Ding Dong. He quickly pulled his tongue in. "Shut it, Butts." And then he shoved the cake into his mouth whole. "See? Gone. Done." He waved at me. "Keep going. This shit is getting real." Several brown cake crumbs came flying out of his mouth.

Jasmine leaned over the edge of the couch and came back with a Dustbuster in her hand. She flicked it on and vacuumed Kootch's crotch for a few seconds before turning it off again and looking at me expectantly, lowering the small machine to the floor by her leg.

I guess I was supposed to pretend she hadn't just vacuumed Kootch's crotch and continue with my story, but I just couldn't. I started laughing.

"What's so funny?" Jasmine asked.

Rae started giggling next to me.

"What?" asked Kootch. "Is it the vacuum thing?" he grinned big. "Oh, you don't even *know*. Jasmine? OCD all the way, man. Dude, just wait. You'll see."

"Just because I don't wallow in filth, doesn't mean I'm OCD," she said, frowning at him.

"How often do you change your toothbrush?" Kootch asked, staring at the ceiling, a smile barely concealed under a fake-serious face. He held up a single finger.

"Once a week. Just like any normal person. There are millions of germs that gather there and grow while you're at school, you know. They reach critical mass and you have to protect yourself."

"Aaaaand how often do you change your sheets?" He held up a second finger.

"Every single day, like normal people who aren't pigs. Do you have any idea how many mites and other crap are living in your bed?"

"Aaaaand how many times to you check doors and lights after you go to bed?" He put up a third finger.

Jasmine rolled her eyes. "Safety! Security! I want to live until I'm at least twenty! That requires a minimum of three checks, just to be sure none were forgotten and no one messed with them while I was checking other places! Duh!"

He tipped his head back down and looked at Rae and then me. "I could do this all night, but I think you get the picture." He jabbed a thumb in Jasmine's direction. "She's been vacuuming invisible crumbs and mites and God knows what else off my body for ten years. *Ten years*. This all started when she was five. The day she kicked me off her swing set and never let me back on it."

"That is *not* what happened, and you *know* it!" she shrieked, hitting him in the face with her pillow again.

"Do you guys think we could go back to the yin and yang thing?" asked Rae. "It's the first thing that anyone's ever said to me that makes any sense."

Rae's hopeful expression was killing me. She wanted answers, a solution. Maybe for her there'd be some, but for me, it was hopeless. No matter what I understood about my problem, it wouldn't change the fact that people who got too close to me died. Love was a death sentence with me, and I didn't want anymore blood on my hands. There was already so much there that I'd never be able to wash it all off, even with a lifetime of scrubbing and praying for forgiveness.

"Okay, as I was saying, yin and yang. Nature in balance." Jasmine looked at me, passion taking over her voice. "Haven't you noticed that when you're together, you and Rae, Kootch acts kind of normal?"

I looked at Kootch, whose face was all puffed out because of the second Ding Dong he'd just shoved in his mouth. Jasmine quickly grabbed the vacuum and sucked up the few crumbs that escaped onto his chest.

Rae was staring at him too. "He looks better now, actually. Since Malcolm came in and punched him in the face."

"Yeah, I think it was the punch that did it for me," said Kootch, talking around the food. He swallowed hard. "A punch to the face always calms me down."

"No, it wasn't the punch," argued Jasmine. "It was Malcolm coming in here. Maybe him touching Kootch made it happen faster, but it was happening anyway."

Kootch frowned. "You're acting like I'm easy to manipulate."

"You and everyone else. Except for me of course." Jasmine smiled and fluffed her hair. "I'm a Neutral." She started jiving in her seat. "Can't touch this, dah, nah, nah-nah .. nah-nah ... nah-nah. Can't touch this."

"Neutral my ass," said Kootch under his breath.

I thought about what she was saying. I didn't know anything about this yin or yang thing, but I did know that today was the first time I'd been able to hang around Kootch without him smothering me. And not only that, people were acting different. They were leaving us alone. Whenever Rae and I were together, people treated us like we weren't even there. A flush crept up my neck as I realized that I never thought about hiding in a bathroom when Rae was around. There wasn't any need to.

Rae was frowning. She had to be running through memories, just like I was. Looking up at me, she had what appeared to be hope in her eyes. "The cop," she said, staring at me.

I shrugged my shoulders a little, not knowing where she was going with this.

She bounced a little in her seat. "The cop!"

I shook my head. "The cop, what?"

"You're the reason why everything got messed up!"

I leaned back into my chair, my heart sinking. Now she got it. Now she knew. I'm always the reason things get messed up. I turned around and looked at the door, wondering how long it would take me to get home from here.

# Chapter Thirty
# Rae

IT ALL FINALLY MADE SENSE. Why the police officer had snapped out of Rainbowland so quickly. Why we'd been able to play basketball in gym class. Why we'd been having so much fun at that party!

"The cop!" I said, barely able to contain myself. This thing was real. Jasmine was onto something amazing, I knew she was.

Malcolm just shrugged at me, like he either didn't get it or didn't care, but that did nothing to dampen my enthusiasm. For the first time I had real hope, something I could grab onto.

I bounced like a little kid, the spring in the seat throwing me up with almost no effort on my part. "The cop!" Pretty soon I was going to squeal. I could feel it bubbling up inside me. The joy. The excitement. I so rarely allowed those emotions in my life because they were so dangerous for others, but here, I was safe. I could be happy and it wouldn't hurt anyone, all because of Malcolm!

He frowned at me. "The cop, *what?*"

"You're the reason why everything got messed up!" I was so *happy* he'd messed it up. Now I had proof that what Jasmine said was right.

Malcolm looked so sad all of a sudden, I had to dial my excitement back and think about what I'd just said. *Oops.*

"*No,* I don't mean it like that. Not messed up. What I mean is that I had this plan and you came up and ruined the plan."

"That's so much better. Thanks," said Malcolm, rolling his eyes, resting the side of his head on his fingers, his elbow propped up on the arm of the chair.

I jumped up from my seat and came over, kneeling down by his right side. I stared him in the face, placing my hand on his arm. He couldn't look away; I wouldn't let him.

"I had that cop in a trance. I can do that if I try really hard. I can make someone forget everything."

His face darkened and he looked down pointedly at my hand on his forearm. "Like you're doing with me right now?"

I frowned, taken aback by his tone. "No. I'm not doing anything to you now. I don't think I even could if I wanted to."

"Sure," he said, pulling his arm away.

I shook my head, ignoring his comment and hurtful detachment from my touch. I had to get him to understand. "When you came walking up to the porch, he dropped out of Rainbowland and came back to reality, and he wasn't affected by me anymore at all. Don't you see?"

"No. Sorry." He shook his head, not meeting my eyes anymore.

"You erase my effects. You balance me out. Together, when you and I are near each other, we can be *normal.*"

Malcolm looked at me again and we stared at each other for a really long time. The room was totally silent. Even Kootch wasn't saying anything.

Tears filled my eyes as my heart swelled in my chest. This was the first time in my entire existence that I'd glimpsed the possibility of a normal life, of being a regular teenager who could just come home and argue with her parents and get a hug from them without worrying about them getting deranged over it. *I can have friends! I can join clubs! I can ... I can... do anything!*

Malcolm broke his gaze away from mine, his face going dark again as he stared off into the distance.

"What's wrong?" I asked, my voice going all weepy. My fantasy world, the one that had been right there in front of me in 3-D color, was slipping out of my grasp. My heart squeezed in on itself and the pain made me almost cry out.

"I have to go," he said. He stood. I fell back onto my butt on the floor.

"You can't go now!" said Jasmine, clearly distressed. "She just poured her heart out and laid it at your feet, you idiot!"

I moved back and somehow made it into my chair, unable to look at anyone. The shame was burning me up from the inside. "It's no big deal. Just let him go." I couldn't say any more or I'd throw up, right there on Jasmine's perfectly vacuumed carpet.

Kootch sighed loudly. "Dude, you know I'm not the most sensitive guy in the world, but you can't just take off after all that. Didn't you hear what she said?"

I'd never heard Kootch sound so sweet before, and I wanted to thank him for sticking up for me, but I couldn't get any words out. I couldn't even look at him or Jasmine. I just stared at the carpet fibers, trying not to imagine the life I could have had with Malcolm at my side.

After the joy completely left my body, all I could think about was how I must have done something really terrible in my last life to have deserved this special kind of hell. To catch a glimpse of a normal life and then have it snatched away...

"I don't mean to be a dick, but I just can't do this. I just ... I've been me for too long. I've been in the dark for so long I don't trust the light. You can't understand. You just can't. I don't blame you for hating me."

He was saying this to me, but I couldn't look at him. It was too awful to bear. The words were already cutting me open, and I was bleeding freely onto the floor. I felt drained and empty.

"No. Fuck that. You're not going anywhere." Kootch stood.

I looked up, wondering what he was going to do. I had to stop him before he and Malcolm got into another fight.

"Just let him go," I said, painful emotions coloring my voice and making the words come out strained.

"No! Don't be such a frigging wimp, Rae." Jasmine stood next to Kootch. "I know you like him, and I know he likes you. You guys were obviously meant to be together. Yin and yang, look it up!"

"That's not us," said Malcolm. "I am darkness personified. She's the light. If we get together I'll eventually just snuff her out like I do everyone else." He sounded angry and frustrated.

"Bullshit. Everyone knows the light is stronger than the dark," said Kootch. "Ever take a shit in the middle of the night?"

The room went completely silent. I'm pretty sure even the clock stopped ticking. I looked up and saw only confusion on Jasmine and Malcolm's faces, probably mirroring my own.

"Please tell me you have a point," said Jasmine.

"I do."

"A *relevant* point."

"It is. You go in the bathroom, take a shit in the dark 'cause it's the middle of the night, and then you have to light a match, right? And what happens?'

He looked around at all of us, like he was waiting for us to catch up. I was totally lost, now picturing Kootch with his pants around his ankles, sitting on a toilet with a lit match in his hand. It wasn't pretty.

"It lights up the whole damn bathroom is what I'm saying. Just that one tiny flame gets rid of a whole damn room full of darkness. And it gets rid of the stink too, so that's a nice side benefit." He smiled at all of us, pleased with his theory.

"As disgusting as he is, and as awful as that image is that is now burned into my brain, he has a point." Jasmine reached over and twisted Kootch's nipple without even looking at him.

He smacked her hand away and pretended like he was going to punch her. Of course he didn't. He just rubbed his chest and scowled.

"I appreciate you trying to help, guys, I really do," said Malcolm, "but I can't risk it. I can't do it. I like Rae and you guys too much."

He turned and walked towards the door.

"So you're just going to let Derek or Holder take her then, is that it?" asked Jasmine. "The dynamic duo of assholedom?"

Malcolm stopped, his back to us.

Jasmine continued. "Ever wonder what the hell is going on with them? Why they're so interested?"

Malcolm turned his head to look at us sideways. "They're just addicted. Rainbows."

"No, they're not," I said. I didn't want to manipulate him into staying, but I didn't want to lie either or let him walk away with misunderstandings between us. "Mr. Holder had never seen me before. And he got more than Rainbowey on me, like, immediately. That's never happened to me. Never. I swear."

Malcolm looked towards the door again and sighed really loudly. His shoulders sagged and his head dropped. He said nothing for five full seconds. I counted them out with the clock on the wall.

Tick.

Tick.

Tick.

Tick.

Tick.

"There's something I forgot to mention," he said, turning back around. He walked over to stand next to the coffee table, looking at me and then the others.

"Well, don't keep us in suspense," said Jasmine, sarcastically.

He put his hand on the back of his chair and squeezed it until his knuckles went white. "I heard something. I forgot about it until you said that, Rae. I'm sorry I didn't mention it or think of it before."

I just stared at him, wondering what he was going to tell us or confess. Whatever it was, he was staying to say it, so there was nothing I wanted more than to listen.

# Chapter Thirty-One
# Malcolm

I FELT GUILTY AS HELL. I was planning to run. That hadn't changed. But now I realized there was more to this picture than just the close-up view we'd been looking at for the past hour or so. The conversation that I'd overheard in the bathroom came back to me in a big rush after Rae said that Mr. Holder had never met her before and couldn't possibly be a Rainbow already. I knew now that it was quite possible there was a bigger picture here. It just wasn't coming in clear enough for me to see the whole thing.

But I did finally realize who the other voice belonged to.

"It was Derek," I said. "In the bathroom with Mr. Holder."

"What?" asked Kootch, confusion written all over his face. "What were they doing in the bathroom together, and why are you telling us this disgusting factoid?"

"I was hiding in the bathroom from ... doesn't matter. And when I was in the stall, Mr. Holder came in with Derek and they were talking about a girl. At the time I had no idea who it was, but they were discussing getting her alone. I can't remember exactly what it was they said ... something like they had to see if she was the one they were looking for?" I said it like a question, searching my memory for the exact sentences they'd used.

"Looking for? Like they knew about Rae already?" asked Jasmine, sounding excited.

"Yeah. But when I was in detention later trying to figure out who they were looking for, I knew right away it wasn't Rae. They already knew too much about her and she's new. There was no way they could know."

"Sure they could," said Jasmine, her arms folded across her chest. She looked supremely confident.

"How?" asked Rae. She looked scared.

Kootch rolled his eyes. "Here it comes. Brace yourselves."

Jasmine didn't even spare him a glance. "This shit happens all the time. People in power looking for people with special abilities. People they want to manipulate. Trust me. This shit is high level, international, government control. They have access to all kinds of info."

"Aaaaand cue the crazy," said Kootch, stepping out of Jasmine's range.

"Shut up, assmunch. I know what I'm talking about. My parents are connected. They have a network."

"And you're all up in their business with them because you're a spy kid and you have like a go-go gadget watch that shoots out grappling hooks and shit," said Kootch, laughing around his words.

Jasmine frowned. "I'll deal with you later, punk." She turned her attention to Rae and me, all seriousness now. "This isn't a game. You guys know what you do is powerful. You can influence people. Not just one at a time, but huge groups. Think about what someone could do with that if they could control it." She paused, letting her words sink in.

They were definitely sinking in deep for me, and the expression on Rae's face said they were doing the same to her. It sounded eerily possible.

"My parents are part of a network of ex-military personnel and scientists..."

"Conspiracy nuts," interjected Kootch.

"...Professionals, who keep track of shit like this. You're not the only ones who've been attacked. Trust me. My parents are out of town right now, but when they get back, they're going to want to talk to you. And they can show you some shit, too. You'll believe it after they show you. I am totally not playing right now."

Rae was shaking her head. "I don't think that can happen. When I go home my parents will already have our stuff packed. I can guarantee you right now, you won't ever see me again after tonight." She hung her head.

Just the words stabbed me in the heart. I'd been planning to disappear myself, but I guess in the back of my mind I'd imagined her staying - being somewhere where I could find her later or communicate with at least. Picturing her just disappearing too made me feel positively ill. I wanted to punch a wall at the unfairness of it all. Several times.

"So, you don't go home," said Jasmine, as if it were so simple.

"Where's she supposed to go?" I asked, getting pissed that Rae was in this position. It felt like my fault.

"She can stay here with me." Jasmine smiled. "I have an extra room, and if anyone comes sniffing around, you can stay in the panic room. It's totally rad."

"It is rad," agreed Kootch. "Inner sanctum shit. Plus lots of Ding Dongs."

"Plus, we have Ho Ho." Jasmine nodded at Kootch and he nodded back.

"Can't count out old Ho Ho," he agreed.

"You really like that Hostess stuff, don't you?" asked Rae, a small smile curving up the side of her mouth, making her dimple show. *That fucking dimple. She could turn me into a Rainbow with that alone.* I had to look away.

"No, man. Not the cakes. The *beast*. The unholy terror of bloodlust that is Ho Ho." Kootch smiled proudly.

"Go get him up," said Jasmine, walking over and pushing some buttons on her alarm keypad.

"Aw, man, do I have to?" Kootch was whining, looking distressed.

"Just do it. But wash your hands first so he doesn't smell the Ding Dongs on you."

Kootch left the room, and the water went on in the kitchen. I had no idea what a Ho Ho was, but I was definitely interested in finding out. Knowing Jasmine, it was probably a turtle.

"You're super nice to invite me, but I can't stay with you, Jazzy. My parents ... you don't know them. They've been around me a long time."

I knew the underlying meaning to her words. They were Rainbows who couldn't be shaken. Time and distance away would mean nothing to them. I had one of those once. A Miserable who died miserable.

"Where else are you going to go?" she asked. "You could go with Malcolm maybe." She looked at me.

I shook my head furiously. "No way. I live in a total dump. Besides, my social worker's coming to move me out on Monday. I have to take off."

"Take off? What do you mean take off?" asked Rae. The sad look was back on her face.

"Leave town. Move on. Start my life somewhere else." I shrugged. It sounded stupid, especially considering I'd just spent my last ten bucks on beer. My mouth twisted up in a sick version of a smile.

Kootch came in from the backyard through the sliding glass door. The fact that he was struggling was clear.

"No ... fuck ... Ho Ho! Stop! No, Ho Ho, *no!* Goddamn it! Butts! Come get this demon, would you?"

Jasmine smiled. "Rae. Malcolm. I'd like you to meet my dragon. Say hello to Ho Ho." She faced the back door. "Ho Ho! Come!"

A gigantic brownish red I-don't-know-what came streaking around the couch to slide to stop at Jasmine's feet.

"Heel!" she commanded.

The beast spun around, its butt slamming into the side of the couch as it wiggled in to sit at her leg. There wasn't enough room there for it to do what it wanted, so it laid its shoulder against the cushions and actually pushed the furniture back a foot. When the beast was finally settled next to its master's leg, it looked up at her, a grin on its face. A giant, slobbery tongue fell out of its mouth and dangled out of the side of it. Drool soon followed.

Rae stared, her face white and her jaw hanging open in stark fear.

"I honestly thought a real dragon was going to come out of your back yard," I said, not moving a muscle.

"Believe me, when Ho Ho farts, you'll think she *is* a dragon shooting fire out of her ass," said Kootch, breathing heavily as he walked back into the room. "Trust me. Nostril hairs are a thing of the past in this house."

He had globs of white goo on his pants.

"Um, Kootch?" Rae pointed to them with a shaking finger.

Kootch grabbed some Ding Dong wrappers off the table, using them to pull the stuff off. "Fucking dog. Drools like a goddamn rabid werewolf." He made an annoyed sound as the plastic just smeared the gooey substance into the fibers of his pants. "Next time you're getting her off the leash."

"A guard dog," Rae said. "What kind is she?"

"Canary Island Mastiff. Baddest badass dragon dog of all time. Trained by my dad."

"The baddest badass human of all time," said Kootch. "Trust. The guy is all kinds of scary." He threw the plastic down on the table, ignoring Jasmine's sharp intake of breath, probably over the germs if her expression was any clue.

"See, the funny thing about Ho Ho," explained Kootch, "is that she's the dirtiest, sloppiest, most disgusting pig of a dog there ever was. So you'd think Miss OCD over there would have a stroke just looking at her. But noooooo. She vacuums my ass crack every time I walk through the door, but Ho Ho? She could take a shit right here on the floor and Jasmine would say it's adorable."

"Hey! Ho Ho would *never* shit on our floor. She is house trained, unlike *some* people." She patted the dog on the head and smiled before looking back up at Rae. "Rae, Ho Ho will keep you safe, I promise. You have nothing to worry about."

"But what about your parents?" Rae asked, not sounding very convinced.

"Oh, trust me. When my parents see what you can do and hear about what happened, they'll insist you stay."

Rae's face fell. "But see, that's the problem. They won't do it because they want to. They'll do it because that's just what happens. And then they'll become Rainbows."

I felt like total crap as soon as the words came out of Rae's mouth. The solution was simple. But I couldn't do it.

Jasmine smiled confidently. Then she looked at me. "That's not going to be a problem."

I shook my head, tensing my muscles all over my body. *Run! Just run!*

"Don't you shake your head at me, Malcolm. You're staying too."

"No, I can't," I said, still shaking my head. "I can't do that."

"Why not?" asked Kootch. "You said you live in a shithole and you're leaving anyway. Why not just come here?"

It made perfect sense on paper. All of it. Except for the part where Holder and Derek were trying to take Rae down; there was nothing I could do to help her with that problem. I have no reason to stay. I should just disappear. That had been my plan all along, the only thing that could work for me.

Until Rae had come along, of course. Until Rae had come and given me another option. The problem is that I didn't know if I could trust it, this illusion of another way. My life had been nothing but one tragedy followed by another. I had no reason to believe I'd have anything but darkness surrounding me, smothering me, until the day I died.

Rae was the light. The yin to my yang or the yang to my yin. Whatever it was, it was nothing I'd ever known before. Joy. Happiness. Rae brought me hope. And hope was a dangerous thing, because it made you dream big and do stupid risky things.

"Fine. Just a few days until we get things worked out," I said. "And only if your parents say it's okay, Jasmine. Can you email them?"

"Yep." Jasmine looked at Rae, beaming. "You in?"

Rae shrugged, looking shyly at me and then more confidently at Kootch and the dog. "Okay, I'm in. It's the only way I'll be able to stay for a little longer." She looked at me again. "And I'd like to stay."

# Chapter Thirty-Two
# Rae

I COULDN'T BELIEVE IT. SOMEHOW Jasmine had managed to convince Malcolm and me to stay with her. I felt like I was walking in a dream. Could this really be happening? Was I running away from my house and my family? Doing the thing I'd dreamed about for as long as I could remember?

"Where will we sleep?" I asked, wondering if it was going to be in the secret room under her house. Maybe I should have been freaked out about that, but the idea of hiding while surrounded by guns sounded like a great idea after dealing with Derek tonight, even though I knew I could never shoot a human being or anything else for that matter.

"I think it's best if you and Malcolm are near each other," she said, all businesslike now. "Kootch, can you take Ho Ho back out?"

Kootch walked to the back door. "Come on, Ho Ho. Out you go. Go light up the night, why don't ya, you smelly beast."

"Go on, Ho Ho. Outside," said Jasmine, nodding towards the back door.

Ho Ho the beast-dog ran out, her drool swinging around her head as she went. There was a special kind of confident sway to her stride, as though she knew she could tear our throats open with little effort. She feared nothing. A shiver of respect ran up my arms. I rubbed them to get the goosebumps off, wishing I could be as brave as she is.

"We can't sleep together," said Malcolm.

My face heated up. "Of course not. No one was saying we would." Total rejection sucked. I was getting the distinct impression that Malcolm wanted nothing to do with me or this whole situation. I couldn't blame him, though. That kiss we'd shared had been mind blowing.

He probably thought he was a Rainbow. I had no idea how I could convince him otherwise, except to have a crappy kiss, and I honestly didn't think any kiss with him could suck, even if I tried to make it bad. But I had bigger things to worry about, namely my parents finding me and bringing in a SWAT team to rescue me, so I let it go. For now, at least.

"I won't put you in the same bed, but I will put you in the same room. It's not to couple you up or anything, because honestly I have no idea what that could do to any bystanders, but we have to be careful about the influence you have on people. If one of you gets around my parents without the other, I don't want them to get hurt, you know what I mean?"

"This is a bad idea," I said, imagining her parents getting injured. Jasmine was the only person in the world who'd ever tried to help me, and I couldn't repay her by hurting someone she loved.

"I agree," said Malcolm, looking at the front door, his hands clenching and unclenching over and over.

"It'll be fine. Maybe they'll be Neutrals like me," Jasmine said. "Anyway, come on. I'll show you to the guest room." She pulled her phone out of her back pocket and pressed buttons on the keypad as she walked down the hall.

Malcolm and I followed her, the glowing screen in her hand and a nightlight near the floor guiding the way.

Jasmine pushed open a door at the end of the hall, still staring at her phone and speaking distractedly. "This is our guest room. There's a trundle bed under the main bed. Just pull it out. It's on rollers. Sheets are folded on top."

Her phone beeped and she clicked a few buttons. She finally looked up, all smiles. "My parents said you can stay."

"You didn't tell them about us," said Malcolm, hesitating in the doorway.

"Yes, I did."

"You couldn't have said all that stuff that fast."

"All I had to do was say one word and that's all it took."

"What word?"

"I could tell you, but then I'd have to kill you." She stopped smiling. "Lights are there, but I suggest you leave them off all the time. Shades are down, so no one can see in, but let's not tip anyone off that the room is being used. Keep your voices low. Bathroom's down the hall. Rae, I'll bring you some PJs. Malcolm, you're on your own."

She left us standing in the doorway.

Neither of us moved at first.

"So," said Malcolm, looking down at me.

"So," I said back, staring up at him.

"Are we really doing this?" he asked, his voice going softer.

"Yeah, I guess. I'm not even sure what it is we're doing, though."

"We're cutting free. That's what I see. It's what it feels like."

"Being free is scarier than I thought it would be." It felt good to admit that.

"Yeah. Me too." He sighed, looking less serious and more just like the boy I'd played basket ball with.

*Had it only been today that we were in the gym together?*

"Did you ever imagine when you saw me in English class that you'd be standing with me here right now?" I asked, unable to stop the hint of a smile from sneaking onto my face.

"Not in a million years," he said, the right side of his mouth twitching up.

I looked at him for a few more seconds before walking into the room. I moved slowly, letting the dim nightlight plugged into a hallway outlet guide me.

"It's dark in here," I said, holding my hands out, trying to feel my way and make sure I didn't bump into anything.

"Story of my life," he said, his hand brushing against mine.

He grabbed my fingers and held on, sliding his around to tangle ours together.

My heart stopped beating for a second or two and then raced to catch up. My ears burned. He was touching me, and it felt so nice. I didn't want it to stop. Both joy and pain warred within me. *Please don't let this be our influence over each other making this happen. Please let this be real.*

"Maybe you just need a little nightlight," I said, my voice trembling.

"Yeah. Maybe I do," he said, pulling me into his arms and holding me gently. "A friend once told me that all it takes is the single spark of a match to light up a whole room of darkness."

"And get rid of the stink at the same time," I said, giggling into his chest.

He tipped his head down, putting his cheek next to mine. It made me feel warm and cared for, wanted for who I am and not for how I make people feel and forget.

And then I knew.

It has to be real.

It just has to be.

## What to read next ...

Read Malcolm's and Rae's continuing story here:
DUALITY: Book 2 (Euphoria).

Being an independent author, I depend entirely on *you*, the reader, to get the word out about my books. If you liked this book, won't you please leave a review online and recommend it to a friend? The more you spread the word, the more books I can write, and nothing would please me more than to put a new book in your hands every single month.

*I read all my reviews!*

*Find more Elle Casey books at the following retailers:*

*Amazon*
*iBooks*
*Barnes & Noble*
*Google Play*
*Kobo*
*Walmart*
*Your Local Library via the OverDrive ebook platform*

Want to get an email when my next book is released?
Sign up here: www.ElleCasey.com/news

# ABOUT THE AUTHOR

*Elle Casey, a former attorney and teacher, is a* NEW YORK TIMES, USA TODAY, *and Amazon bestselling American author who lives in France with her husband, three kids, and a number of horses, dogs, and cats. She has written more than 40 novels in less than 5 years and likes to say she offers fiction in several flavors. These flavors include romance, science fiction, urban fantasy, action adventure, suspense, and paranormal.*

## A personal note from Elle ...

If you enjoyed this book, please take a moment to leave a review on the site where you bought this book, Goodreads, or any book blogs you participate in, and tell your friends! I love interacting with my readers, so if you feel like shooting the breeze or talking about books or your family or pets, please visit me. You can find me at ...

www.ElleCasey.com
www.Facebook.com/ellecaseytheauthor
www.Twitter.com/ellecasey
www.Instagram.com/ellecaseyauthor

# Other Books by Elle Casey

## CONTEMPORARY URBAN FANTASY

*War of the Fae* (10-book series)
*Ten Things You Should Know About Dragons*
(short story, The Dragon Chronicles)
*My Vampire Summer*
*Aces High*

## DYSTOPIAN

*Apocalypsis* (4-book series)

## SCIENCE FICTION

*Drifters' Alliance* (ongoing series)
*Winner Takes All* (short story prequel to Drifters' Alliance,
Dark Beyond the Stars Anthology)
*The Ivory Tower* (short story standalone, Beyond the Stars: A
Planet Too Far Anthology)

## ROMANCE

*By Degrees*
*Rebel Wheels* (3-book series)
*Just One Night* (romantic serial)
*Just One Week*
*Love in New York* (3-book series)
*Shine Not Burn* (2-book series)
*Bourbon Street Boys* (4-book series)
*Desperate Measures*
*Mismatched*

## ROMANTIC SUSPENSE

*All the Glory: How Jason Bradley Went from
Hero to Zero in Ten Seconds Flat*
*Don't Make Me Beautiful*
*Wrecked* (2-book series)

## PARANORMAL

*Duality* (2-book series)
*Monkey Business* (short story)
*Dreampath* (short story standalone, The
Telepath Chronicles)
*Pocket Full of Sunshine* (short story & screenplay)